A New Arrival In Port Berry

ALSO BY K.T. DADY

A New Arrival in Port Berry

K.T. DADY

Port Berry Book 4

Choc Lit
A JOFFE BOOKS COMPANY

Choc Lit, London
A Joffe Books company
www.choc-lit.com

First published in Great Britain in 2025

© K.T. Dady

Cover art by Dee Dee Book Covers

ISBN: 978-1781898543

Compassion changes the world.

CHAPTER 1

Spencer

'Lobster? You're allergic to lobster?' Spencer Jordan frowned at the boy gazing up at him.

'I had it on a cruise ship last year, and Mum said my cheeks turned pink.'

Spencer scribbled in his notebook. 'I'll make a note. Anything else, Leo?'

Leo pushed the dangling cord of his red cape into the corner of his mouth as he shook his head.

That was a relief. Being placed in charge of three ten-year-old boys with anxiety was going to be tough enough, without adding allergic reactions into the mix. Spencer was pretty sure Leo wouldn't come across any lobsters while out and about earning Sunshine badges.

Spencer's new setup at the Sunshine Centre to help build confidence was off to a good start, and he was so pleased some of the kids there had agreed to his idea, thinking it fun.

The woman in charge of the centre, Debra, smiled warmly as Spencer glanced her way. He hadn't long joined as a health care worker, helping to mentor children, and couldn't

1

help out full-time due to his work commitments at his flower shop. He sighed inwardly, wishing he could help the children lose their anxieties straight away, but he knew it would be a process. Even though he was soon to turn thirty-six, he could still remember the fears he had as a child, especially when he was placed into the care system.

Spencer had yet to learn everything about the kids under his watch, knowing only some parts of their backstories and concerns. One thing he did know for certain was, children needed support, and that was something he could offer buckets of. They had joined the respite centre to help bring them peace, and Spencer was keen to be part of their healing.

'I'll leave you to it,' said Debra quietly, her bright eyes offering reassurance.

'What colour are the badges?' asked Leo, still chewing on his cape.

Spencer's plan was to get his friend Luna to rustle up some on her sewing machine. He glanced around at the array of colours in the arts and crafts room where they sat. 'All different.'

Leo looked over at the accordion doors that led to a large patio in the back garden, where a small nature reserve resided along with an allotment. 'Will any involve nature?'

'I like nature,' said Jax, his dark eyes only focused on Leo.

Spencer nodded at the boy while putting his notebook away in his brown satchel his sister had bought for him for his new job. Lottie was extremely proud of him the day he came clean about his secret studies in mental health care for children. He'd kept his evening course to himself, letting people think he was doing what he used to do with his life: hitting the town most nights just to have one-night stands. He just wasn't comfortable letting anyone know his plans until he had them set in stone. It was a new chapter in his life, and he wanted to enter it gently, without fuss.

He turned to the third boy in his care. 'What about you, Ryan? Any badges you're looking forward to receiving?'

Ryan shrugged. 'As long as it's not swimming,' he mumbled.

Leo flapped a corner of his cape so it covered part of Ryan's knee. 'Wish I could swim.'

Jax wrinkled his nose. 'You go on cruises with your mum every year.'

'I'm not in the sea. I'm on the ship.'

That didn't seem to help Jax. 'What if you fall in?'

Leo's grey-blue eyes held the softest of smiles. 'A mermaid would save me.'

Jax scoffed as Ryan frowned. 'You don't actually believe they exist, do you?'

'Have you ever seen one?'

'No, but—'

Leo interrupted his friend. 'Then how would you know?' Ryan grinned.

'We can start earning badges today if you like,' said Spencer, interrupting the conversation he knew was about to go off in all directions.

'I don't mind.' Leo shrugged at Jax. 'If it's easy.'

Spencer glanced around the room, thinking it best to start where they were. 'Arts and crafts badge.'

The boys visibly relaxed, making Spencer realize he had his work cut out for him when it came to taking them outside their comfort zones.

Ryan pointed at the easels. 'Can we paint? I love painting.'

It was a good start, so Spencer agreed and watched as the boys went about their business quietly. It was nice seeing them at peace, even more so feeling his own serenity. He was pleased he had made the decision to finally do something else with his life. It took his sister getting knocked off her bicycle a couple of years back and ending up in a wheelchair to change his mindset. His poor excuse for a life couldn't continue down mundane roads. He couldn't keep blaming his childhood for his misery.

'I'm going to draw a picture for my aunt,' said Leo. 'She's always at our house. Mum says she needs cheering up.'

'Why is she sad?' asked Jax.

Leo raised a pencil to his sheet of plain white paper. 'I don't know. I heard them say something about her husband, a secretary, and a cliché, but I don't know what that means.' He glanced up at Spencer. 'Mum said you lived with your aunt.'

Just the thought of Rebecca made Spencer smile. What a godsend she had been in his life. 'That's right. When I was your age.'

Ryan frowned. 'Why did you live with your aunt?'

'His parents were sent to prison,' said Jax, shading in the tail of an aeroplane.

Spencer wasn't that surprised. Most knew his backstory, as it was big news at the time. Still, he didn't think it appropriate for grown-ups to fill the lads with such old stories or any part of his story.

'What's it like in prison?' asked Leo.

'Don't know. I've never been,' replied Spencer, pondering over how to change the subject. It was obvious the boys would be curious about him, but some things weren't meant for small ears. 'So, how are we all getting on?' he asked joyfully, raising his tone a notch too high.

Ryan gestured at his outline of a nearby flower arrangement. 'Mine's okay.'

It was more than okay. Impressive to say the least. Spencer encouraged him to continue, then sent a quick text to his friend Alice to ask her to remind her grandmother to make a start on those Sunshine badges, seeing how Luna rarely used a phone, let alone read text messages.

It was February, and Spencer and the boys had a busy year ahead. After being bullied at school, Leo needed to be able to trust more kids than just Jax and Ryan, Jax had to start talking to people outside his circle, and Ryan had dropped out of swimming competitions because he had started to freeze with nerves at the start of each race, so he wanted a break from the pool.

'When do we get our badge, Captain Spencer?' asked Leo.

'End of the week.' He was sure Luna would get her friends on the case if she couldn't manage a whole heap of badges in a short time. 'And just call me Spencer.'

'I think we could have a mermaid one,' said Leo, pushing his silver round glasses up his button nose. 'You said we could help choose badge ideas.'

Spencer nodded. 'Yep.'

Jax didn't look best pleased. 'You want us to go looking for mermaids?'

Leo shook his head. 'No. It can be our magical badge.'

Jax still looked confused. 'What are we going to do that's magical?'

'My mum said it would be magical if I went back to school.'

'So what does that mean for me?' asked Jax.

Leo offered a warm smile. 'You can get yours when you buy some sweets.'

Jax broke the tip of his pencil on the easel, he'd pressed it that hard. 'You want me to shop?'

Leo turned to Spencer. 'That's why we're here, isn't it? My mum said Jax has to talk to people.' He looked back at his friend. 'It's easy, Jax. You just go to the counter and speak.'

'It's easy to go to school, Leo, but you're home-schooled, so why don't you just walk through the school gates like the rest of us have to?' Jax huffed, flopping back into his chair.

'It's all right, Jax,' said Ryan softly, placing a hand on his shoulder. 'My coach says it's mind over matter.'

Jax frowned. 'Then how come you don't race anymore?'

Ryan sighed. 'I'm not sure I want to swim, but my mum wants me to. It's my talent, and she says I shouldn't waste it.'

That was a lot of insight for Spencer. He stepped closer to Jax. 'We won't be rushing into anything here. In fact, we're not even going to think about swimming or schools or speaking to people we don't know. All we're going to do is learn some new skills, have a bit of fun, and take each badge as it comes. Like right now. Let's get these pictures ready to take home later.'

Jax went back to his easel, but the atmosphere had changed in the room, and Spencer knew the boys were nervous again.

'We'll even go camping one day,' he added, hoping it might light a spark.

Leo was the first to smile. 'Like proper Scouts?'

Spencer nodded. 'Of course. We're the Sunshine Centre. We even offer rock climbing.'

That perked Jax up. 'I want to go rock climbing. Will it be as high as a mountain?'

'Probably not,' replied Spencer, pleased to see the mood lift.

'Can we do photography?' asked Ryan, hazel eyes fixed on his picture.

'Don't see why not.' Spencer already knew that Ryan's dad worked away a lot as a wildlife photographer, so he could see why the boy would be interested in such an activity.

'And dig for fossils,' said Leo, flapping his cape over one shoulder.

'We can do that over the road from my shop in Port Berry.' Spencer mentally searched the harbour, figuring out the best section for the task.

'Or here in Penzance,' said Jax, pushing his dark hair out of his smiling eyes.

'We can explore both places.' Spencer beamed on the inside at their enthusiasm. 'And while we're near my shop, you can earn a badge for flower arranging.'

It didn't hold quite the same level of excitement as the fossils, but still, it was something Spencer always found calmed him, so it was something to add to the growing list.

Debra appeared, waving him over. 'How's it going?'

Now the boys were talking activities, rather than about prison or anxieties, he felt it was going quite well. Raking a hand through his copper locks, he smiled. 'Good.'

They both knew it wouldn't always be that way, as life at the large building designed especially for people with disabilities, those in need of emotional support, and anyone wanting respite often had its hiccups along the way. Both Spencer and Debra knew the lads weren't entering some sort of get-well-quick scheme. The whole centre was created to help and calm, not pile on pressure. There was even a sensory room and soft play area.

Leo, Jax, and Ryan had willingly joined Spencer's badge scheme, and he was on a mission to help keep them grounded at all times while reducing their anxiety levels as best he could through the art of fun. There wasn't an endgame as such. Just time with someone understanding and compassionate, like his aunt had been. He'd made a plan, hit the ground running, and was already off to a great start. Yep, this year was going to be all about peace, balance, and harmony.

CHAPTER 2

Beth

Beth woke drenched in sweat again. It was still dark out, and her exhausted body refused to get out of the damp bed, as shivering seemed a better option. Her eyes could barely open, and all thoughts of having a great start to her day evaporated the moment she realized she'd hardly slept at all.

The bedroom was small and dull, pretty much how she felt as she forced her weary limbs to move. Perhaps if she just changed her nightie she could grab another couple of hours before her baby woke for a feed.

Turning to face the sleeping boy, she held nothing in her brown eyes but weariness. How were other mothers glowing? Catching a glimpse of her tall thin frame in the floor mirror as she stood, she was sure all she held about her was death warmed up. Not what she expected the start of her thirties to look like.

Archie murmured, causing her frown lines to deepen. He was three months old. He had to sleep through at some point. If only he could sleep some more right now.

Clutching the end of the white cot, she waited, praying he'd settle, as she needed sleep. So much sleep.

The baby appeared peaceful enough, so she set about getting changed into another cotton nightdress, wrapping a cream dressing gown over the top.

The bed was still damp, and it would have to stay that way, as she was exhausted. She covered the bottom sheet with the quilt, then flopped on top, closing her eyes, hoping for more rest.

What if something happened to her in the night? Her heart could stop beating, or her body could spontaneously combust like that woman in the magazine she had read about the day before. Perhaps a brain tumour was to blame for the shakes she felt when trying to sleep. Something was sure to happen. She would be gone and her baby taken away to who knows where.

She turned to Archie, but she couldn't smile. He had the most adorable chubby cheeks, and when his blue eyes smiled her way he was beyond cute. Everyone told her how lucky she was to have a baby who only cried to be fed, changed, or cuddled. One woman at the baby clinic told her that her own baby didn't stop whingeing.

Archie wasn't the problem. She was. If her heart wasn't racing it was fluttering. If her body wasn't in a panic it was because she was manically cleaning anything in sight. If only she could sleep more than every other night, she was certain life would be bearable again. It was only exhaustion knocking her out in between the night sweats. Her appetite was poor, her head often light, and oh how her back ached. At least she had a doctor's appointment next week and was sure she would receive an asthma pump for the tightness she kept feeling in her chest.

She pressed her head into the plump headboard and gazed at the netting up the window. The light would break through soon. She imagined all the other mums out there, full of rise and shine and ready to roll. They'd be putting on their ironed clothes and tying back their shiny hair, all smiles for their gorgeous husbands and perfect kids. Breakfast would be ready and schoolbags lined up at the door.

Beth couldn't remember the last time she'd applied lippy, let alone brushed her hair with care.

The fridge creaked in the kitchen, the other end of the passageway. It was a familiar noise but still made her mouth twitch. Why couldn't she hear noises involving a loving man singing in the shower, or her own voice sounding happy once more?

There was no one to blame for her new single-parent life but herself. Ticking off a one-night stand from her bucket list wasn't as hot and steamy as she had imagined. More a stupid drunken fumble in the darkness of a hotel room at a conference, of all places. Had her life not been so lonely, she wouldn't have gone down that road.

Beth had given up saying, 'Why me?' a long time ago. It was in her past. A past that left her with a future in the form of a son.

She wished her parents were alive to help and support her in her time of need, even though she was used to being on her own. She used to be able to hold her own hand quite well, but she often felt it would be nice if she didn't have to.

Oh, how it was going to be so easy. Loads of people got on with parenthood, so why not her? Why did it have to go so wrong? It wasn't fair she had no one in her corner helping.

She glanced at Archie again. He was fine. All that pregnancy drama, and for what? Nothing. He was perfect in every way, and now alone with her. She'd been through hell with worry before the birth and it had left her feeling as though she might die each day. Could she go back and tell the hospital staff? How could she tell anyone about the state she was in? They would take her baby away. Section her, possibly. Something bad would happen, because she was certain she had lost the plot at some point during her pregnancy, and not much had changed since the birth. At least that part went well.

A light hue sat in the window pane, and the sound of birds entered the room. Beth closed her bloodshot eyes and tried for a calming breath. Part of her brain told her to make a bottle up ready, but the tired part told that side to shut up. Sleep was needed. Lots and lots of sleep.

Archie made the smallest sound but it seemed to roar through the room, snatching away Beth's respite. She jolted, not wanting to move a muscle, but she had no more choices. Her son was awake and hungry.

It was a struggle clambering to the kitchen to get on with her morning chores. Not only were there many unpacked boxes in the way from her recent move, but her weakness slowed her movements. The day after night sweats was always the worst. At least Archie would settle for a while after his nappy was changed, which she got on with while his milk cooled.

His little face showed signs of happiness as he stared up at the small teddy bears dangling over his head. Beth was a caring mum, that much she knew about herself, even if she had lost so much that she hardly recognized the woman staring back at her each morning in the bathroom mirror. If she wasn't panicky and exhausted every day, they would have a normal life. Archie would see quality, not Beth Horton vampire meets zombie mum.

'You deserve better,' she whispered, cuddling her boy to her chest while lightly brushing over his wispy strands of strawberry-blond hair.

Maybe things will improve now we've moved to Port Berry.

She hoped.

CHAPTER 3

Spencer

Spencer was on shift duty at the Happy to Help Hub with his friend Alice. It had been a quiet morning, so he mostly spent time making up food parcels in the back room.

'You doing deliveries later, Spence?' asked Alice, popping her head around the door frame.

'I've got two booked in after lunch. Why's that?'

'Just got a call from Mrs Bradshaw.'

Spencer nodded. 'Sure. Add her to my list. It's by the fruit bowl.' He stood, stretching his back. 'We need more tinned veg,' he added, stepping into the shopfront that made the drop-in centre along Harbour End Road.

Alice waved a notepad in the air. 'Yeah, I have another list.'

Spencer yawned as he approached the street door. He gazed across the road at the dark sea. 'Bit choppy out there today.'

'Mum always says Cornwall is only beautiful in the summer, but Nan disagrees. Reckons Mum isn't looking properly to say that.'

Spencer smiled at the harbour. 'I'm with Luna on that one. I can see the beauty here in each season.'

Alice joined him her light-brown eyes almost glazed over. 'I don't need to go outside to know what season we're in. My body tells me.'

'Your fibromyalgia playing you up today, Al?'

'It's not too bad.'

Knowing she rated her pain levels on a scale of one to ten, he asked which level she was at today.

'Three,' she announced happily. 'Pretty good for this time of year.'

'You could go jogging with Robson tomorrow morning.'

Alice laughed. 'No thanks. I might be turning thirty-one at the end of the month, but I feel about seventy-one right now. That activity is strictly for summer.' She nudged him in the ribs. 'You could do with some exercise.'

'I do enough running around. Anyway, now I'm part-time at the centre, I've not much time to add anything else.'

'You back at the shop after deliveries?'

'Yeah. You?'

'No, Mum and Nan have got the newsagents covered today. I'm helping Mabel at the B & B.'

Spencer gazed down the road, even though he couldn't see around the bend to where Seaview B & B was. 'Can't remember the last time I had a holiday.'

'Volunteering here is my holiday.'

He could see her point. 'I'm taking the kids camping in the springtime, if their parents sign the consent forms. Hopefully the weather will be on side.'

Alice hugged his arm. 'Aw, Spence, you're really enjoying your new mentor role already. I can see those baby-blues of yours gleaming.'

He had to laugh. 'I really want to make a difference.'

Alice pointed at the window. 'You already make a difference when you create beautiful bouquets of flowers.'

'Wasn't my life though, was it? Rebecca opened Berry Blooms. Lottie and I just carried on with the shop after she died.'

'You not keen anymore, Spence?'

'Oh, don't get me wrong. I love the shop. It's part of me. It's just with the kids, I feel I have purpose.'

Alice nodded slightly. 'I get that. I feel the same about my Benny. It was one thing when he was just my nephew, but after my sister died and I became guardian, well, it was life-changing in more ways than I imagined it would be.'

They stepped away from the door as Spencer opened it for the middle-aged woman outside. A gust of cold air blew Alice's long dark hair backwards as the lady came forward.

'I have a donation for the food bank,' she chimed.

Alice took the bag from her. 'Thank you so much.'

'Would you like to come in for a cuppa?' asked Spencer. 'It's nippy out there today.'

'I'm good,' replied the lady. 'Got lots on today.'

Spencer closed the door as she walked away. 'I'm so glad our little food bank has taken off.' He turned to watch Alice empty the shopping bag onto the light-wood table. 'Not that I want people to need one.'

Alice sighed, raising a carton of long-life milk. 'I know. It's not right.'

He'd lost count of the times the volunteers at the Hub had discussed the cost of living. It wasn't something he had the energy to think about, knowing it was best spent raising funds to keep the Hub open and finding ways to assist those in need in all areas. 'Ooh, I forgot to tell you. Mick from the hostel called when you were getting us cake. Said Yuri has settled in nicely, and Shaun has got the fella a labouring job at his company.'

Alice clasped her hands. 'Aw, that's great. I knew Yuri would be okay once he had a roof over his head and a job. He was so eager the moment he walked through the door.' She pointed at the street. 'I'm glad we could help.'

Spencer gazed at the harbour once more. 'Makes you wonder who out there needs help. You see people pottering around, but you don't know what troubles they might have.' His phone rang, interrupting his thoughts.

'You get that, Spence. I'll see to Len.' Alice gestured to the elderly man plodding their way.

Closing the door to the back room, where all the food was kept, Spencer answered the call from Debra. 'Hiya. Everything okay?'

'It's Jax, Spence. Won't go to school again. Said he'd run away if his dad tries to force him. He can't keep faking illness either. It's all getting a bit much now. Thought I'd let you know in case his anxiety levels are raised next time you see him.'

'Thanks. Hopefully his school will find a solution.'

'His dad is in talks with them, but he also wanted to update us. Bless Jax, his social anxiety has flared, but he's taken a shine to our centre, so at least we can help with his confidence when he's with us. It all helps.'

'Thanks for letting me know.'

'Bye, Spence.'

Spencer went back outside to see if Alice needed any help. She was sitting in the big blue comfy chair having a chat with Len, who often liked to come in just for a natter to ease his loneliness since his wife passed away. Leaving them to it, he went back to making up food parcels while worrying about Jax. The boy looked in good spirits over the weekend, but then again they were having fun.

* * *

Spencer scooped up the last morsel on his dinner plate and sat back, satisfied. 'Thanks, Lottie. That went down well.'

Lottie laughed. 'Didn't last a minute. Have you eaten at all today?'

'Yes, I was just hungry, that's all. Had a lot of running around to do.'

His little sister's sea-blue eyes held concern. 'Have you taken on too much?'

Spencer waggled a hand while the other raised a glass of water to his mouth. 'I'm okay.'

Lottie manoeuvred her electric wheelchair around the kitchen table so she was closer to his face.

Spencer laughed. 'What you looking for?'

'Any worry lines.'

'Got plenty of those just from being your brother.'

'Oh, ha ha.'

'Seriously, Lott, I'm fine. Just a busy day. Plus, I was worried about Jax. Poor kid isn't doing too well at school.'

'Aww, does he need extra help?'

'No. He has social anxiety, and it affects him in class. Chris, his dad, let us know.'

'Something like home-schooling might suit him or smaller classes. The school will probably make those suggestions.'

'Leo loves being home-schooled.'

Lottie started to clear the table. 'I think that would have suited you.'

It was true. Spencer had little in the way of happy memories from his school years. He decided to change the subject. The last thing he wanted was to go back to his own past. So much of it still haunted him, so he preferred to ignore it altogether. Besides, he had more people to occupy his mind now.

He glanced at his sister stacking the dishwasher. She was all he had left in the way of family. When he'd heard she'd been knocked off her bike by a car, he was sure his heart left his body. There was no one in the world more important to him than Lottie.

'Do you want to stay over tonight, Spence?' she asked, glancing his way. 'We can watch a film.'

He looked at the clock over by the window. 'What time is Sam due back?'

'He shouldn't be too long. He's faffing about at the new headquarters. No doubt his rumbling tummy will bring him home soon.'

Spencer smiled. He loved how much his sister was settled with a loving partner. Samuel Powell was a good man. She was in safe hands with that one, he was sure. Still, it didn't stop him being there for her like he always had been.

A flashback hit him of a time when she was two and he'd wrapped a blanket around her while he read her a book from his school library. She liked the pictures, and he liked trying to teach her things. A shiver met his spine as he remembered what happened the next day.

It was scary being eight years old and surrounded by police officers. His dad had always told him not to trust them. It wasn't them he was worried about. Lottie was screaming as a strange woman carried her away, and he couldn't get to her, as he was being led off to a different car. There were so many flashing lights, but the noise of the chaos around him seemed muffled somehow.

It wasn't the first time he'd been taken away from his parents, but this time was different. He could tell. He wondered where Jordy was and told the woman next to him that his six-month-old brother was still inside. Jordy was so small and often so quiet, Spencer worried the baby might go unnoticed. Almost a week had passed when he found out where Jordy was.

'Spence, you okay?' asked Lottie, her hand on his arm.

He hadn't even noticed her approach. 'Hmm? Oh, yeah. In a world of my own for a minute there.'

She seemed to be studying him, and he was certain she could often see his thoughts. 'Stay over tonight,' she said softly.

Samuel was due back soon. She didn't need her big brother much anymore. 'I'm a bit tired, so I'll head off. Do you need me to do anything before I go?' He knew she wouldn't, being the independent type, even more so since losing the use of her legs. If there was one person who oozed inner-strength and positive vibes, it was Lottie.

He kissed her cheek at the door and ruffled her strawberry-blonde hair, making her laugh, then he glanced at the wide hallway. It was so different to how it looked when he was growing up there. Aunt Rebecca had a quaint lemon-washed harbour house up Berry Hill. Now, three of the houses in a row had been knocked together, with renovation work still being carried out, thanks to Lottie and Samuel.

Walking down the steep road, he wondered what Rebecca would have thought about her home, now so large. At least there was more room for Lottie. Samuel was making sure she had it easy at home, installing everything she needed.

He paused to stare out to sea. All was quiet. Just how he felt.

CHAPTER 4

Beth

Being told by the doctor that she didn't have asthma just stress and to take up yoga wasn't exactly helpful.

Beth inhaled sea-salty air as she pushed Archie's pram along the harbour. It was a fresh morning, but she needed the nip in the air to clear her stuffy head. She was sure she had something wrong with her chest. After all, it kept tightening, making it hard to take a proper breath.

Feeling rather deflated and still confused, she flopped onto a bench for a moment. Archie was fast asleep, snuggled in his blanket, not a care in the world.

'It's all right for some,' she mumbled, smiling softly.

A seagull cried, gaining her attention, and Beth wished she had the ability to fly away. Where to exactly, she wasn't sure. She'd only just completed a home swap with someone, so she had another bedroom. She couldn't see herself flying anywhere else too soon.

Pulling her scarf up to her chin, she wondered what was happening in the primary school where she worked. Maternity leave was boring. She much preferred teaching the little ones, although, the way things were, she was grateful for the time off, as she wasn't sure her rattled mind could cope with much else.

The dullness of the sky matched her mood. She tried to visualize sitting there in the summer. The warmth on her face, a spring in her step. It always cheered her. Maybe she would feel better by then.

'Valentine's Day soon,' said an elderly lady, plonking herself at the other end of the bench, making Beth jump.

Beth smiled politely. She didn't care about that silly day.

'Nice flower shop over the road,' added the woman.

Beth scanned Harbour End Road until she spotted Berry Blooms.

I bet it's her shop. She's trying to draw in customers.

'They always look so pretty, don't they?' Beth said, gesturing at the place.

Midnight-blue eyes seemed to study her for a moment before turning towards the sea. 'I'm Luna.'

'Beth.'

'You're new to the area.'

Beth smiled to herself. 'I am. Know everyone around here, do you?'

Luna gave a sharp nod. 'Pretty much.' She thumbed behind her. 'That's my family's shop there. Treasure Chest.'

Beth glanced at the newsagents.

'And that's the Happy to Help Hub,' she added, thumbing a few doors down. 'The volunteers help with all sorts. Have a nosey at the noticeboard. Might show some local groups you could join.'

'Groups?'

Luna gestured at the grey pram. 'Parent and baby groups.'

That was the last thing Beth wanted to be part of. All those mums with their heads screwed on right, then her . . . a mess. What if they noticed? Told social services she was falling apart? Best to avoid any interactions for now.

'Thanks. Good to know,' was the only response she was willing to give.

Luna's head bobbed slightly, then she stood and walked away.

Beth narrowed her eyes, focusing on the old woman's white bun. 'Goodbye to you too,' she mumbled.

A grizzle came from Archie. He'd want a bottle soon. Part of Beth didn't want to go home though. Harbour Light Café looked like a good place to settle her son for a feed, but she didn't want to be around people. That was so unlike her. Nothing was the same anymore.

Beth rocked the pram, sending her baby back to sleep for a bit longer.

I can't sit here all day.

As usual, there wasn't much else she felt strong enough for, so she made a start on the long walk home, pausing briefly at the Hub. There was a small woman inside, dressed as though she were a land girl from the Second World War.

Beth lowered her eyebrows and walked away. There wasn't any point dawdling, getting ideas about baby clubs.

A man's loud voice calling out to someone made her turn her head. It was just someone loading a van belonging to the flower shop. He was obviously talking to whoever was inside.

She mentally shook her head at herself for jumping so easily at noises. She was becoming super-sensitive lately. Just as she went to carry on her way, something sprang to mind, making her take another look at the man with the van.

No. It can't be.

Pretending to faff about with the bag hanging on the pram, she stole another look at the medium-built man with the ginger hair. He had an armful of red roses close to his chin, but his face was revealed enough for her to see quite clearly.

It's him.

Just for a moment, she froze. There was no way she was standing on the same street as the man she had slept with a year ago. He'd been at the bar. All smiles and something resembling heartache. It was no big deal. Two adults keeping each other company just for one night. So what if she wanted more than the brandy to warm her. Why couldn't she do something wild and out of character for a change?

Beth's brain was slowly starting to wake from the trance she was in with the florist.

No, no, no, no, no.

She hurried away, picking up speed until she turned a corner. At last, she could take a breath, not that it went anywhere. Her chest was doing its boa constrictor thing again, refusing to allow air to fill her lungs. She tapped below her neck. How could it just stop there? Was there a wall or something that she didn't know about? What the hell was her breath doing?

Archie was still happily in the land of nod, and Beth so wished she was too. With everything going wrong with her mind lately, perhaps she'd imagined her one-night stand holding red roses in the street. After all, it was plausible.

Should she go back and check? It seemed the logical thing to do, but somewhere back during her pregnancy logic had left her, and she still hadn't tracked it down.

Beth shook her head, checked Archie once more, then headed home, not knowing what to do.

He's Archie's dad. I have to tell him.

But she couldn't. She didn't know how. Would he believe her anyway? It had been a year since the conference. Who was he? Another teacher or health care worker, or was he the man who had delivered the flower arrangements for the foyer, then stuck around for some free food?

There was she thinking herself wild and carefree. No names, no numbers. The last night in the hotel. Home first thing. She'd stopped grinning to herself about her escapade the moment the pregnancy stick said *positive*. If only she'd had the guts to ring around some of her colleagues to ask if they knew of a ginger man at the conference. As far as she could remember, there were a few men there sporting the copper colour.

The walk home seemed to take longer than usual, but that was because she had slowed, deep in thought. She had found him. Archie's dad, and he wasn't some child psychologist, as imagined. He sold flowers. In Port Berry.

Just as she questioned what she had witnessed down by the harbour, a small white van came into eyeshot. *Berry Blooms*, it said along the side, and, just as quickly as the vehicle appeared, it was gone.

Well if that wasn't a sign from above to confirm she wasn't dreaming, she didn't know what was.

Beth's jelly legs normally got her home, but today her racing heart and light head were freaking out about something else. At least this time she could understand why her nerves were playing up. The panic often came out of nowhere for no reason, adding confusion into the mix. Still, the feeling had her hurry home, because if she was going to be afraid of whatever was happening to her body, she wasn't about to do it in public.

Bumping the hefty pram up three flights of stairs to her front door, while the lift was being fixed, only caused her chest to constrict even more. The back of her lungs felt so bruised, and the fluttering in her heart couldn't be healthy.

Relieved to finally be indoors, Beth cried, covering her mouth to hold in any possible noise she might make. She fumbled her way around the small kitchen, dropping things and losing count of the scoops of baby formula. But still she rushed, hoping the activity would ease the fear she was feeling. If she just kept going, it would fade. How else could she make it go away? She didn't even know what was happening to her.

CHAPTER 5

Spencer

'Flower arranging badge?' questioned Leo. 'I didn't think you were serious about that.'

Spencer held back his laugh. 'It's still arts and crafts. I find it quite relaxing. Afterwards we can pop in the café and have hot chocolate.'

'I'm for the hot chocolate part,' said Jax.

Ryan quirked one eyebrow. 'It's Valentine's Day tomorrow?' He turned to his friends. 'It's the busiest time for flower shops. My dad told me.' He motioned towards Spencer. 'We can help you with that.'

'That's two badges then,' said Leo.

'How is it two?' asked Spencer.

Leo flipped his cape off his shoulder. 'One for flower arranging, and one for being kind by helping you.'

Spencer chuckled. There was no arguing with that. 'Yes, great idea. A kindness badge it is.'

Jax removed his coat. 'So, what do we have to do?'

Lottie came out of the back room of the shop. 'Ooh, hello.'

Spencer raised a finger. 'And . . .'

On cue, the lads started singing 'Happy Birthday', making her smile stretch as wide as possible.

'Well, thank you,' said Lottie. 'But my birthday is tomorrow.'

'But we won't see you then,' said Leo, chewing his cape.

'In that case, and after that wonderful performance, you can all take a small bouquet home with you later.'

Leo and Jax followed her into the back room while Ryan stayed in the shopfront with Spencer.

'There is so much red in here.' Ryan was gazing up at hanging paper love hearts.

Spencer grinned. 'It doesn't always look like this. We're just getting ready for the big day.'

Ryan gestured at the back room. 'Not sure Jax will like it out here when the customers come in. You know he has to get to know people first.'

'We're making flower arrangements out back, and it's only Lottie working today. He won't be asked to do anything else or be out the front.'

Ryan nodded his approval, then joined the others, leaving Spencer feeling proud of how the boy looked out for his friends. They were a small circle but had bonded well at the Sunshine Centre. There was real trust between them, and it was nice to witness, especially seeing Leo put his trust in any child.

Debra had told Spencer that Leo wouldn't make friends with any children at first. His nerves were too rattled from being bullied at school.

Spencer remembered the fights he'd get into himself, and how often his aunt was called to the school. Rebecca was so lovely, talking things through with him, rather than shouting. Sometimes he was sure it was only the love from her that held him together.

He entered the back room to see the boys gathered around the large table, with Lottie handing out instructions. She too was a member of the Sunshine Centre, so it was easy for the children to settle with her, having seen her around often.

Had it not been for Lottie's accident, he would have never entered the place. He'd heard of it, most had, but it wasn't something he'd thought about. Perhaps he should have joined a long time ago so he had somewhere to go to help clear his head, rather than a pub and a one-night stand. He was so glad he had moved on from that chapter of his life.

'We've had another idea for a badge,' said Leo.

Spencer was loving the enthusiasm. 'Let's hear it then.'

Leo let the cord from his cape slip from his mouth. 'Festival badge.'

Spencer had to laugh. 'You want me to take you to a festival?'

Ryan shook his head. 'No, he means we organize one.'

That idea was even more bizarre.

'Hear them out,' said Lottie.

Leo raised his index finger. 'There are lots of people at the centre who need help.' He moved his finger to his chest. 'So we could have an awareness day. Mum always says the world needs more love. So how about a kindness festival?'

Jax agreed. 'I wish everyone was kind.'

'A kindness awareness day,' said Lottie.

Leo beamed. 'We can make noise at our festival.'

Spencer raised his brow. 'Noise?'

Leo shrugged and started cutting some ribbon. 'Mum says you have to make noise sometimes to be heard. She likes to go on protests at times.' He turned sharply to Jax. 'Oh, my mum's going to give your dad information on home-schooling for you. She's been speaking to your dad.'

Jax turned to Ryan as though asking for his thoughts.

'It's up to you, Jax,' he told him.

Jax nodded. 'Yes, I'd like to do that.'

Spencer pulled some of the stems towards him as he sat. 'That's nice of your mum, Leo.'

'Wish I could be home-schooled,' said Ryan. 'My school is boring.'

Jax frowned. 'Your school has its own swimming pool.'

Judging by the scowl on Ryan's face, Spencer thought it best to change the subject.

'So, Lottie, where you off to for your birthday?'

The boys all looked up.

'Once we've finished here on Valentine's Day, we're off to a hotel in Devon for a couple of nights. But I already can't wait to come back and help you lot organize the festival of the century.'

Leo giggled. 'Mum knows a man who plays in a band. Has a banjo and everything. We can ask him to play songs at the festival.'

'Good idea,' said Lottie. 'And we can put up a notice in the Hub asking for volunteers.'

'And set up stalls,' said Spencer. 'I'll talk to Debra first. See if we can make our festival part of the Sunshine Centre's fundraising events.'

Leo fist-bumped the air, then stayed in a superhero pose for a moment before reaching out for some flowers.

Spencer made a mental note to tell Luna more badges had been invented.

'We're better than any other team,' scoffed Jax.

'Yeah,' cheered Ryan. 'We're the . . . What are we called?'

Silence loomed for a moment while everyone put their thinking caps on.

'The Sunshine Superheroes,' said Leo, looking mighty chuffed with himself.

Jax turned to him, frowning.

Ryan laughed. 'I'm not wearing a badge that says that, but if it makes Leo happy, we can have that name.'

'Yes!' cheered Leo, once more adopting his pose.

Spencer looked around the table and smiled. He was so happy with his life now, and having a kindness awareness event to organize lifted his spirits just that little bit more, especially as the idea had come from the children, who seemed happy to make plans, even Jax.

Lottie caught his eye and smiled. 'Remember the pop-up stand we had for the Hub at the Port Berry Craft Fayre? We could have more of those dotted around filled with info on all sorts. The more educated people are about things, the easier it is for them to have compassion.'

He had to agree. 'Yes, we can have information on mental health as well as physical disabilities, and let's not forget those with invisible disabilities, like Alice. She has to wear a badge asking for a seat when she's using public transport, as no one can see how she might be feeling that day from fibromyalgia.'

'She can't always stand for too long,' Lottie told the boys.

'My mum had a row with a woman on the bus once about those badges,' said Leo. 'Another woman told a boy off for not giving up his seat to the lady with a badge, and his mum had a go at her because her son had problems with his hips. That's why he didn't get up. Hypomobil-something.' He shrugged. 'Anyway, my mum told the woman not to judge people. They might have their own reasons for not giving up their seat. The driver got involved in the end because there was lots of shouting.'

Spencer sighed, louder than he'd intended. 'It makes me feel as though we should all have badges.'

Lottie blew upwards at her fringe. 'If people were less judgemental and more kind, we wouldn't have these problems.'

'We should ask Debra to have the kindness festival at the centre, then more people will see how helpful being kind is,' said Ryan. 'I'm always happy there.'

'That's a good point,' said Spencer, 'but she'd have to close the quiet areas down for the day, and she won't want to do that in case they're needed. No, best we ask Councillor Seabridge for use of Old Market Square and Anchorage Park, once we've got Debra on board, that is.'

'She'll say yes,' said Leo. 'She loves kindness.'

The boys started to mutter among themselves about the festival while Spencer and Lottie shared a smile. He could tell by the way she looked at him that she was proud of him too. It was a good feeling, finally having purpose. What with the Happy to Help Hub and the Sunshine Centre, Spencer felt he'd found somewhere he was needed.

Once Rebecca had taken over as their parent, Lottie no longer needed him to feed and wash her. It was good for his little sister. Two-year-olds needed care, and even though his aunt fussed him, making sure he never had to lift a finger in her home, part of him was at a loose end. It seemed to stay with him as he grew. He spent many years feeling useless, and nobody knew.

CHAPTER 6

Beth

It was quiet outside. Cold and dark. Beth pulled away from the window, glad to see the back of another day. It was bad enough watching couples walk hand in hand the previous night for Valentine's Day. She didn't want to see love. It didn't belong to her, and now she was slowly losing her mind, the chances of having that sort of love in her life was slim to none. Who'd want her? A broken mess of a woman.

Beth couldn't get Spencer out of her head. She knew his name now, thanks to an online search of his shop. She felt so intrusive looking, but she had to. A family-run business, and just that line alone in the info section made her scoff. A rush of adrenaline had hit her heart when she saw Lottie's name, but she soon settled when it became clear Lottie was his sister not wife.

Another search later, and she discovered he lived above the premises. He also had ties with the Happy to Help Hub in Port Berry, and the Sunshine Centre over in Penzance. Seemed he was one of life's helpers, not just a florist. He was in the mental health care profession for children. There was so much about him she didn't know. Everything in fact. Her heart pounded each time she set eyes on something about him on the screen. She was sure her finger would slip, hit the wrong key, and somehow let him know someone was online stalking him.

Closing her eyes as she slouched onto the sofa, she took a minute to dissect her life. She was beyond tired, in every way, and couldn't function properly. Why, oh why couldn't she just be like other mums? Everyone else seemed to cope.

She sat up, glancing at her son sleeping in a cream Moses basket on the living-room floor.

Poor Archie. You deserve better.

Numbness held off any tears.

Grabbing the phone, she decided it would be for the best if she called her cousin, if only to help clear her head.

'Hello, Pearl.'

'You okay, Beth? You're calling late.'

Beth glanced at her phone to see it was half eight. The noise of Pearl's children in the background met her ears as she returned to the call. 'Sorry, lost track of time.'

Pearl's voice softened. 'How's it going in the new place? You unboxed everything yet?'

'Still waiting for you, aren't I?'

'Sorry, yes, I know I said I'd be over, but what with the kids, work, and Raj, I don't know where the time's gone.'

Beth let her off the hook. 'It's done, stop flapping.' She glanced at one stack by the telly. Telling a small fib would ease her busy cousin, so what did it matter?

'I got you to move this way so we'd be closer now the baby's here, and there's me never around.'

'I'm okay, Pearl. I was just calling for a chat, that's all. Archie's fast asleep, but I can hear yours are still up.'

'Raj is on bath duty tonight, that's why the pair of them are running around like it's Christmas Eve night.'

'Don't blame me,' called out Pearl's husband.

Beth listened to their conversation involving quiet time, too many bubbles in the tub, and the kids giggling. She smiled at their happiness, always loving being in Pearl's home. The whole atmosphere of the place was as soothing as hot chocolate on a snowy night.

Beth's living room suddenly looked bleak. Was that how her life would be from now on? Lifeless. No laughter. No bubble baths. No one to kiss her cheek, as she heard down the phone before her cousin came back to her.

'Sorry about that, Beth. So, how's the little man?'

Archie looked his adorable self, peaceful with his dreams. She'd ignored his cries at five a.m. the other day, as sleep was needed, not his racket ringing in her ears. *How much longer could she hold out before he was silent?* Not long, it turned out. She'd seen to his needs, then spent the rest of the day feeling guilty she'd left him to cry for a solid ten minutes. What kind of mother did that? His nappy was dirty. He wasn't asking for much. He needed her, and she'd clasped her hands over her ears and buried her head in the pillow. The shame of the moment still haunted her.

'He's good.' Beth hesitated, wondering if she could confide in Pearl about how lousy she was at motherhood, or what was happening to her mind. At the very least she could mention seeing Spencer Jordan.

Pearl's children were close to the phone again, causing Beth to pull back a touch. Their high-pitched screams weren't the calm chat she was expecting.

'Look, Pearl, I can hear you're busy. I'll call another time.'

'Sorry, babe. Honestly, it's all go here tonight.'

'Speak soon.'

'Bye, Beth. Love you.'

'Love you too.' And with that, Beth ended the call.

It was as though someone just dumped a whole heap on darkness on her head, as the feeling of emptiness hit hard. If it weren't for the low light from the lamp in the corner of the room, she would have been sure there was no light left in the world at all.

I want to be normal again.

She gazed at her son.

You deserve a life like Pearl's kids have. I can't give you that. I can't give you anything.

Slowly and calmly Beth set about packing Archie's pram bag. She filled it with some clothes, nappies, and a tub of baby milk. His bottles were packed, as was his washbag. She added an extra blanket to the pram, then sat at the small dining table squashed into one corner of the living room and started to write in the notebook she used for shopping lists.

As much as she knew Archie would be safe and loved with her cousin, she also knew Pearl would be on her case if she dumped the baby on her.

Carefully, she cradled Archie, placing him gently in his pram. He stirred slightly, wriggled his arms, then drifted back to sleep.

What was she doing? She knew exactly what she was doing. She just couldn't stop herself. Even the bitter cold air failed to wake her from the trance she seemed captured in. Her feet moved by themselves. Her body forced to join the trip. Her mind unable to comment or complain.

The journey down to Harbour End Road seemed to take all of five minutes, and if one person passed her along the way, she didn't see them.

Beth steered the pram to the harbour wall, looking out at the blackness of the sea. It looked deadly out there tonight. No stars or full moon to romanticize the scene. No jolly sailors singing sea shanties while aboard their vessels. Just the low hum of moving water.

She turned to face the shops on the other side, closed up for the night. Lights from the flats above were dimmed by drapes or blinds, and no shadows passed the windows.

Glancing over her shoulder, she wondered if the upturned dinghy could be another option. The shingles surrounding it were damp but accessible. No boulders or slippery seaweed to cause obstruction in the dark. How easy it would be to sail away to wherever the tide decided.

A gust of wind caught her mousey hair, flicking a long strand close to her eye, making her blink. It was enough to get her moving her weary limbs.

Checking the street and the windows up high for signs of life, Beth took a calming breath. No one was about, so she headed over to the door beside the flower shop.

Archie was snuggled, unaware of his fate. He was her life now, and she loved every inch of him, but it wasn't fair he had a mother who was broken. Perhaps if she just had one week to herself to sleep, she would be able to think clearly, not feel scared, and figure out what to do.

If I left him, would he die? Would I?

Heart palpitations took centre stage. The hand reaching towards his warm cheek shook, and not from lack of gloves. Beth could feel parts of her cracking under the strain of what, she couldn't say. It was just torture. Day in, day out. How was she still standing? How was she still alive when the fear that ran through her daily felt like death was upon her? Nothing made sense. Nothing but one thing.

She leaned into the pram, pushing a note into the side of the mattress. 'I'll not be far, baby boy,' she whispered. 'I love you so much.' Closing her eyes, she raised her face to the sky, taking a moment to just breathe.

Something clanked over by the boats, and Beth looked around her once more. She wasn't sure how she raised her index finger to the doorbell and pressed it. She felt as though she'd left her body and it was functioning on its own, under its own steam. She sprinted across the road and dipped low behind the harbour wall.

Each second passing could have been hours. Beth could barely breathe. Then it happened. The street door opened, the backlight revealing golden copper-brown streaked hair.

Beth peeked from her hiding spot, knowing the lack of lamps where she shivered would keep her hidden.

Spencer had one arm around the back of his neck as he stepped out to the pavement searching the street. He looked in doorways, then over to the boats. Shaking his head, he dipped low to the pram, then called out, 'Hello?'

Beth lowered.

Take him. Take him inside.

She closed her eyes, willing the man to do what she asked. Not one part of her said it would be for the best if she just popped up and explained her situation.

Another call filled the air, then silence.

Beth slowly raised her head just in time to see Spencer lift the pram and carry it up the stairs to his flat. She waited awhile, knowing he would appear again to close his front door.

He peered down the street once more, hands on hips, and Beth could only imagine the scowl on his face. After what seemed like forever, he went back indoors, closing his world on hers.

Beth slumped to the cold ground and stared out to sea. If God should strike her down, she hoped it would be with immediate effect.

CHAPTER 7

Spencer

Having just opened his laptop to browse through pictures of past events on the Sunshine Centre's website to grab some inspiration for the kindness festival idea, the doorbell rang.

Spencer sighed to the ceiling. 'Typical.' He'd just got comfy as well, snuggling on the sofa, a hot chocolate to his side, and a blanket on his legs.

The idea to ignore the caller, knowing it wouldn't be Lottie because she was still in Devon with Samuel, didn't last long. It still could be important, so begrudgingly he got up, sliding into his navy slippers.

Plodding down the stairway while stretching his back, he yawned. Who on earth was knocking for him at gone nine o'clock at night?

It took two looks to register the pram on his doorstep, and even then he was sure he must be seeing things. Checking along the street for the owner, he called out, but no one answered.

Bags and boxes were often left of a night outside the charity shop, and someone had placed a box of non-perishable food items in front of the Hub one night. Maybe the pram had just rolled his way. Although, why the owner had rung his bell was anyone's guess.

Spencer gazed in the pram, expecting to see such items. His jaw hung loose as he came face to face with a baby. An actual real-life baby.

What the hell!

It didn't matter how many times he looked, nothing changed. A sleeping baby was in a pram on his doorstep and there was no sign of anyone else in the street.

After confusion faded, Spencer thought it best to take the baby into the warmth of his flat and call the police. He checked once more before closing his door, but still there was no one about.

Grabbing his phone, he peered down at the cute infant. 'Aww, bless. Don't worry, I've got you,' he whispered. He went to straighten, then noticed the note wedged along the side. Straight away his stomach flipped and he felt pity for the child.

Please don't tell me this is what I think it is.

He sat on a chair close to the pram and unfolded the paper, shoulders sinking immediately, as it became quite clear from the first line that it was exactly what he thought. Someone had purposely dumped their baby. But why on his doorstep? Why not somewhere else, like the church? It wasn't far.

With little brain power to enter the mind of the mother, Spencer continued to read the letter out loud so he absorbed each and every word.

'*Please look after my baby. His name is Archie, and he's three months old. He likes cuddles, and his favourite toy is the small panda in his pram.*' Spencer took a moment to control his breathing. His heart was already broken for the poor little thing. '*I just need some time. Please don't tell anyone. I'll come back, I promise.*'

The watermark made Spencer visualize a teardrop falling on the page. He glanced at his phone, wondering if a call to his friend Henley would be the best idea. Henley was a social worker, after all, and he worked closely with the Hub. He'd know the right channels to go through for this sort of situation.

Perhaps he could call January Riley. As a therapist she might be able to track down the mother and offer help. Jan was brilliant like that. He'd seen her help many people who came into the Hub.

Little Archie was none the wiser, and Spencer was still utterly gobsmacked. He read the next line on the note and all colour drained from his already pale face.

That did not just say that.

He double-checked. Reading aloud to help the words sink in. '*He's your son, Spencer. Please believe me. He's yours, and I just need you to care for him a little while.*'

Not much else happened for a few beats after that discovery, as Spencer fell into some sort of trance with the pram.

A low grumble came from the baby, causing Spencer to jump to his feet, arms splayed in front as if telling the child to halt.

Archie settled, and Spencer inhaled deeply, feeling his chest tighten.

This isn't happening. No, no, no.

He held the letter high to his face, staring at it blankly until his brain woke and caught up with the moment. The next part of the letter told him the baby would want feeding at around eleven, then should settle till early morning.

The large grey bag hanging on the handle caught his eye. It was bulging but sealed. Moving it to the table to unpack, one of the first things he saw was the large tub of powdered milk. He hadn't made up a bottle since he was eight. Had much changed? The bottles looked clean, but had they been sterilized? It was a relief to see a box of sterilizing tablets in the bag. Quickly, he pulled out a bowl from one of the lower cupboards in the kitchen and got on with the task, following the instructions as best he could with a frazzled mind.

Archie was still enjoying his snooze time, which was a small mercy. What would he think when he woke to find his mother gone and some strange man holding his food?

Raking a hand through his locks, he flopped back onto the chair. 'What the hell am I going to do?' he mumbled.

Something needed to make sense so he could take the next step, but his head was in a whirl. He glanced once more at the snuggled bundle, noticing little Archie had a touch of Lottie about his features. Was this really his child? Not that it mattered to his current situation. A boy needed care, and care he would get, whoever he was.

Spencer chewed the inside of his cheek as he contemplated calling his sister. Lottie would tell him to call social services, as most would, but most hadn't been whisked off to live with strangers like he had as a child, so why would they understand his reluctance to hand the kid over?

Still, he felt the need to talk to someone, and Lottie was the one he trusted most in the world.

I can't. She's enjoying her birthday trip.

Well, that was one excuse, and a pretty solid one at that, but he knew he was going to have to tell her at some point, especially as it appeared Archie was sticking around for a while, and Lottie would notice when he turned up for work pushing a pram.

Best get it over with.

'Spence? Is everything all right?' Lottie said before he'd had a chance to say hello.

It was late, after all, and she knew he knew she was in Devon, sharing a romantic break with her partner.

Spencer swallowed hard while trying to find the right words for the job. 'Something's happened. I have a guest. Well, the thing is . . . So, what happened was . . . erm.' His shoulders drooped along with his voice.

'Spit it out, Spence. You're making my nerves rattle.'

'It's a baby. He's here. Archie. He's right here.'

There was silence for a moment, then Lottie cleared her throat. 'Okay, Spence, you need to take a breath, then explain using a proper sentence.'

Inhaling deeply only made him lightheaded. 'Someone left a baby on my doorstep just now.'

Lottie's gasp caused him to move the phone from his ear. 'What! Have you called the police?'

The memory of officers dragging his parents off to a police car hit.

'Spencer!' Lottie shouted.

'No,' he snapped, not meaning to.

Her breathing had settled, he could hear, but he knew she was still annoyed by his lack of action.

'What's going on?' came Samuel's muffled voice in the background.

Spencer listened while his sister explained. It wasn't long before she was back to talking to him.

'Look, Spence, I know how you feel about foster homes and such, but if someone's left their baby, the police have to know, or at least call Henley. He'll know what to do for the best.'

'He's my son.'

Silence loomed.

Lottie must have mouthed the information to Samuel, because Spencer heard him say, 'Oh.'

'I'll be there as soon as I can,' said Lottie. 'Sam's already packing our things.'

'No, you don't need to come here. Enjoy your last night at the hotel. I'll see you tomorrow.'

Lottie scoffed, cracking the line. 'Oh, yeah, because I'm really going to sleep soundly tonight with this on my mind.' A loud sigh followed. 'How do you know he's your son?' she asked quietly, sounding somewhat suspicious.

Spencer explained about the letter, then read it out when she asked to hear it. There was another round of silence, which was good, as he needed the break to wrap his head around the facts too.

'Do you know who she is?' asked Lottie.

The question made him cringe at his old self. He'd had way too many one-night stands, but as far as he was concerned, he'd always been careful. While shaking his head at himself, Lottie repeated her question, this time with a snap to her tone.

'No,' he mumbled.

'Oh, come on. Surely you must have some idea. The letter said Archie's three months, right? So add that to the nine months in the womb, assuming she went full term, and that's twelve months. One year, Spence. What were you doing around this time last year?'

'How can you expect me to remember what . . .' He trailed off as his cogs started to turn. Yes, yes he did know what he was doing in February the year before. He was at the childcare conference, as it was helpful to his course. 'Bloody hell,' he muttered, eyes widening at the memory.

After Lottie's accident, he'd made the decision not to sleep around anymore, but he caved that one night at the hotel. The regret he'd felt the next morning waking in his room had him leaving for home before the sun came up. He'd been so thankful he'd left her room the night before. At least he didn't have to see her ever again.

He gazed at Archie.

'I honestly thought you'd stopped all that, Spence,' said Lottie, waking him from his memory. 'You said you had when you *finally* told me about your new chapter.' The disappointment in her tone didn't go unnoticed.

'She was the last time,' he said, wallowing in his own disappointment. 'I haven't been with anyone since. And now I'm thinking clearly, it has to be her.'

'Do you know her name?'

Even though she couldn't see him, he still shook his head. His lack of reply told her the answer.

'Oh,' said Lottie. 'Well, where did you meet her?'

'A conference.'

Lottie seemed to perk up. 'That's good. We can track her down from there. Was she staff, a delegate? A—'

'I didn't see her on any panels, so I can only assume she was there to learn, like me.' He flopped his head to the table. 'Oh, I don't know.'

'It's okay, we'll figure it out.'

'We don't have to do anything, Lott. She said she'd be back soon. I can speak to her then.'

'No, Spence. We need to find her as soon as possible. She's obviously not well or struggling somehow to dump her baby. She needs help. Maybe she's in a dangerous situation or something. We can't just wait around to see if she pops back up.'

Spencer straightened. He'd been so preoccupied with finding out he had a son, wondering what to do next, and talking to his sister, he didn't stop to think the mother might be in danger. He glanced once more over her written words. 'She said she just needed some time.' Saying the words out loud somehow comforted him. 'He's so young, she probably got a bit overwhelmed with it all.' He hoped it was something as simple as that.

Lottie sighed. 'I'll be there soon.'

'No need. It's late, and he'll want a bottle in a couple of hours, then we'll all need some sleep. I'm not doing anything about this till morning, so you might as well come round then.'

'Spencer, please call someone.'

'In the morning. Just let him settle here tonight. Like I said, it's late.'

'But what if she's hurt?'

A pain hit his temple. He couldn't think about that. A baby needed him. His baby, by all accounts. And something told him the mother would return. Maybe it was hope, but it was what he held on to as he hung up his call and turned once more to stare into the pram.

CHAPTER 8

Beth

'I can't believe this!' yelled Pearl.

It had been the worst night of Beth's life. She was sure her mind had left her altogether. Not much else could explain the madness.

Pearl's dark hair was almost touching her cheek, she was bent over so close, and Beth wanted to flick it away. Flick her cousin away, but she had made the mistake of calling her, and now she had to suffer the consequences. Not that anything Pearl said mattered. She could scream the building down and yell out all sorts of insults, but nothing would make Beth feel as bad as she already did.

'Beth, you need to get up. Do you hear me?' Pearl tried to drag her off the sofa, but Beth groaned and pulled away.

'Please leave me,' she whispered, a wedge of guilt lodged in her throat. 'I don't want to do anything.'

'You have to do something. You can't stay in this state.' Pearl gave up tugging and flopped to the other end of the seat. 'You left your baby with a stranger. I need you to talk to me so I can go get him back.'

'He's safe. With his dad.'

Pearl's dark eyes widened. 'What do you mean, *his dad*? You told me you didn't know who his dad was. One-night stand, wasn't it? You being footloose and fancy free, right? Flipping heck, Beth, wake up!'

Beth groaned to an upright position, sinking her body as close to the arm of the seat as possible so she wasn't touching Pearl. It was understandable her cousin would be fuming, but there was no way Pearl would understand the reasons for the abandonment. Beth couldn't understand it much herself.

All night, she thought she'd be able to breathe more freely, but that didn't work. The long, cold walk home hadn't snapped her out of zombie mode, and staring at the ceiling for the best part of the night only drained her even further.

Beth looked to the door, half expecting men in white coats to burst in and carry her away. If only someone could make her mind work properly again. Perhaps feel. She was so numb, tired, lonely, and quite possibly the worst person on the planet.

Pearl's words weren't sinking in much. Everything fading in and out. All Beth wanted was to curl up and be left to die. She didn't deserve any kind words or sympathy from her cousin. She just needed quiet.

'That will be Jan,' said Pearl.

Beth became alert. 'Who?' Her bloodshot eyes moved to the doorway as she realized someone was knocking on her front door.

'I told you I called Raj's friend, January Riley. She's here to help.' Pearl moved to open the door, and Beth felt too exhausted to care. 'She's a therapist,' added Pearl. 'What you need right now.'

Before Beth had time to blink, a middle-aged woman with dark eyes was smiling gently down at her. Beth focused on the woman's mass of blonde curls, thinking them pretty against the woman's dark skin. Her own head was greasy and no doubt smelled.

'Hello, Beth. I'm January Riley, but everyone calls me Jan.' She sat on the sofa while Pearl announced she was off to make some tea. 'How you feeling?'

If I knew that, I could help myself, thanks!

Beth took a calming breath as best she could, then burst out crying, which really was unexpected. Pearl came running in, tissues in hand, and cradled her into her arms.

'I don't know what's going on,' Pearl mumbled to Jan, but Beth heard.

'Whatever is going on,' said Jan, a little louder so Beth could definitely hear over her slowing sobs, 'we're going to figure it out, and I can promise you, everything's going to be all right.'

It was reassuring to hear, but that was all.

Beth loosened Pearl's grip, then wiped her nose when her cousin stood to fetch the tea.

'Why don't we start at the beginning, Beth. See if we can spot the trigger for all this.' Jan's voice was as soothing as the lullabies she'd sing to Archie.

Oh no, she couldn't start crying again. How dare she feel sorry for herself after the stunt she had pulled last night? She needed to reach for some focus. Talk to the woman. It could hardly make matters worse.

Thinking back, Beth recalled the day fear overtook her mind, body, and soul. It wasn't hard to remember.

'You can pinpoint the moment, can't you?' said Jan, offering a reassuring smile.

Beth gave a slight nod. 'I was in my last stage of pregnancy.' She continued to share her nightmare, wondering what the therapist would make of the journey from hell she'd been on. She was still figuring it out herself.

'Ah, I see,' said Jan, once more had been explained. 'What happened to you during that time were panic attacks. What's happening to you now is PTSD.'

Beth didn't mean to scoff. It just came out. Jan was making her sound like she was ex-forces or something. 'I haven't been to war,' she said quietly, even though part of her felt she had. 'I don't have flashbacks.'

Jan smiled softly as she closed a notebook on her lap that Beth had only just noticed. 'People always think that's what PTSD is all about. But there is so much more to the condition, and it's not just linked to the military. It's caused by all sorts of trauma, and what you went through was traumatic. It didn't help not knowing what was happening to you. It's always worse when you have no label for your problem.'

The therapist was right, just handing out medical terms had made things slightly clearer.

'But I do know some stuff about anxiety,' said Beth. 'I'm a primary school teacher, and I've had a few kids in my class who suffer with their nerves.'

'Knowing about it and having a full-blown panic attack swipe you off your feet are two very different things.' Jan thanked Pearl for the tea she passed over. 'You now know what it feels like, and you have discovered there is so much more to the issue than just the fear it causes.'

'So, that's it?' asked Pearl, sitting on the chair opposite Beth. 'Trauma is causing this?' She turned to Beth. 'I wish I had known about your pregnancy problem. I would have tried to help you.'

'I didn't know what was happening to me. I assumed I was cracking up. I wouldn't let the doctors near me at first. I wasn't just afraid, I was petrified, and I couldn't do anything about it because I kept freezing. It was such a weird feeling. I felt stuck.' Beth glanced at Jan.

A wave of gentleness flashed through Jan's eyes. 'Well, now I know your story and what led you to where we are today, we can work on getting you better.'

Beth swiped away a tear. 'I thought I'd gone insane. I lost my voice, Jan. I couldn't communicate with anyone, and I just wanted the world to leave me to die. Are you sure that was just anxiety doing that to me? I honestly thought the condition was just about fear, not irrational behaviour and feeling lost.'

'Oh, there's a lot more to all mental health problems than most people think. Look at you just now with the PTSD subject. Like most, you linked it to the armed forces, and all you knew about its symptoms was flashbacks. Your night sweats, hypervigilance, thinking you're going to die, your baby might die. It's all increased alertness, keeping you triggered at all times. That's PTSD.'

Pearl folded her arms in a huff. 'Why didn't the hospital staff tell her that?'

'I wasn't having most of that then,' said Beth. 'Just the panic. It waved through me whenever they came near me, wanting to induce labour, but I didn't know what was happening to me. I wanted to give birth, I really did, but it was as though a wall appeared from nowhere and just brought me to a stop. I couldn't get past it. I couldn't even speak.'

Pearl turned to Jan. 'But why wouldn't the doctors and nurses recognize that?'

Beth shook her hands, clutching her fingers to calm the tremble. 'Not one person in that hospital mentioned anything to do with mental illness.' She cast her mind back to clarify. It was true, no one said a word. 'I guess they just thought I was scared.'

'Okay,' said Jan. 'At least we know how this started, so let's take some time to work out a recovery plan for you, Beth. It's for the best if we stay focused on your healing.'

The thought alone made Beth feel as though air was back in her lungs. From the way Jan was speaking, it might just be possible she'd be able to get back to normal at some point. Hope filled her from head to toe. It was a start, and way more than she'd had for months.

'We need to talk about Archie now,' added Jan, and that small light in Beth suddenly dimmed to a dot.

'It's okay, Beth,' said Pearl. 'We'll get him back.'

'I think he's better off where he is for now,' she told her cousin, then looked to Jan for her reaction.

Jan still held the warmest smile. 'I need to know where he is, Beth. I know you're safe, and now I need to make sure Archie's in the best place.'

'He can always stay with me,' said Pearl.

'He's safe,' snapped Beth, not meaning to. 'Sorry.'

Jan's head bobbed. 'It's okay, Beth.'

'He's with his dad.'

'Who she doesn't know,' said Pearl.

Beth locked eyes with her. 'I do now.' She turned to Jan. 'It was a one-night stand. But recently I bumped into him again, sort of. Anyway, once I knew his name, I looked him up. He works with kids, which means he's been vetted.' She took a moment to explain that to herself again, then glared at Pearl. 'I wasn't thinking straight, okay.'

Pearl sipped her tea, obviously deciding not to respond.

Jan leaned a touch closer. 'It would be helpful all round if I knew where this man lived.'

A flutter hit Beth's solar plexus. 'No. You'll take Archie away or someone else will. He'll be put into a foster home.' She swiped away another tear.

'No, not at all,' said Jan. 'Archie has two parents, and if one of them wants him, then he'll have a home with them. Children aren't taken from their parents for no reason.'

'But I have a reason. I left him on a doorstep.'

Pearl looked at Jan. 'For all we know, Archie's dad might have already called social services and handed him over.'

A cold chill came over Beth. 'But I wrote him a letter. I told him he was Archie's father, and I said I'll be back soon. Surely he wouldn't . . .' Another tear fell.

'Best thing we can do right now is find out,' said Jan. 'Do you think you could tell me his name, Beth? I promise everything I do from this moment forward will be in yours and Archie's best interests. Hey, I'm on your side. If you need some time, that's fine. If you want your son back, I'll make it happen. But I will feel a lot better knowing Archie is safe right now.'

'Tell her, Beth. I'm worried about Archie too, you know,' said Pearl.

Beth took a deep breath, trying to loosen her tight lungs. 'His name is Spencer Jordan.'

Jan's eyebrows lifted. 'Spencer?'

'You know him?' asked Pearl.

'Yes, I work closely with the Happy to Help Hub where he volunteers. He's one of the creators of the place.'

Pearl nodded. 'Not seen it myself, but heard of it. But I thought he worked with children.'

'His name came up linked to the Sunshine Centre as well,' Beth told her.

'That's right,' said Jan. 'He's trained in health care for children.'

'And he's a florist,' Beth told Pearl, whose eyes had gone as wide as they could go.

'Flipping heck, he gets around.'

Jan smiled softly. 'Spencer is a good man.' It sounded as though her exhale was filled with relief, which lightened the load for Beth a touch.

'He is?' she asked, earning an eye roll from her cousin.

Jan's curls bounced as her head bobbed. 'He is. Archie is in good hands. At least we don't have to worry about that.'

'How do you know he hasn't called in a social worker?' asked Pearl.

Beth narrowed her eyes at Jan's expression, as it seemed to hold a secret.

'Because I know Spencer,' replied Jan. 'He wouldn't give up Archie for all the tea in China.'

Instead of feeling reassured, Beth was suddenly worried. Had she lost her son to the stranger? Was she about to go into battle with more than her mental health?

CHAPTER 9

Spencer

There were so many nappies lining the supermarket shelf, Spencer felt a little overwhelmed. He clutched the shopping trolley, wondering which was the best brand to buy. Things had changed since he was eight, and the corner shop never did have much in the way of choice anyway, so it was easy for him to know what to buy when his mum sent him off with a few quid and plastic carrier bag.

Homing in on the nearest packet, he widened his eyes at the price. 'What!'

'Shocking, isn't it?' said a female voice.

Spencer turned to the pretty lady around his age. 'Oh, yes. They cost a fair bit.'

'And the milk.'

Spencer glanced down at the two large tubs in his trolley and wondered if Archie's mum was struggling financially. 'Hmm,' he muttered.

'Do you need any help?' she asked, edging closer.

He politely declined the offer and carried on examining the guides on the nappies until he found ones suitable for Archie.

He checked his phone before seeing what else he could buy. Lottie hadn't messaged him, so he assumed she was doing okay looking after Archie with Samuel.

He had told them not to come back last night, but they had anyway, and thank the lord they had. Poor Archie was ever so distraught on seeing a stranger trying to feed him, and no matter what Spencer did, it wasn't soothing enough to comfort the child.

Archie had spent most of the night wailing, only settling when in Lottie's arms, and Spencer had managed a few hours' sleep.

There were some colourful toys along the aisle that caught his eye, and he was sure they would catch Archie's too, so they went in the trolley. He was glad the supermarket catered for most things a baby might need, and within minutes the trolley was full to the brim, with a cream baby bath lying on top.

Spencer looked twice at the checkout till. How could one tiny human cost so much? He blinked hard, paid, then packed the lot away in the back of his van, feeling quite pleased with himself.

It had been a weird night and even stranger morning, but all in all, he felt he was handling the situation well enough. The flower shop was fully staffed for the day, the Sunshine Superheroes in school, and no shift at the Hub. Now all that was left was a proper chat with his sister about the baby, because they hardly had time for anything other than seeing to Archie all night.

All the way home thoughts of fatherhood consumed him, bringing him back to his childhood when he was the main carer for his siblings. He never saw himself having kids. He never saw himself settling with anyone. But Archie was in his life now, and protecting and providing for the baby was at the front of his mind, just as looking after Lottie and Jordy had been all those years ago.

He opened his front door and called up to Samuel to ask for help bringing in the shopping, completely forgetting that

Archie might be asleep. Slapping his hand to his mouth, he shook his head as he went back to the van.

Samuel came down quickly, his amber eyes widening at the load. 'Wow! I thought you were only buying nappies and milk.'

'I figured he'd need more than that for his stay.'

There was something about the way Samuel looked that caused a tremble in Spencer's stomach.

'What?' he asked, looking towards his street door.

'Jan's upstairs.'

Spencer's blood boiled immediately. He thought Lottie had agreed not to call anyone, but the moment his back was turned she had gone and done that. How could she? He would never do something like that to her.

As though reading his mind, Samuel said, 'It wasn't Lottie.'

'You?' asked Spencer, glaring.

'No. She just turned up. Said she needed to speak to you about Archie.'

'How does she know about him?'

Samuel gestured towards the flat. 'Why don't you go find out.' He grabbed some more bags and headed upstairs.

Spencer took some breaths, inhaling the fresh salty air from the sea. There was something about the scent that always calmed him. It reminded him of his aunt. He glanced in the direction of Berry Hill, looking up at the pastel-coloured harbour houses.

It wasn't scary the first time Rebecca brought him to her home to live. She'd decorated his room in light blues and white, giving him a safe space to call his own. He didn't have to lift a finger for Lottie or himself and didn't know what to do with himself for a good few weeks.

His aunt's neighbour, George, used to take him down to the harbour to look at the boats, but it was of little interest. Still, the air smelled nice and the view was peaceful.

He knew what his aunt would say about Archie. If Rebecca was around, the baby would have so much fuss made of him, he'd never shed another tear again.

The thought made Spencer even more determined to care for the baby, just as his aunt had for him.

Marching up the stairs, arms full with shopping, Spencer forced a smile towards his friend. 'Hello, Jan, and what brings you here?' As if he didn't know, and Jan's reaction said exactly that.

Lottie went to speak, but Spencer got in first, playing it cool.

'Archie all right?' he asked Lottie.

She smiled as she gestured to the spare bedroom. 'Sleeping, bless him. I think he finally got fed up with Sam singing.'

Samuel frowned. 'Hey, he liked my voice. Eventually.'

Ignoring Jan, Spencer started to unpack.

'Do you want a cuppa, Jan?' asked Lottie as Samuel edged towards the open plan kitchen.

'No, ta. I think it's time I spoke to Spencer.'

Spencer stopped faffing with a pack of yellow bibs. 'Who told you about the baby?'

'His mother,' replied Jan.

He caught his sister's sympathetic smile before turning all his attention to Jan. 'Is she all right?'

Jan looked surprised that was the thing he asked. Perhaps she thought he'd be angry. Well, part of him was, but that could wait.

'She's okay. Well, she will be.'

'What happened?' asked Lottie. She looked at Spencer. 'Jan wouldn't tell us until you got back.'

They all stared at Jan, wanting answers.

Jan linked her fingers on her lap. 'I can only tell you what Beth has allowed me.'

'Beth?' questioned Spencer, earning him a disappointed glare from Lottie. Ignoring his sister, he went back to listening to Jan.

Jan continued. 'The short version is, she had a rough time of it at the end of her pregnancy, and it has affected her mental health.'

Spencer watched Lottie and Samuel look to each other. He wasn't quite sure what they were thinking. He didn't know what to think himself.

Jan added, 'I know leaving Archie on the doorstep suggests otherwise, but I want you to know that Beth is stable. She was having panic attacks but didn't know what was happening to her. And a problem with her pregnancy left her with trauma. Having a newborn baby while suffering with her mental health has been difficult, but she's going to be fine now she's getting the help she needs.'

Spencer clenched his fists. 'What the hell happened during her pregnancy?'

'That's her story to tell,' replied Jan.

'Is Archie sick at all, Jan?' asked Lottie softly, holding Samuel's hand.

'No, he's fine.'

Spencer needed to calm down. He didn't even know why he was so wound up. Was it because Beth had left the baby on his doorstep? Was it what happened to her during pregnancy, maybe? He was agitated about something but couldn't quite put his finger on what was annoying him the most.

'I'm glad you're helping her, Jan,' said Samuel, breaking into the silence.

Jan smiled. 'I'm going to make sure she gets all the help she needs.'

'And meanwhile?' asked Lottie, glancing at the bedroom.

Jan turned to Spencer. 'She's asked if you would look after Archie for a couple more days.' She looked at Lottie. 'She just needs some rest.'

Lottie sighed. 'We've only had him one night and I know how she feels.'

Jan nodded. 'It's tiring looking after a baby, isn't it? And Beth's not long moved homes. Can you imagine doing all that while feeling so incredibly ill?' It looked as though Jan was going to say more, but she stood instead, gathering her handbag.

'Jan?' asked Lottie. 'Do social services need to be involved?'

Spencer went to snap, but Jan interrupted him. 'No. This is a private arrangement between Archie's parents. He's not in any danger, but if you would like them to step in, I—'

'No thanks,' said Spencer sharply.

Jan headed for the door. 'How do you feel about meeting Beth in my office in a couple of days to talk, Spence?'

He nodded. 'Sounds like a plan.'

'Yes,' agreed Lottie. 'It'll give Beth some breathing room, and Spencer some time to bond with his son.'

Jan smiled her warm smile. 'I have to say, after seeing him while waiting for you to get back, Spencer, I think he looks a lot like Lottie.'

Spencer had the same thought.

'He has her hair and eyes,' said Samuel, resting a hand on Lottie's shoulder.

Spencer watched them beam at each other.

'We'll take good care of him,' said Lottie quickly, facing Jan.

'We?' questioned Spencer.

She blew up at her fringe as though it suddenly offended her, but Spencer could clearly see it was he who had insulted her. 'Of course, *we*. I'm not going to leave you to it, am I?'

He admired the love she always threw his way. No one but Lottie, Rebecca, and George cared for him in such a way. Sure, he had a great circle of friends, who he knew would soon be the next ones on his doorstep to help with baby duties, but the love his sister and aunt gave him was the purest of all. And George was the only father figure he'd had. It was a shame he and Rebecca were gone, because they would have made wonderful substitute grandparents for Archie.

Jan eyed the pile of baby goods on the table. 'Seems like you're sorted for a while. I'll leave you to it. Call me if you need me. Meanwhile, try not to stress over this too much. I know it's a bit sudden, but I believe things will work out well in the end.'

'Can we have her phone number?' asked Lottie. 'We can text her updates about Archie. It might be helpful.'

Jan shook her head. 'Best leave that idea for now. I'll let her know how much love he's surrounded by. That'll help.'

'Yes,' said Lottie. 'Tell her we'll do our very best by him.'

Jan said her goodbyes and left.

Spencer followed her down the stairs and waved her off. His friend Sophie was just entering the Hub to do her shift, so he waved to her as well, knowing it wouldn't be long before the whole of Port Berry knew he had a kid, because he wasn't about to hide the fact.

CHAPTER 10

Beth

Beth woke after a long nap, surprised she'd slept at all. It felt strange not having Archie around. She kept feeling as though she had forgotten something. It was nice to rest and not feel so on edge, but she was missing him so much already.

Walking around her flat wasn't helping to lift her mood. The whole place needed a facelift, and there was still some unpacking to do. Perhaps if she made it feel homelier, it would help settle her too. Jan said clear the clutter, clear the mind. Only thing was, she hadn't unboxed much to make a mess.

It was Archie's room she wanted to decorate but she hadn't had the energy. Cute ducks and rabbits was her design, but all he had was his cot squashed up to her bed in her beige room.

There was definitely a lighter air about her since meeting Jan, and just saying everything out loud had made so much of a difference, she couldn't believe it. Pearl had finally left her alone, and Jan had made herself available twenty-four seven. The last person who was there for her like that was her dad. Oh, how she missed him. Named her son after him. Hopefully her dad would be watching over her baby. Although, since hearing back from Jan that Archie was in loving hands, a weight had fallen.

'Right!' she told the room. 'How about a spring clean?'

Ever since she started feeling ill, cleaning had helped. For some reason, whenever she felt panicky, she'd start cleaning, it didn't matter what, but by the end of the chore, her nerves had settled.

The day seemed to drag, and she knew it was because Archie wasn't there keeping her company. She wondered while unpacking some of his clothes if he missed her. Would he notice she wasn't around? How quickly would he adapt?

All day he filled her head, even when she took a long hot soak in the bath to relax. It was laughable, as she couldn't remember the meaning of the word, but it worked just a little.

She wished she could bottle Jan and carry her around all day. Every time she called to check in, they'd talk for a while and everything was clear. It was a good feeling, but having Archie out of sight wasn't.

It had been agreed she would meet with Spencer at Jan's office in a couple of days. It seemed so far away.

I need to see him.

She paced the room, wondering what to do for the best. Arrangements had been made. Why must she be the one to rock the boat? Because she missed her son so badly, it hurt.

I could call Jan.

Better still, she could just go to Spencer's and . . .

'And what?' she asked the room.

The feeling of being the stranger in Archie's life, trying for access, fuelled her enough to wrap up in some warm clothes and head off to Harbour End Road.

It was a cold brisk walk that cleared her head and nostrils. Anything could have been going on around her and she wouldn't have noticed. Her mind too occupied with what to say to the man she was about to face.

She figured she'd have to take the hit at some point, as it was highly unlikely he wouldn't have something to say about the way she had handled his introduction to his son.

The shops were closed by the time she made it to the harbour. It was cold and dark, even the seagulls had settled for the night.

Beth stood in the same spot she had contemplated leaving her son. The boats bobbed in the calm sea behind her, and the lights of the flats over the road were once more dimmed by drapes or blinds.

Archie's up there.

Determined not to cry, or wait any longer, she made her way across the road and inhaled deeply.

Do it, Beth. Just knock.

One more breath for courage, and she rang the bell, feeling all life drain from her face as her eyes welled.

Just like before, it took a moment for Spencer to open the door, and she had a moment where she worried he might have left Archie in the bath.

She stared up into curious blue eyes, momentarily losing her words. He didn't seem to recognize her, not that she was expecting him to. 'I'm Beth Horton,' she blurted.

The greeting left his face immediately, but she daren't remove her eyes from his glare. Whatever he or anyone else had to say, she'd deal with it. They hadn't a clue what she'd been through, so who were they to judge? Was he judging her? She couldn't be entirely sure.

'You'd better come up,' he said softly.

She didn't need to be asked twice. Archie was up there somewhere, along with her breath. She walked towards a gentle tinkling musical sound coming from the top of the stairs.

'He's just had a bath and is settled in his pram . . .'

Whatever else Spencer said faded away with the tune as Beth noticed the pram as soon as she entered the living room. Archie was mesmerized by the rotating farm animals and pleasant noise coming from the baby mobile attached to his bed for the night.

'Hey, baby boy,' she whispered, lightly stroking his cheek.

Archie wriggled, waking fully from his trance, and Beth lifted him immediately, bringing him close to her cheek. He smelled of fresh laundered clothes and baby shampoo.

A hand placed a blanket over Archie's back, covering part of her too, reminding her Spencer was in the room. He stepped back and gestured to the sofa, so she sat, snuggling her baby into her some more.

It took a moment for her nerves to settle, her heart to stop weeping for her son, and for her to feel the courage needed to look her child's father in the eye.

'Thank you,' she said quietly.

Spencer didn't reply, but a small nod was offered, followed by making tea.

Beth had no idea where to start. Archie was back in her arms, closing his eyes, showing he was the only relaxed one in the room.

'I thought I'd see you in a couple of days,' said Spencer, standing over in the kitchen, not looking her way.

'I know. I'm sorry to intrude like this, but I couldn't . . .' She dipped her head, not having the energy to explain.

'It's okay,' he said, turning but still not making eye contact.

Beth could feel Archie's slow and steady breathing as he drifted off.

'First time I've seen him fall asleep so fast,' said Spencer softly.

Guilt hit hard. Had she not abandoned her child, he would have been enjoying his usual naps. She could imagine him fretting, wondering where he was and who the stranger was. Did he call out for her inside his mind? Her heart cracked.

'It was wrong what I did,' she said, finding her words. 'To you both.' She glanced up, knowing she had to face him.

Spencer was staring back, his expression blank, but his posture relaxed as he sat on a kitchen chair. 'Jan explained.'

'Everything?'

His head tilted a touch. 'No.' Silence sat between them for a few beats, but she knew he hadn't finished. 'Will you tell me?' His voice was low, gentle. Perhaps for the sleeping baby's sake.

'It's not a happy story,' she replied, still reliving the trauma.

'That's okay. I'm used to sad ones.'

The kettle clicked off, but Beth shook her head as Spencer gestured towards the worktop. She didn't want to talk and sip tea as though they were friends passing the time. Truth be told, all she wanted was to curl up on the sofa and fall asleep with her son cradled in her arms. However, it was in Archie's best interest to lie flat in his pram, so she settled him there, then herself back beneath his blanket, taking comfort in his scent embedded in the soft material.

'You don't have to talk about what happened right now,' added Spencer. 'But I would like to know one day.'

As much as she wanted it left in the past, she knew if she just got it over with now, it would be easier to move forward.

'Everything was fine at first,' she said, raising her gaze to meet his. His eyes didn't hold the same warmth as Jan's, but she could tell he was paying attention. 'It was in the last stage of my pregnancy. I was told Archie's stomach wasn't growing as fast as the rest of him, so they wanted to start me off. Get him out early. So they booked me in a few days later to be induced.'

Spencer gave a slight nod, which was to be expected. It was easy for anyone to understand that part of the story. But what would he make of the rest? She still had trouble believing it herself.

Beth swallowed dryness. 'I was so worried. My thoughts started to go all over the place. When it came to inducing labour, something happened to me that I've never experienced before. I didn't know what it was at the time, but Jan explained I had a full-blown panic attack.' She took a deep breath. 'I locked myself in the bathroom and refused to come out, so no one actually saw what I was going through, as I didn't want anyone to see me freaking out. Obviously I came out in the end, but it was late in the day, so they said they would try again in the morning.'

Spencer seemed frozen. She was sure he didn't even blink.

'The doctor asked if they could start me off the next day,' Beth told him. 'Then she added that they couldn't force me. I could say no. It was as though she woke me from the nightmare I found myself in, so I said no, and she walked away.' She lowered her gaze. 'But it wasn't over.'

'Did you go home?' he asked quietly.

Beth shook her head. 'I was kept in for a week, and each day one of my doctors would come and ask the same question.'

'And you kept saying no.'

'Yes, but I didn't know why. I wanted my baby to be safe. I wanted to give birth, but this wall kept blocking me from acting. It was so strange . . . and filled with fear.'

'Sounds like a long week.'

'Longest of my life. Everything about it was bizarre.'

'Because of the invisible wall?'

Beth met his curious eyes. 'Yes, but then I had another scan. They didn't tell me anything, and I was too numb to ask, then after that, something snapped in me, and I let them induce me. All I kept thinking was Archie's stomach wasn't growing, and it was my fault. My nerves were rattling each minute of every day.'

'And you didn't tell anyone?'

'I didn't know how to express myself. It was as though someone had stolen my voice. All I knew was my baby needed to come out, and I couldn't do it.' She took a calming breath, desperate to hold back the tears threatening.

'It sounds like you were very much alone, Beth.'

It was surprisingly comforting hearing him mention her name. She smiled softly. 'I'm not sure I felt alone. I was too busy feeling insane. I wasn't even sure I could feel emotion anymore. Like I said, I had no voice.'

Spencer shuffled in his seat, losing his relaxed demeanour. He got up to switch off Archie's mobile. The baby was sound asleep and didn't need it, but Beth missed the soothing music instantly. He moved to sit at the other end of the sofa. 'I would have been your voice, Beth.' His words were sincere, and part of her warmed.

'It's a strange feeling when you just shut down. Jan said it was the anxiety taking control, but when I see myself in that hospital bed, it looks like I have depression.'

'Maybe you slipped into that state because your situation wasn't improving. If you think about it, you were kind of running on a loop.'

Beth bobbed her head.

She watched him bite his lip. 'They all knew me up there, and one time, I got the feeling a team of nurses were talking about me. They were huddled together by the desk, shooting daggers every few seconds.'

'Seriously!'

She looked over at him. He seemed as tense as her. 'I don't know. Maybe I was just paranoid. I just wanted to go home.'

Spencer's lip twitched. 'And how was the birth?'

Beth relaxed into the blanket, her jaw loosening a touch. 'All right. My midwife was lovely, so was the doctor who attended the birth, and I handled the pain as well as can be expected. The woman giving birth in the next room was screaming, but I was more into gritting my teeth. I had gas and air, and a ventouse was used, and Archie was born. All six pounds four of him.'

'And how was his stomach?'

Beth's anger tried to rise, but she settled herself, knowing calmness was needed in her life now. 'The doctor who was at the birth came to see me with a chart. There were guidelines and dots. The line that represented Archie's stomach had a dot attached underneath. That's what the concern had been. I asked her if that was it, because I couldn't believe how close the dot was to the guideline. I just stared at it in disbelief. I was shocked to see it touching the line, as I was expecting it to be halfway down the page.'

Spencer looked confused, and she knew how he felt. The chat in the hospital about the baby-development chart was so confusing. 'So there wasn't anything wrong with his stomach?'

'Nope. The doctor gave me a sorrowful look, told me on behalf of her team they were sorry, and that the scans aren't a hundred percent accurate. Those were her words. I was utterly gobsmacked.'

'Then what happened?'

'Nothing. That was it. The whole conversation lasted barely five minutes. She was just sent to explain that his stomach was perfectly fine and to say sorry. It was a short, polite apology. No fuss, no frills. And I was speechless. My mind was yelling, "That's it! That's where the dot is! I went through hell for that!". They didn't even test his stomach when he was born. In fact, they didn't do any tests on him. The next day, I was sent home.'

'Bloody hell, no wonder you have trauma.' Spencer seemed to chastise himself. 'Sorry, I didn't mean to blurt that. I can just see why the experience affected you.'

Beth could see it too now Jan had made certain things clear. 'It went on to affect me in the form of night sweats and hypervigilance. But I still didn't know what was wrong with me until Jan explained.' She smiled, thinking of her therapist. 'She's a nice lady. She simplified everything.'

Spencer gestured at the pram. 'I noticed he eats well.'

'There's nothing wrong with him, that's why.'

He flopped back, and she heard his sigh. 'What a nightmare.'

'Jan says I'm healing now. That's what I have to focus on. If I keep going over it, I'll just stress and make myself worse.'

Spencer turned, facing her full on. 'It's not easy healing when you have a lot going on.'

'You mean Archie?'

He nodded. 'Newborns are hard work. Plus, I heard you moved home recently. It's a lot.'

Tell me about it!

Beth twiddled with the blanket. 'I'm just glad I know what I'm dealing with now, and that I have help.'

'You've got me too.' His expression was serious, only his eyes showing a gentleness about them.

'I thought you would hate me.'

Spencer reached for a piece of the blanket, and she wasn't sure if he was going to hold her hand but had decided against it at the last second. 'I don't hate you, Beth.'

CHAPTER 11

Spencer

It was shocking to hear what had happened to Beth during the last stage of her pregnancy. The frustration of not being there to help was sitting heavy on Spencer. He was sure with the right frame of mind she would have been able to navigate the situation better. Had he known, he would have asked a ton of questions, and got her the best care.

Beth seemed a little more comfortable in his presence now. She was still clutching one of Archie's blankets to her lap, and he wondered if she would up and leave any moment, taking his son with her.

The time spent with Archie was short, but it had been enjoyable, and even the baby had settled. Spencer wasn't ready to say goodbye. He liked having his son around all the time.

'Let me get you that tea,' he suggested, removing himself from her big chocolate eyes. He pottered around in the kitchen as quietly as possible, not wanting to disturb Archie, glad of a moment without needing to fill the space between him and Beth, then handed her the tea and sat back down.

'Thanks,' she said softly.

'So what now?' he asked, needing to get it off his chest. 'How do you want to play this?' He flapped one hand between them. 'You and me?'

She was hiding her face in the cream mug. 'I, erm, I'm not sure.'

'Do you want me to look after Archie for a bit longer?' He hoped she'd say yes, as he wanted time to bond.

Those dark eyes were on him again. He could see the sadness sitting there. 'I'm not sure. It was nice having a break, but at the same time, it felt strange not having him around.' She breathed out a small laugh. 'I'm not sure if I can get much rest. When he was here, I was still worried about him.'

'That's understandable. But I want you to know he's in good hands. Even my sister came to help with her partner.'

Beth smiled. It was weak, but a smile all the same. 'You could be Mary Poppins, and I'd still worry. I can't help it. I overthink and imagine all sorts of things going wrong. Jan said I won't always feel this way.'

Spencer took a mouthful of tea, not really wanting it, but it gave him time to think. The last thing he wanted was to say something that had the potential to make matters worse. She'd been through enough, and Jan was right, Beth needed respite.

'I'm surprised you haven't asked the big question,' she said, pulling his attention back.

'What's that?'

'If he's really yours.'

Spencer glanced at the pram. 'He looks like my little sister. Besides, I'd still help you and Archie if you needed it.'

'You're one of life's helpers, aren't you?' Her soft smile widened. 'I looked you up. Saw you and your sister on your shop's website.'

'We all need help from time to time.' It wasn't something he wanted to focus on. He liked helping people. It wasn't a big deal.

Beth leaned towards him. 'I want you to know Archie's definitely your son. The last person I slept with before you was

66

over two years before, and there was no one after. Now I've had more time to study your face, I can see he favours your side of the family.'

Spencer was sure his cheeks flushed a little. Should they talk about their shared night in the hotel room? 'Erm, about that night we spent together.'

'We're grown-ups. We had a one-night stand. It happens. No point going over it.'

'Right.'

They both sipped their tea, avoiding eye contact.

'So,' said Spencer, the silence getting the better of him. 'How about we get to know each other properly?'

Beth nodded. 'Tell me some stuff about you.'

That was his least favourite topic. He only felt he found himself after Lottie's accident. Anything prior wasn't much to write home about. Catastrophe sprang to mind.

Spencer gulped some tea, then sat back. She deserved to know his truth. Scratching his head, he wondered where best to start.

Beth laughed. 'That bad?'

'Complicated.'

'We don't have to do this now. Perhaps we should slow down.'

Spencer lowered his arm. 'It's okay. I'd rather you know the rest of me.' His face flushed. 'Wait, that came out wrong. I didn't mean because you've had my body, not that you really had my body as such, what I mean is . . . I was talking about what you already discovered about me by yourself. Alone. Not with me.'

Beth's laugh was muffled by her hand. 'I knew what you meant.'

'Good, because I got a bit lost then.'

'Yes, that red tint creeping up your neck told me that.'

Spencer touched his neck. 'Dead giveaway, isn't it?'

Beth shuffled in her seat, pointing at her feet. 'Would it be okay if I took my boots off?'

'Yes, of course. You might as well get comfy if you're going to listen to my story.' He waited for her to settle again, pleased to see a hint of peace in her eyes.

'I'm ready for your epic tale.'

Spencer breathed a laugh out of his nose. 'Epic could be one word, but I'm going to give you the short version, or it's quite possible we'll still be here this time next year.' He followed her gaze around his flat.

'That's okay. It's nice here.'

He'd always thought it practical.

'Has a homely vibe,' she added.

'It's pretty plain.'

'I can feel positive energy here.'

Spencer smiled. 'I do try.'

'My flat is cold. Feels like someone died there. Probably my spirit.' She shook her head, then met his eyes once more. 'Have you lived here long?'

'A while, I guess. The flat came with the shop, and my aunt owned both, but we lived in her house up Berry Hill. That's where I grew up. Aunt Rebecca adopted us.' He paused, letting that part sink in before he hit her with the main story.

'What happened to your parents?' she asked quietly. A question he'd answered numerous times, mostly as a child.

'Okay, what I'm about to tell you is the kind of stuff you hear about on the evening news. Excuse me if I sound nonchalant, but it's an old story, and I'm quite detached from it now, especially because of how many times I've repeated it over the years.'

'Oh, you don't have to tell me, if it bothers you.'

'It doesn't, but before I start, I want you to know that my past will never come into contact with you or Archie. Basically, what I'm trying to say is, he doesn't have grandparents to visit on my side.'

'Nor on mine.'

Spencer lightly tapped her hand, then pulled back quickly, not wanting to do anything inappropriate. 'I'm sorry for your loss.'

Beth's eyes said a thank you.

'Right, let me spit this out. I don't normally make a pig's ear out of it. My parents were heroin addicts, and when my little brother was six months old, they killed him because he was crying. I was eight at the time. Lottie two. We were placed in care, then my aunt came and, well, I guess she rescued us from our nightmare. So, you see, Beth, I know what it's like to live with fear. I also know how to take care of a baby because I had to look after my siblings, and I know what love looks like, thanks to Rebecca.' He motioned towards the pram. 'I'm not my parents. I'm my aunt. Archie would never live the life I had to. He will always be loved.'

Beth was still for a moment, no doubt absorbing his childhood. 'I'm sorry you lived through that, and I'm glad you had your aunt.'

'Me too. I dread to think where I'd be now if it wasn't for her. Didn't put me on the straight and narrow for a long while, and even as a grown man I never settled.' He lowered his eyes for what he was about to say next. 'I used to sleep around a lot. Not thinking much of myself. Lottie would say I needed to up my self-esteem, but I ignored her, not wanting to put myself in a position where I might allow someone to hurt me. So, I'd love them and leave.' He felt the need to apologize. 'Sorry.'

'Don't apologize to me. I wanted a one-night stand too, but just so you know, it was my only one, and nothing I care to repeat. Oh, no offence. Nothing to do with you. You were . . . I just mean, it's not the road I wish to travel.'

Spencer smiled. 'Don't blame you. After my sister was run off her bicycle and lost the use of her legs, I decided to change my life. The man you see now was only invented a couple of years back. What happened with you was a setback.' He slapped one hand to his head. 'That sounded terrible.'

'Don't stress. I know what you mean. How crazy though. There's you, not wanting to do that sort of thing anymore, and me thinking it worth a try, and now look at us.' She turned to Archie. 'Maybe he was supposed to be born. Perhaps he's destined to go on to do great things.'

'Well, let's hope so.' Spencer met her gaze as it slowly came back his way. 'I think we should agree to make up something magical about how we met, because we can hardly tell our boy about our one-night stand when he's older and asks how we met.'

'Are you trying to say our moment of madness wasn't magical?'

Spencer dropped his smile, then realized she was joking. 'Hmm. Well, where were we? Ah, yes, me and my epic life. Actually, I think I came to the end. Now we know each other's nightmares. I guess you know the rest about me. Where I work and volunteer.'

Beth gave a firm nod. 'Spencer Jordan, helper.'

'So, what about you? Did you have a good childhood?'

Beth shrugged one shoulder. 'I guess. My mum died when I was a toddler, so I grew up with my dad and his mum. He moved us down this way from Bristol, then Gran passed away when I hit twenty, and it was just me and Dad until a couple of years back. Pearl's my only cousin, and most of my friends are work colleagues.'

'What do you do?'

'Primary school teacher.'

'Ah, so that's why you were at the conference.'

She nodded. 'Been thinking about becoming a SEN teacher, perhaps after maternity leave.'

'Speaking of which,' he said hastily. 'I want you to know I'll help with child support.'

'Oh, that's not why I brought him to you.'

'I know, but I want to do my part. I want to be in his life, Beth. I want to help you both.' He tried to steady his breathing while she mulled it over.

'I didn't know what I was doing when I left him on your doorstep.' She pointed at the window. 'I watched him. Waited for you to take him inside. I thought he'd be better off. But Jan told me I wasn't a bad person, and, well, you know the rest. Anyway, now I'm here, I can see he's been looked after, and I can tell you already think a lot of him. So, yes, I'd love you to be part of his life, but I don't expect you to do anything for me. Just Archie.'

'If it makes you feel any better, you could help me too.'

'In what way?'

Spencer was pleased he'd caught her interest. One of the things he'd learned from helping to build the Hub was, helping others helped you. He figured if he could get Beth in there it might just benefit her too. 'You could assist me when it's my shift at the Hub.' He pointed at the pram. 'We can take little man with us. He won't tear up the place, I'm sure.'

Beth smiled. 'What would I have to do?'

'We have a small food bank there. You could help make up some parcels to hand out.'

'I can do that. Okay, it would be nice to do something.'

'Yeah, I got the feeling you've been cooped up most days.'

'Feels like forever.'

Spencer wondered if he should tell her his other idea.

'You look like you've something to add,' said Beth. 'After tonight, I think we can clearly say honesty works for us.'

He nodded. 'You're right. It certainly came easy. So, I was thinking, and please don't feel obligated, I'm just throwing it out there, but how would you feel about moving in here for a few days?' He gestured to the bedroom closest to the bathroom. 'I have a spare room. No funny business or anything, just you getting to be around Archie all the time but resting as much as you like. I'll help until you feel stronger, and you can come out and about with me whenever you like to the Hub or the flower shop. It's just an idea.'

'I can't expect you to give up your life.'

'I'm not. I'm just adding two into the mix.'

Beth scoffed. 'You make it sound as though looking after a baby is easy.'

He shook his head, remembering how he cared for Jordy and Lottie when he was so young himself. 'I know it's not, but it has to be easier if there are two of us doing it. You're not alone anymore, Beth.'

Beth looked to be mulling over the idea.

'Just a few days,' he added quietly.

The wait was more nerve-wracking than expected, leaving him questioning his idea more than once. Was he being a fool? No, he was sure he wasn't. She needed help, and he was there, stepping up. He rolled his shoulders back, clicking his stiff neck. Even if she declined, he would still find a way to reschedule his diary so he'd have time for Archie. With more staff at the flower shop, he could take time off in the week, as there was no way he could push back the Sunshine Superheroes at the weekend. They needed him too.

Beth shifted, capturing his attention. 'Okay,' she replied softly. 'Let's give it a try.'

CHAPTER 12

Beth

The Happy to Help Hub held a warmth about it that Beth had found in Spencer's flat. She gazed around at the framed affirmations on the wall, reading each one slowly to let the helpful words sink in, appreciating the boost. A waft of sea air blew in as the door opened quickly.

'Sorry, can't stop,' said a young man. 'Just wanted to pop this up.'

She watched him head to a noticeboard and pin a small card in place before darting off.

The door didn't close properly behind him, so Beth went over to shut out the draught. She took a moment to stare over the road at the harbour. It certainly was a pretty sight even in the cold light of February.

Spencer was suddenly by her side. 'Archie's settled in the back room. He does like his sleep.'

The memory of waking that morning in Spencer's spare room, covered in more blankets than the baby's one, caused a slight temperature rise, or perhaps that was the heat in the room making itself known since she had closed the door.

'What would you like me to do?' she asked, eyes fixed on the boats.

Spencer went over to a light-wood table and gestured towards a small stack of cardboard boxes. 'You can put some of these together, then fill them with some food.' He handed her a printed shopping list. 'Just bits that you see here. We don't always have everything, and sometimes people ask for certain things, so be prepared to be flexible.'

Beth glanced at the noticeboard on her way to a green high-back chair. 'There are a lot of different ads on here.'

Spencer looked up from the table. 'Yeah, we encourage the locals to advertise here.'

'Someone's looking for a home swap. I remember when I was doing mine. Not as complicated as I'd first thought.' She prodded a finger into a small flyer. 'There's a parent and baby group held at the church hall once a week.'

'You want to check it out?'

Beth moved away from the board. 'Not sure.'

'I can come with you if you don't fancy going on your own. A load of parents and kids can be a bit daunting when you don't know anyone, I guess.'

Sitting down, she started to assemble a box. 'I'm used to being around parents and kids. Comes with my job.' They shared a smile before he headed off to the back room. 'I'll think about it,' she added quietly. She didn't exactly want to be judged by the other parents no doubt doing a wonderful job, and what if anyone there had heard she'd dumped her baby on a doorstep? They would hate her for sure.

Spencer was taking his time, probably checking on Archie, snuggled in his pram in the corner.

She looked to the storage room, feeling grateful her son's dad was a good man. It had turned out to be easier than expected talking to him all night. Their conversation had gone well into the small hours, and it was nice to spend the night actually sleeping. Archie had been fed and was having his morning wash by the time she'd surfaced.

The Hub door opened and in walked a woman dressed as though she lived in the 1940s. 'Morning, chick,' she greeted cheerfully. 'I'm Ginny. Beth, right? Thought you might like some cake.'

Beth eyed the slice of lemon drizzle placed before her. 'Thank you,' was all she could think to say to the petite woman around her age.

'I've not much time today.' Ginny thumbed towards the street. 'I'm getting my tea shop ready to open next month. Just left my partner in there, decorating. I'll introduce you to Will soon enough.' She nudged Beth's shoulder. 'Come to dinner with us at Robson's at the weekend. Might as well meet the team.'

'She means at the pub,' said Spencer, leaning against the storage room door. 'The Jolly Pirate. Just on the bend.'

Ginny pointed at the table. 'I brought Beth some cake.'

His eyebrows lifted. 'So I see. Lottie been on the phone to you, has she?'

Ginny flashed him an innocent smile. 'I don't know what you mean. But if I happened to overhear Sam talking to Lottie on the phone earlier, well, that's hardly my fault.' She bobbed her head his way. 'Is it true? Are you a dad?'

Beth didn't know what to say. Should she intervene and save him? Did he need saving? He looked happy enough, even had a touch of proudness in his eyes.

'It's true.'

Beth gestured at the back room. 'Would you like to see him?'

Ginny clasped her hands, squealing quietly. 'Ooh, is he back there?'

'Come on.' Spencer waved her closer.

'Aww, look at his little face. Bless him.' Ginny rubbed her stomach as she straightened from the pram. 'I'm in my first trimester,' she told Beth, smiling. 'We weren't going to tell anyone till further along, but Will was fit to burst from excitement, and once you tell one person around here, the whole of Port Berry knows by the next day.'

'Congratulations,' said Beth, wishing she held the glow Ginny had about her. All she had was a ghostly complexion. Subconsciously, she touched her cheek. Perhaps some vitamins were needed. She made a mental note to buy some.

'I'd better get back,' said Ginny. She gave Spencer a light squeeze around the waist. 'I'll see you two later.'

Beth followed her to the door to wave goodbye. 'Does that mean everyone knows our business now?' she asked as she turned.

He hunched his shoulders as he plopped into a big blue chair. 'People will find out soon enough.'

Beth sat next to him. 'She didn't say anything horrible to me.'

Spencer laughed. 'Why would she? Ginny's not horrible to anyone.'

'I meant because of what I did with Archie, and you, and—'

'Hey.' Spencer's hand rested over hers. 'No one will be told about that.'

'But she said she overheard Sam talking.'

'It doesn't matter what she heard. Ginny wouldn't judge you nor would she spread that news. She's one of the founders of this place. All Ginny Dean has ever done is help people.' He motioned at the street. 'She runs the café next door. Well, she did. She did a shop swap with Will, as she wanted his tea shop, but now they're partners, I think they're just sharing everything. They're good people. Please don't worry.' He sat up straighter. 'Besides, if anyone says anything to me about Archie being left on the doorstep, I'll tell them he was simply spending the night at his dad's, and they should mind their own business.'

Beth smiled as she grabbed another box. 'You're a nice person, Spencer.'

'I'm not that nice. I'm thinking of pinching some of your cake.' He winked, making her laugh.

She offered him the small fork that Ginny had left with the slice. 'So, how many people run this place?'

Spencer declined the sweet treat, getting up to put the kettle on instead. 'Me, Lottie, Ginny, Robson, Alice, Sophie, and Sophie's grandad, Jed. We started it, then invited Sam on board. He's a rich business dude that has a trust and everything. He owns the Food Bank Café. You might have heard of it. Over in Penzance. He's opening more around Cornwall. He's now a partner in this place. Plus we have Will helping out and Sophie's partner, Matt. He was the first person in need to walk through that door.'

Beth followed his finger to the window. 'How long have you been open?'

'Springtime last year. We wanted a place where people could pop in if they needed help with anything, so we got the community involved. Take Matt, for instance. He was able to get free dental treatment and health care. There are loads of small businesses signed up with us. It wasn't until we visited Sam's place that we started our own small food bank. Now we have more people come in for food than anything else.' He pointed at the noticeboard. 'Although we get a lot of eyes on that as well. Got quite a few people jobs that way. We know what's available around here before the job centre.'

Beth smiled at the thought of such a small place doing so much. 'I can see why you were so quick to help me now.'

'Ah, you're different. You're family.'

His casual comment went deeper than he'd ever know. Beth was quite taken aback. It was best to tuck in to the lemon drizzle slice and perhaps change the subject.

She went to say something about the weather when the door to the Hub opened again.

'Hello,' said a young woman. 'I was wondering if you had any free nappies by any chance.' She glanced back at her pram she was holding outside.

Beth jumped up. 'Come inside. It's cold. Here, let me help.' She held the door open for the woman to roll her pram inside.

'Ooh, thanks. And there was me thinking it was going to be a bit milder today.'

Spencer handed over the tea he had just made for himself. 'Fancy a cuppa?'

'No thanks,' she replied politely. 'I've got an appointment to get to. But as I was passing, I thought it worth an ask. I know some of the food banks have baby food. Wasn't sure if this place had any baby bits.'

Spencer shook his head. 'Sorry, we don't have anything like that, but I do have some spare nappies in my son's baby bag. I only have size three.'

'My boy still fits that size, for now. But I couldn't take from your own kid. Wouldn't feel right.'

'It's okay,' said Beth, rushing off to collect four nappies from Archie's bag. 'Here, please. We've got more at home.'

Home?

She quickly shook off calling Spencer's flat her home. She hadn't even moved in yet. All they did that morning was bring a few bits over from hers, and most of that was Archie's.

'Thank you so much,' said the woman. 'I don't get my money till tomorrow, so was caught a bit short.'

'No worries,' said Spencer. 'Happy to help.'

Beth opened the door for her, then watched her stroll down the street. She stood there for a while, shivering but unable to look away. What if that was her one day? An arm came around her shoulder, guiding her back into the warmth.

'Come and finish your cake,' said Spencer's gentle voice. 'I've made you tea.'

She sat in the comfy blue chair, staring at the steaming mug. 'So far I haven't had that worry,' she said quietly.

'And you never will.' Spencer had turned back to the small worktop, stacking fruit into a colourful glass bowl. His tone was firm but gentle.

Beth picked up the plate. 'Do you think we could ask for donations for babies, Spence?'

I just called him Spence.

She quickly shovelled some cake into her mouth to hide her blush as gleaming blue eyes peered her way.

'It's a good idea. I'll call a meeting, and we can discuss it. After seeing the price of nappies, I can understand why people struggle to afford them, and the milk! Jeez, that costs some.' He took his tea and sat opposite her. 'If you feel up to coming out for dinner with the team, we can have the meeting then. Robson serves some nice grub at his pub.'

'Do you have all your meetings in there?'

'Mostly. There's a big beer garden out front, so we sit out there when the weather's nice, and we found ourselves sitting outside more and more or going to one of our homes once Matt joined us. But he goes in the pub now, so we're back to talking there again. More room, you see.'

'Why didn't Matt go in the pub?'

'Oh, he's a recovering alcoholic. And as he was homeless when he first arrived, he hadn't tested the whole pub atmosphere for a long while. He's okay now. He'll be two years sober this year.'

'Wow, people really can change their life.'

Spencer smiled. 'And get better.'

She figured that statement was for her benefit. It did lift her a touch. If this Matt fella could conquer an addiction, surely she could beat her trauma.

'I knew it was a good idea bringing you in here,' said Spencer, leaning forward to chink his mug with hers. 'Here's to our newest member. You fancy being in charge of the baby bank?'

'Me?'

'It was your idea.'

'But I don't know how to do what you do.'

Spencer chuckled as he sat back and sipped his tea. 'You just did exactly what I do here.'

'I just gave her some nappies.'

'You showed kindness, Beth. You helped her. That's all we do at the Hub. Try our best to help.' He lowered his drink, losing his casualness. 'But I know you're supposed to be resting, so I won't put pressure on you.'

79

'Actually, I've been having a good day today, and I don't feel pressured at all. I feel blessed.'

Spencer bobbed his head. 'Gets you like that.'

'Do you think I could be one of the helpers? I'm not sure someone with my problems is in a position to help others.'

'Anyone can show kindness. But you take your time. Ease yourself into the role if you like. I'm not here full-time.'

Beth glanced at the noticeboard. 'You know, if I went along to the parent and baby group, perhaps I could find out how much a baby bank is needed around here. Maybe some of them could become donators.'

Spencer raised his beverage. 'I like your style there, Beth.'

And she liked the way he said her name, but that was enough of that. There was a baby bank idea rattling around in her head, and she was sure it wouldn't disappear any time soon. 'I want to come to the meeting with your team,' she said happily.

'Consider it arranged.'

Archie murmured, and Spencer had her finish her drink while he went to fetch him. He really was showing he'd be a hands-on father, and as she'd never been one to sit around all day twiddling her thumbs, she was glad she had something else to occupy her time.

Spencer came back, a sleepy baby snuggled into his chest. 'He's so perfect, isn't he? Melts my heart each time he looks me in the eye.'

She couldn't argue with that. 'I don't feel I've been able to enjoy him, what with being so ill.'

Spencer sat by her side, bringing Archie towards her. 'Hey, things will change now,' he said quietly. 'You'll see. So, no stressing, okay? And no getting too involved with this place if it's too much for you to handle.'

Beth lightly stroked Archie's fine hair. 'I think it will be good for me, but I'll speak to Jan first, just to make sure.' She met the concern in his eyes. 'I'll take it in my stride, okay?'

'You can be a lady of leisure if you want. I've got this covered.'

Beth breathed out a small laugh. 'Sounds lovely, but I've always been active. Perhaps it would be best for me to get back to that. Little man here keeps me busy, but mostly tired.'

'You'll feel better now you can sleep all night.'

'And what about you? You'll need sleep too.'

'True, but I've always been more of a six-hour-a-night, rather than eight, person.'

'Left to my own devices, I think I'm more nine.'

'Archie will sleep through the night soon enough, and if you want to be really active, I can always arrange for you to go jogging each morning with Robson.' He winked, making her laugh.

'Jan mentioned exercise too. But I don't think I'm quite ready for that yet.'

'Don't blame you.'

'But the more I think about the baby bank, the more I know I'd like to help arrange that.'

Spencer handed her the baby. 'You're a good person, Beth.' He pulled the blanket around them, then lightly brushed back a strand of Beth's hair as it fell towards Archie.

Beth warmed at his gentle touch.

'Sorry,' he said quickly, pulling away. 'Your hands were full. I . . . Erm, I'll make him a bottle.'

She bit her bottom lip, trying hard not to allow the feeling of his soft touch to melt her heart. He was the last man to touch her, and now his hand had found her hair once more.

CHAPTER 13

Spencer

'Been a bit busy today, have you, Spence?' asked Lottie as he entered Berry Blooms.

He parked Archie's pram to one side in the back room. 'Still had time to bring you lunch. Here.' He passed her a foil-wrapped plate. 'Compliments of Ginny.'

Lottie smiled. 'Ooh, lovely.'

Spencer sat at the large table with her and unwrapped his own plate, but just as he was about to take a bite, Archie whined.

'Has he had his lunch yet?' asked Lottie, stretching her neck to take a peek at the baby.

'Yes. He just wants a cuddle, don't you, mate?' Spencer carefully lifted him and sat back down, juggling baby and a slice of onion quiche.

'Let me eat some of my lunch, then I'll hold him and you can eat yours.'

'No, I'm good. You tuck in.'

'Are you sure about all this, Spence?'

'Of course. I think I can manage with one hand.'

'Not that. You inviting Beth and Archie to live with you.'

Spencer gave up trying to stab a piece of cucumber and picked it up with his fingers. 'It's just a few days, perhaps a couple of weeks. Beth needs some rest, but she struggled not being around little man here, so it made sense to me. She gets to be around Archie and have some help.'

Lottie lowered her fork. 'As long as you're sure. It's exciting having Archie, but I don't want you ending up stressed by trying to do everything.'

Archie's big eyes peered straight at Spencer, making him smile. 'I'm not stressed.'

'Just call me or Sam if you need help.'

'He doesn't do much yet.'

'What about on Saturday? You're supposed to be taking the boys out to earn another badge.'

Spencer glanced at the shopfront. 'It's litter picking, Lott. Archie can come with us. He likes going out in his pram.'

'And what about when you take them camping, fossil hunting, or setting up the festival with them? Archie can't go along then.'

'Beth will be okay on her own during those moments. It's just too much for her doing everything alone while she's unwell.'

Lottie reached over and tapped his arm. 'Let her know she can call me though.'

'I will, and I'm sure she'll be happy for you to help. I don't want her thinking we're taking over, but I'll let her see how much support she now has, and I know you want to make a fuss.'

Lottie sighed. 'He's so gorgeous.'

Spencer glanced down at the snuggled bundle in his arms. 'He looks like you, especially when you were his age.'

'You remember so much about your childhood.' She smiled softly. 'I don't think I have a memory before six. In fact, I think my first memory is of Rebecca planting flowers in the back garden.'

'She loved her flowers,' he said, looking across at some boxes of ribbon.

'We were lucky to have her, and Archie is lucky to have you.' She stroked the part of the blanket where the baby's foot was tucked beneath.

'And a lovely aunt like you, Lott.'

'How did Beth get on at the Hub this morning? Were you busy?'

'It wasn't too bad during our shift, and Beth aced it. She came up with adding a baby bank to the food bank. We're going to discuss it with everyone at dinner on Sunday down the pub.'

'Great idea.' Lottie's smile turned to a frown. 'You haven't left her in the Hub alone, have you?'

'No. As soon as Sophie and Alice came in for their shift, I introduced Beth and Archie, then we left. She's with Jan now in the café. I thought it best to let them have some time alone so brought little man here. She'll be along soon.'

'So should Sam, once he's stopped faffing with his new office. I swear, ever since Ginny cleared her old flat, he's been nonstop trying to turn it into the Trust's headquarters. Almost there. Would have been finished by now had he left walls alone. Wait till you see it, Spence. Looks so much bigger now.'

Spencer's mind drifted to the farmhouse Ginny and Will had recently moved into. 'That's just reminded me. Aren't we supposed to be having a painting party at Ginny's one day?'

'Ooh, yes.' Lottie snaffled some of her food. 'She's flat-out with the tea shop at the moment though, so who knows when she'll ask for help with that!'

'A lot has changed, hasn't it?' He peered down at his son.

'Life always changes. Not much we can do but try to keep up.'

Spencer managed to spear some quiche. 'When Beth comes over, perhaps you could suggest she hangs out here for a bit with you while I go see Debra. She's got a couple of people she wants me to talk to about the festival. With a nod from these fellas, we should be good to go in April.'

'Yes, that's fine. It's been so quiet in here today, I sent Sarah home early.'

Spencer rolled his eyes. 'You're not supposed to send the staff home. What if it picks up?'

'Then I'd call Sam. It wouldn't take him a minute to get here. Stop fussing.'

He'd been making sure Lottie had help his whole life. It was a hard habit to break. One of the things at the forefront of his mind was always her. It was just ingrained in him from the moment she was born that she was his responsibility. He'd done nothing but make sure she led a happy, carefree life, even hiding things from her to keep her in a world filled with rainbows and sunlight.

Had he been right, though, to keep her in the dark about things that were part of her life? Looking down at Archie made him think about responsibility once more. So much had changed, and he had made the decision to better himself in every way. Perhaps it was time to tell his sister the truth about their parents.

'Lottie, there's something I need to tell you.'

Her eyes were straight on his, paying full attention. He knew she knew all his tones so was looking as serious as him.

'What's happened?'

'Nothing recent. It was just before you went into hospital after your accident. I was going to tell you, but with everything going on, I left it be. And you know how it goes, the longer you leave something, the harder it is.'

'Seems you want to spit it out now though.' She was annoyed already, he could tell.

'Yeah, well, what with Beth and me swapping some tough tales, I figured now might be the time to talk to you. It's just, I found something out, and I wasn't going to tell you, but then I was, and that battle went on for a while, then I—'

'Get to the point. You're making me nervous.'

'It's about *her*.' He grimaced at the mere thought of using the word. 'Mum,' he forced out through clenched teeth.

Lottie was clearly shocked. It was rare Spencer spoke of their parents. 'What about her?'

'She died.'

'Oh.' Lottie's voice was small, unsure.

He waited for her to process the information. It hadn't bothered him at the time, but it might her. 'Cancer.'

She looked up from her plate. 'I understand why you keep things like that from me, but I don't appreciate it when you treat me like a child. You should have told me at the time.'

'Does it make that much difference?' He wasn't sure why he'd said that, but it was out there now, hanging between them like a bad smell.

'Of course it makes a difference. What if I wanted to go to her funeral?'

He glared her way for even thinking such a thing. 'You wouldn't have been able to. You were in hospital.'

Lottie flicked away some greenery on the table. 'I might have wanted to send her flowers.'

Spencer's blood started to boil. 'Is that right?'

Lottie's mouth gaped for a moment before she pursed her lips. 'It would have been my choice to make. Not yours,' she said, clenching her fists.

Archie murmured, and Spencer wondered if he could pick up on the adrenaline pumping, so he took a calming breath and met his sister's death glare again.

'I wouldn't have,' she added quietly, softening her features. 'But it would have still been my choice to make.'

'I understand.'

'Actually, you don't. You're bossy, Spence, and always think you know what's best, but you don't. You don't get to be in charge of what I should and shouldn't know. It's none of your business what I do about situations involving my life.'

Spencer controlled his sigh. 'I was just protecting you.'

She scoffed. 'From what exactly? I'm a grown woman, and my bio-mum died. Why do I need protection from that?'

'I don't want you to have anything to do with them. Not even knowing if they live or die.'

Lottie tapped her chest. 'Again, my decision.'

'If you don't know, it doesn't mess with your head.'

She leaned forward. 'Don't you get it? This is part of my life. I have every right to know what's happening in it, good, bad, or downright ugly.'

'It's easier if you don't think of them at all.'

'For you,' she said, shoving a finger his way.

Spencer glanced at his son. 'Let's not argue in front of the baby, Lott. He'll pick up on negative vibes.'

Lottie shook her head. Clearly showing she still had the hump even if her voice was now calm. 'Suddenly the expert?'

'No. Not suddenly. Funnily enough, I discovered that snippet of information way back when you were his age.' He let that sink in. Perhaps if she knew the half of it, she'd be a bit more understanding of why he felt the need to shelter her from the big bad world.

Lottie visibly relaxed in her wheelchair. 'Look, Spence, I know you had it tougher than me, and I know you tried your best to keep me and Jordy safe, but you don't have to do that anymore.' Her watery eyes met his. 'I'm safe now.'

Spencer attempted to swallow the lump wedged in his throat. It was easy for her to tell him to let go, but perhaps if he'd been a better big brother, Jordy would still be alive. He daren't look down at Archie in case a tear escaped.

'I'm sorry, Lott. I shouldn't hide things from you.'

'You're the best brother anyone could ask for, Spence,' she added softly. 'But you have to let me deal with *them* my way.'

'Okay,' he managed. Taking a deep breath, he looked her way. 'She was cremated and scattered in the memorial area of a cemetery. If you did want to lay flowers, they have a communal spot there.'

'Thank you, but I don't. You see, even though I went through stages growing up where I was curious about them, I never wanted to cross the line that led me back into their lives. Rebecca told me years ago that our dad would never get out after he was convicted of that other murder he'd committed in prison. So, if he's also dead, you might as well spit that out.'

'I've not heard anything, so I assume he's still alive, rotting hopefully.'

Lottie sighed. 'You can't control everything. So stop trying to get your ducks in a row. Life is messy, and we just have to figure it out as we go. There is no straight path. I honestly believed you'd changed last year. That you'd finally had a breakthrough and stood up to your demons.'

'I have changed. That's why I wanted to get that off my chest. I'm not the person I was, and I don't carry baggage around with me anymore. Well, not as much. I see you happy with Sam, and I know he loves you, and that settles me. I watched you take back control of your life after you were told you'd never walk again, and your strength gave me courage. I am different now, Lott, and I'm liking this man I see in the mirror.'

Lottie huffed quietly. 'Well, it's about time.'

He watched Archie's eyes fluttering to a close. 'I know I'll probably struggle not to be one of those helicopter parents, but I won't raise him the way I did you, because I'm not afraid for him. He's safe.'

'And he's loved.'

He smiled her way.

'And you're loved, Spence,' she added. 'And worthy of love. Don't forget that when you're getting to know Beth.'

'Oh, there won't be anything like that between us. This is just about being helpful and giving support.'

Lottie smiled. 'Just in case. It's worth knowing that you can have a long-lasting, loving relationship with a partner.'

'I'm not looking for love.'

Lottie picked up her fork to finish her lunch. 'Perhaps it's time you let your heart take over from that busy mind of yours. It'll be interesting to see what happens then.'

'No thanks. I've seen the way you and Sam go all dreamy-eyed every time you look at each other. I mean, seriously, Lott, anyone would think you're living in a fairy tale.'

Lottie beamed as the bell above the shop door jingled and Sam announced his arrival. 'I am. And one day, you will know exactly what that feels like.'

Yeah, right!

CHAPTER 14

Beth

Being invited out for a walk in Anchorage Park while Spencer was litter picking with three boys from the centre where he worked part-time felt more of a big deal than it should have. It was nice he wanted to introduce her and Archie to the lads, but she also wondered if he was simply keeping an eye on her.

She sat on a bench, watching some ducks huddled beneath a weeping willow hanging low to the pond. The weather had turned mild, but she still snuggled her chin into her green scarf.

Archie was content and warm, staring at his pram mobile bobbing before his eyes.

Two of the boys and Spencer were having a chat with a man who had stopped by to ask about the badges attached to their lanyards. They were quite animated in their discussion.

Beth glanced to her side as the boy who wore a red cape sat down. The lads had taken to her quite quickly as soon as they found out she was a teacher. She remembered his name at once. 'Hello, Leo. How's it going?'

Leo raised his litter grabber and clicked it a couple of times. 'Boring.'

'But you're doing a splendid job being a Sunshine Superhero.'

'I bet superheroes don't pick up rubbish.'

'I bet they would if they saw someone could slip on something. A superhero would swoop in and save the member of public from harm.' She saw his eyes widen at the thought. 'Take that man Spencer is talking to.' She gestured that way. 'He looks elderly, right?'

Leo nodded as he plopped one arm over the top of the wooden bench.

'Well,' added Beth, 'you wouldn't want him to topple over on a crisp packet, would you?'

Leo looked along the pathway. 'No, but he's safe here.'

'Yes, because you cleared the way.'

It didn't take long for the statement to sink in. Leo shoved his glasses up the bridge of his nose, sniffed, clicked his litter grabber, then darted off towards a tissue he spotted curled around a nearby bin.

Spencer came over, peered in the pram, then smiled her way. 'All good?' he asked quietly, one eye on Leo.

'Yes, we're having a lovely restful day. Bit like the ducks. Have the boys earned their litter-picking badge yet?'

He grinned over at Ryan and Jax having a sword fight with their grabbers. 'Erm, excuse me,' he called.

The lads lowered their weapons and went back to hunting down rubbish.

Spencer nodded at Beth. 'Almost. Another ten minutes should do it.'

'And this was your idea, was it? All this badge malarkey?'

He was watching the boys while talking. 'It all started with a comment Leo made, really. He wanted to be a Scout, but he's too nervous to be around a lot of kids, so I figured we could have something similar at the Sunshine Centre. There aren't many kids there his age, and they were the only three to sign up. Their parents gave consent, and here we are. It's great seeing the boys out and about, laughing.'

Beth smiled. 'Perhaps you should consider becoming a primary school teacher.'

His eyes momentarily flashed her way as he laughed. 'No, thanks. This is enough for now.'

'You look as happy as them.'

He went to reply, but Leo came sprinting over, his face as white as a ghost.

'What's wrong?' asked Beth, as the boy practically squashed himself into her side.

Ryan and Jax approached, and Beth watched Ryan fold his arms tightly, with the grabber poking out. Everyone seemed to be glaring down the pathway, except Leo, who she could feel trembling.

Beth followed Spencer's gaze to see a man followed by a group of six boys about the same age as the ones around her. A park-keeper was with them, and judging by what they were carrying, they all seemed ready for a spot of gardening. Due to the time of year, she figured they were having a bit of a tidy of twigs and such.

Leo's head was low, but Ryan's held high as the group passed. Spencer said a cheerful hello to the head of the team, but got some sort of crooked smirk in return, which Beth thought odd. Just when she thought that was the end of it, the leader came back, two boys in tow.

'I heard you're working with the Sunshine Centre,' he said, sounding as though he had the hump about that fact.

'Yes,' replied Spencer, staying neutral.

Beth felt she was in the middle of a stand-off, the tension was that strong.

The man waggled a finger in circles at Ryan's lanyard covered in Luna's handmade activity badges. 'I got wind of this nonsense. Bit daft, don't you think?'

Beth wasn't sure who raised their eyebrows the highest. She was sure she won her own badge for that.

It was only Spencer's mouth that smiled. Beth could see his eyes were far from going to that happy place. 'We're building confidence.'

The man scoffed. 'Please! They should just volunteer to help their community, like my team, not this . . .' His fingers waggled again.

'We like what we do,' said Ryan.

One of the boys by the man snorted. 'That's because you're too thick to do anything else. Oh, except your stupid swimming. And you're no good at that either.'

Ryan unravelled his arms. 'Shut up, Donkey. What would you know? You didn't even get picked to race.'

The lad practically growled at Ryan, but Ryan was unmoved.

'Erm, that's no way to speak,' said Spencer.

'Quite right,' said the team leader, turning to flap a hand at the lad.

Beth glanced at Leo, who was as quiet as a mouse. Maybe she'd got it wrong about which boy didn't like to talk in front of strangers. She was sure it was Jax, and she was good at remembering traits about kids, thanks to her job.

'We'll leave you to it,' said Spencer, but the leader didn't get the hint.

His grin was almost sinister as he leaned closer to Spencer. 'Or we could have ourselves some friendly competition.'

Spencer shook his head. 'No thanks.'

'Oh, stop pampering the boys. My team is ready for anything.'

'We're happy doing some quiet litter picking to help the community,' Spencer told him, sounding quite firm about it.

'Let's see who can collect the most rubbish around here in one minute.' The man turned to the boys with him. 'Twigs included.' They nodded eagerly, but Beth was watching Spencer shaking his head.

'I said no.'

'They wouldn't win anyway,' said one of the other boys.

'We did win,' snapped Ryan, holding his grabber aloft. 'We already cleared the path.'

'Right, well, we're off now,' said Spencer. 'Good luck with your gardening. Nice and mild for it.' He turned his back, but Beth could see he had his eye on Ryan.

She was glad to see the group take the hint and walk away. 'Well, he was just charming,' she muttered.

'Old school enemy of mine,' Spencer told her, not sounding too bothered. 'We used to get into a lot of fights. Guess he still doesn't like me.'

Beth turned as Leo had sniffled. 'Hey, are you okay?' she asked softly, trying to lift his chin.

Leo was still so pale. He pointed to his chest, then tapped a couple of times. 'My anxiety levels are rising,' he replied, gasping. 'Mum says to tell a grown-up when it happens.'

Beth managed to meet his watery eyes. 'Focus on me, Leo. We're going to take some deep breaths, okay?'

He nodded but didn't look hopeful.

'In through the nose,' said Beth, joining in with the breathing exercise. 'Out through the mouth.'

Jax was doing it too.

Spencer went to wrap an arm around Leo, but Beth stopped him.

'Give him some space,' she said quietly. 'Now, Leo, keep concentrating on your breath. We're going to count to three as we inhale, then hold it for two seconds, then count to six as we exhale. Count in your head. Ready, and . . . In through the nose two, three. Hold. Out through the mouth, two, three, four . . .' She trailed off, giving him some peace to count.

Poor little Leo. He was staring at her with such hope. It was all she could do to stop herself from wrapping him up in her arms.

'More breaths, Leo. Well done. You're doing great. This technique will calm you.'

'It's calming me,' said Jax, and his words alone made Leo smile. Oh, how it was a sight for sore eyes.

Beth smiled at the boy taking his breathing seriously while Spencer stood to his side, as stiff as a soldier standing to attention. It took a while, but the colour started to slowly creep back into the lad's cheeks.

Leo's head bobbed slightly. 'Anxiety levels decreasing, Miss Horton.'

'You can call me Beth.'

'Doesn't seem right when you're a teacher.'

Jax poked him in the arm with his grabber. 'Hunger increasing yet, Leo? You ready to leave?'

It killed the tension immediately, especially in Spencer, Beth could tell. His shoulders drooped and his lips parted.

Ryan came around the bench to face his friend. 'Come on, Leo. Let's get out of here.' Beth watched him curl the cape further around Leo's shoulder, then point his litter grabber out in front. Jax placed his on top, then Leo did the same. 'Sunshine Superheroes,' he roared, making Leo snort.

Beth placed her cold hands on the handle of the pram as she stood, as it seemed lunch was next for them. She turned to Spencer at her side as the boys headed off in front. 'That could have gone a lot worse.'

Spencer nodded. 'Where did you learn the breathing technique?'

'Jan has been teaching me ways to relax and take back control. That one is the natural art of sedation. Longer breaths out, shorter ones in. I can teach Leo another one later.'

'You can teach me. I think I need it after that.'

'That horrible man scared him so much.' She took the brake off the pram and started to follow the boys out the park.

Spencer shook his head. 'It wasn't him. Shouldn't be head of a group of kids with that crappy attitude though.'

Beth kept her eyes on the boys in front, seemingly in good spirits now. 'If he didn't scare Leo, what did?'

'Rufus Doncaster.' Spencer thumbed behind him. 'The mouthy boy. He was one of the kids that used to bully Leo. Got so bad at one point, Leo ended up in hospital, and another kid was arrested, but Caster got away with it. He's that alpha type that gets his mates to do the dirty work for him.'

'Caster?'

'His friends call him that. Those that hate him call him Donkey.'

Beth muffled her laugh with one hand. 'Oh, that explains that name. I thought Ryan was just insulting him.'

'He was.'

Beth felt her heart go out to Leo. What a terrible trauma he had to face. 'Do you think he'll be okay?'

Spencer shoved his hands into his pockets and pulled out a pair of dark gloves. 'Hope so. He loves being home-schooled, and he's happy at the centre.' He handed over the gloves. 'Here, wear these. Your fingers look blue.'

They were starting to feel in need of some warmth, and Spencer's gloves certainly provided that, apparently in more ways than one, seeing how her heart just fluttered. Probably the adrenaline from helping Leo stay calm.

'Thanks for helping, Beth.'

She smiled over at the boys. 'It's okay. I know how it feels. Let's thank Jan for teaching me some coping strategies.' She certainly was grateful for them when Leo was in need. How she remained calm was beyond her, as she was sure her own panic might have wanted to join in.

Spencer leaned playfully into her arm. 'You did good, Miss Horton.'

That silly heart flutter was back again.

CHAPTER 15

Spencer

Debra called Spencer over as soon as they were back at the Sunshine Centre. 'All okay? You look a little—'

'Excuse me.' Ryan's mum, Annette, interrupted them. 'I brought Ryan here to help him get over this swim fright he seems to have acquired lately. The respite is supposed to help him feel calmer.' She folded her arms in a huff. 'His coach said he's not seen any improvements poolside.'

Ryan's cheeks flamed. 'Mum!' he said through gritted teeth.

One pink fingernail waved him away. 'Shush, Ryan. Mummy's talking.'

Debra gestured at her office. 'Would you like to come inside for a chat, Annette?'

'Not really.' She pointed at Spencer. 'I want to hear what *he* has to say.' Turning to bring the other parents into the conversation, she added, 'I'm sure we all want to know how these silly badges are helping our children.' Ryan's lanyard was flicked, causing him to step back and frown.

Leo looked down at his own. 'They're not silly,' he said quietly, then glanced at his smiling mother.

'Quite right,' she told him. 'Leo has been all smiles since he started here.'

Spencer sank on the inside, knowing he would have to inform Bonnie of her son's close call with a full-blown panic attack in the park earlier. He swallowed hard, thinking it best to deal with one parent at a time. 'Annette, Ryan is doing really well. He enjoys the activities and has no problem getting involved with any task set.'

Annette scoffed. 'Of course he doesn't have problems. There's nothing wrong with him.' The glare in her cool eyes as she looked at the other children was somewhat rude. 'My son is gifted. He'll be an Olympic swimmer one day.' Her glare moved to Ryan, who shied away.

'He's doing really well,' said Beth, pushing her pram closer to the huddle. 'I saw nothing but confidence in him today.'

'And who are you?' snapped Annette.

'She's Miss Horton,' said Leo. 'A teacher.'

'Well I don't need a school teacher to tell me about my son, thank you.' She pointed at Spencer. 'I left him in *his* care because Ryan's coach recommended this place to help reduce stress.'

Spencer moved to Beth's side. It was nice of her to step in, and he knew she had the experience to handle aggravated parents a lot better than him, but he had to deal with the issue himself. 'I can assure you, Ryan is doing really well.' He spotted the boys out the corner of his eye, nodding.

'I hope so,' said Annette, turning her back on Debra when she tried to speak. She placed a hand on Ryan's shoulder and guided him towards the main entrance. 'If I don't see results soon, I'll try some other form of therapy. One way or another, he's getting back in the pool.'

Spencer opened his mouth to speak, but she'd stormed off. It was time to deal with Leo's mother. 'Bonnie, may I have a word?'

Leo took her hand. 'It's all right, Mum. I just got triggered in the park, but Miss Horton made me better.'

Bonnie's gaze was on Beth. 'Erm . . .'

'We did some breathing exercises,' Beth told her.

'I calmed myself,' said Leo.

Bonnie pulled him in for a hug. 'And it worked?' As soon as he nodded, she beamed at Beth. 'Thank you so much. We've been working on some techniques at home, but it's always good to have more in the toolbox, right, my little lion?'

Her cub held a look of proudness.

Bonnie turned to Spencer. 'What triggered him?'

'Donkey,' said Jax, glancing at his dad.

Everyone knew what that meant, and Bonnie cupped Leo's face as though checking him for marks.

'I'm okay, Mum.'

'One day that kid will get his karma,' she told him.

'Meanwhile,' said Chris, Jax's dad, 'how about we buy some comics at the sweet shop to celebrate your wins today?'

Jax pointed down the hallway. 'We wanted to do some painting.'

'But comics sound good,' said Leo.

Chris nodded. 'Okay, let's do some artwork and then go shop.' He looked at Bonnie for confirmation, waited for a nod, then led the boys away.

Bonnie turned to Spencer. 'Was Leo really okay? We don't see any of the bullies often, but whenever we do, it's a trigger. We're thinking of moving away. In fact, it's only this place that is keeping us close. Leo absolutely loves it here.'

Spencer smiled warmly. 'He did really well with the breathing Beth taught him, gaining back control, and we think he's an asset to the centre. We're lucky to have him.'

Bonnie looked relieved. 'He's so excited to be part of the festival, and he can't wait to go camping.'

'That's good to hear,' said Debra. 'We just want the centre to bring peace for people.'

Bonnie nodded. 'It does. Take no notice of Ryan's mum. Everyone flourishes here. You're all doing a wonderful job.'

'Thanks, Bonnie,' said Spencer. He watched her head off to the arts and crafts area, then turned to Debra, wondering if she had anything to say about Leo or Ryan.

Debra lightly patted his shoulder. 'You okay?'

'Yeah. I'm fine, thanks.'

Debra peered into the pram. 'So, this is Archie, eh?' She smiled up at Beth. 'Good to put a face to both your names. Spencer told me all about you when he came to collect the boys earlier.'

He saw Beth's footing shift. He hoped she didn't think he was going around telling people about the pram on the doorstep business. 'I might show Beth around while she's here. Give her a proper introduction to the centre.'

Beth's smile looked a tad nervous. 'I might like to join myself,' she told Debra.

'You are more than welcome.' Debra left them to it, heading back to her office.

Spencer whispered close to Beth's ear. 'I didn't tell her our business.'

'Oh, erm, thanks. I appreciate that.'

He smiled softly, motioning one hand forward. 'I think you'll like it here.'

'You do feel welcome as soon as you hit the car park and see the large colourful flowers painted on the walls.'

'Yes, they really stand out on the white building. Here, let me show you my favourite room first.' He opened a honey-coloured door, revealing an indoor tranquil garden. Tall leafy plants and a trickling water feature were by one wall. A large silvery orb twinkled in the constant stream of clear liquid.

Beth parked the pram by a big cheese plant and stroked over the top of one of the two large cream comfy chairs.

Spencer encouraged her to sit while he flicked a switch by the door that sent the soft music of wind chimes into the room.

Beth's eyes widened. 'Ooh, these are the kind of chairs you fall asleep in.'

'I have done.' He laughed and joined her.

'It really is peaceful in here. It's giving me ideas for my flat. My cousin's house is quite colourful, but I think I prefer these earthy tones.'

'Bring some nature home. That's what Debra says.'

Beth slipped off her boots and curled her feet up on the soft seat. 'Are you really okay, Spence? It was a lot today, what with Leo, then Ryan's mum.'

He removed his own footwear and relaxed back, stretching his arms above his head. 'Yeah, I knew it would come with the role.'

'Knowing and experiencing are two different things. Parents, another thing altogether.'

They shared a smile.

'Ryan's mum is the type to expect instant results, but it's early days for the kids. I won't rush their process here. The whole point is to have fun, chill for a bit, and show them they can do whatever they want to when they put their mind to it.'

'Not sure Ryan has a lot of choice.'

Spencer rolled his head her way and smiled. 'I'm glad you were with us today. They like you.'

'I like them too. They're a nice bunch.'

'If you do want to join here, you can as a member or volunteer. Some people here are both.'

'It does seem like it would be beneficial.'

'I don't want to put too much on you. I know you want to talk baby banks with my friends at dinner.' He followed her gaze over to the trickling globe.

'I don't want to volunteer here, just come visit this room from time to time.' She laughed for a moment. 'I never thought about how healthy peace could be before my head cracked up.'

'Your head didn't crack up. You were just put through something traumatic.' He reached over and lightly tapped her hand, wondering why he felt the need to touch her at all. 'I know it's early days for you as well as the boys, but how are you feeling lately?'

'Much better now I have a label for my condition. That helped massively. I'm sleeping soundly since being at yours. Not sure if that's me or your comfy mattress. Perhaps it's just because I don't have to do any late or early feeds for Archie.'

'You don't have to do any of them. Lady of leisure, remember?'

It was nice to hear her chuckle. 'Thank you, but I like holding him while he drinks his milk. He always looks so content, and it feels kind of special having him in my arms.'

It was a feeling that had grown on Spencer quite quickly. 'I know how you feel.'

'Has the shock of finding out you're a father left now?'

He shrugged. 'I suppose. It's still a little surreal, if I'm honest, but I'm taking it one day at a time. How was the shock for you when you found out you were pregnant?'

'It took a while for me to come to terms with it, but then I settled in to the idea of becoming a mother and started to get excited, and a little scared of what was happening with my body. And I had some moments where I felt alone.'

Sitting up straighter, he took her hand. 'I'm glad we're in this together now.' He gave her fingers a gentle squeeze. 'And I'm looking forward to working side by side with you at the Hub.' Her smile seemed warmer than usual, or maybe he was looking too deeply.

'Your team haven't agreed yet.'

'Oh, wait until you meet them. They'll be all over it. The cost of living is terrible, and babies cost a fair bit.'

They both stared at the pram.

'I hope they say yes, because I'm looking forward to getting started. Since I met Jan, I've received a lot of support. It would be nice to give something back to the community.'

Spencer realised he was still holding her hand. He casually slipped back into his marshmallow of a chair, trying to look composed. 'Shall we just have a kip here until little man wakes for his bottle?'

Beth grinned. 'I like your style, but won't Debra mind?'

'Nah, she has a snooze in here too sometimes. I think everyone here has at some point.'

'Well, if it's the done thing, then why not!'

He watched her curl up into a ball and close her eyes before closing his own, relaxed once more in her company.

Archie whined, and they both sat up and laughed.

'Well, it was good while it lasted,' he told her, standing to fetch him. 'Go back to sleep,' he whispered, reaching for the baby bag. 'I'll be back soon.'

It seemed as though she was going to dispute the suggestion, but her eyes fluttered to a close, and she snuggled back down. With the bag slung over his shoulder and Archie secure in his arm, he managed to place a baby blanket over her lap before heading to the kitchen to sort his milk, where he knew his son would receive a ton of fuss from the cake-decorating class taking place. He glanced once more at Beth as he closed the door, warmth fluttering through him.

CHAPTER 16

Beth

Beth found herself gravitating towards the open fireplace as soon as she stepped inside the Jolly Pirate. The large pub was busy hosting Sunday dinner, the roasting meat wafting through the air, taking over any beer-infused scent. A large Jolly Roger flag behind the long bar caught her eye, then some pictures on the wall of ships and pirates. She could just imagine how the old tavern once served such buccaneers.

Looking around, one of the ladies she noticed first was the elderly woman she'd met on a bench, Luna.

'Hello, love. Heard you moved into the harbour.'

Did everyone know her business? It was starting to look that way.

'Only for a while.'

Those prying eyes of Luna's were boring into her soul once more. It was as if she could read each and every fleeting thought.

Luna peered into the pram, and Archie seemed to smile. Beth was never quite sure if he was happy when he made that face or just had wind. Luna's mouth twitched to one side. 'Is that right?' she said to him, making Beth frown.

A man around the same age as Luna approached. At least his slate-blue eyes held friendly vibes, unlike Luna's stare, which spoke of a million questions and answers.

'Hello, Beth, right?' He didn't wait for a reply. 'I'm Jed Moore. Sophie's grandfather. You ever need anything, my girl, you come see me.' One hand pointed at the main doors while the other rubbed over his grey wiry beard. 'Got me a couple of vessels out there. You want to blow away the cobwebs anytime, I'll take you out to sea. Does wonders for a soul.'

Do I need cobwebs blown away. Do I look that ill? They all know about me, don't they?

Beth told herself off for the bout of paranoia. She had to stop thinking everyone she passed on the street knew she had left Archie on Spencer's doorstep. Would the guilt ever go away? She tried for some sort of neutral expression. Anything to hide how she really felt, although she was still sure the old lady could read her mind.

'You want a drink, my girl?' asked Jed, thumbing to the bar.

'Spencer's already getting me one, but thank you.'

He bobbed his head. 'So, how you finding Port Berry so far?'

'I've not been out and about that much yet, but from what I've seen, I love the harbour the most.'

Jed stood proud as though he owned the lot and she'd just complimented his land. 'Best part of Cornwall.' He winked, placing a finger lightly over his lips. 'Shh! Don't tell everyone I said that. Myrtle over there comes from next door.'

'He means Penzance,' said Luna.

Beth followed his eyes to see the elderly woman in question sitting in the corner, supping a pint of stout.

'Did you both grow up here?' she asked, thinking small talk would take her mind off Luna, who had placed her finger in Archie's palm.

'Yep,' replied Jed. 'All us lot from the Hub did. I come from a long line of fishermen, and Luna's family have always had the newsagents along here for as far back as I can remember.'

'The one called the Treasure Chest?'

'That's right, love. Pop in whenever you like. My daughter does the tarot in there sometimes. You just have to wait your turn.'

Beth looked at Jed to see if that was a joke, but apparently not.

'Speaking of family,' added Luna. 'Here's my granddaughter. Here, Alice. Come say hello to Beth and Archie.'

Beth smiled at the tall slim woman heading over. 'Hiya, we met at the Hub.'

Alice lightly touched Beth's shoulder. 'Yes, I remember. I'm glad you're joining our meetings. This is what happens when you help out at the Hub. One minute you're in there handing over a cuppa to someone who has just popped in for a chat, the next, you're breaking bread with the team.'

'It was nice helping out. I didn't realize how much I would enjoy it.'

'Gets you like that,' said Jed.

Alice waved over a well-built man in his forties. 'Have you met Will yet? He's part of the team. Ginny's other half.'

'I would say better half, but she'd argue that,' joked Will, grinning at Beth before poking his nose in the pram.

Beth was surprised at how well Archie was taking to so many strangers. Perhaps being dumped on one gave him the courage to face anyone. She had to move on from that.

'Nice to meet you, Will. I hear you're going to be a dad soon.'

His dark eyes filled with delight. 'Can't wait. We're so busy this year, trying to get a tearoom and a farmhouse ready before the little one arrives. I'm trying for some sort of organization.'

'Will's ex-navy, so he knows how to be organized,' said Alice.

Will chuckled. 'I won't lie. I do feel better when everything is in place.'

Beth remembered when her life held a form of structure and routine. She thought it best to leave Will to find out for himself how that would go out the window once his baby was born. Although, looking at him, for some reason he looked the capable type, unlike her, who had fallen apart at the first signs of stress.

Jan had told her not to be hard on herself, but it was difficult to remember sometimes, and so much easier to simply lay blame.

Spencer finally came back with some drinks. He handed Beth an orange juice, checked on Archie, then greeted his friends. 'We sitting down or what?'

Beth followed them over to the restaurant part of the pub, where they had secured a long table.

Spencer grinned, pulling out a chair for her, then motioned with his head to the man he'd placed her next to. 'This is Matt, Sophie's partner.'

Matt smiled. 'Have they mentioned I was the first guest at the Hub yet? They tell everyone.'

'He's the celebrity around here,' called Alice, moving to sit near Will and Ginny.

Matt shook his head. 'Ignore her. So, Sophie tells me you did a shift already. You're game.'

What with Matt's London accent and Will's Welsh one, Beth stopped feeling like an outsider. 'I even got an idea for something to be added to the food bank.' She figured it was best to throw her idea out there, as it seemed the team were all seated at the table now.

'Ooh, what's that?' asked Sophie, leaning over Matt.

She looked to Spencer, wondering if he might like to take over, but he gave her the nod to continue. 'A baby bank.'

'What's that exactly?' asked Will.

'I know,' said Lottie. 'People donate baby items instead of food. I mean they can donate food too, but unlike our food bank, there would be clothes and even soft furnishings. Things people might take to the charity shop.'

'Or throw away,' said Ginny.

An athletic man with dark hair and the most piercing blue eyes Beth had ever seen placed a plate of food in front of her. 'You get fed first, as you're new.' He had a handsome smile. 'I'm Robson. Good to meet you, Beth.'

Ginny threw her hand in the air. 'I should get fed next, as I'm eating for two.'

Everyone laughed as the pub staff started to hand out dinners.

Beth leaned closer to Spencer, who was twisted to one side, hand inside the pram. 'Your friends are so lovely.'

He glanced her way with smiling eyes. 'Yep, and they're your mates now as well.'

She slid his arm away from Archie, telling him to eat his dinner before it got cold.

'When do you want to make a start on the baby bank?' asked Samuel, raising his fork Beth's way.

'Oh, I wasn't sure. Spencer suggested I mention it today, and I figured we'd brainstorm.'

'All we need to talk about is advertising to the locals,' said Sophie. 'We're so on board with this idea, Beth.'

Beth saw Spencer smiling out the corner of her eye. 'Erm, I'm going to join a parent and baby group at the church hall. I was thinking I could ask there. See if I can find out how much need there is around here.' She felt Spencer's arm press against hers, but she daren't turn his way for fear of smiling too widely. She was already starting to feel a bit goofy around him, the last thing she needed was to show that in front of his friends.

'Great idea,' said Robson, finally sitting down.

'If we end up with any big items, we can store them in HQ,' said Samuel, making Lottie laugh. 'What?' he asked her.

'You and your HQ.' She looked down the table at Beth. 'He always worked from home, but then Ginny wanted to sell the flat above her café, so this one here snatched her arm off. I've never known someone to love their office so much.'

Samuel frowned, clearly amused. 'It was needed.' He glanced at Beth. 'I have more staff now.'

Sophie laughed. 'Yeah, Sam just about hired half the county last year.'

'I'm building the Les Powell Trust, and now we can add baby banks into the mix.' Samuel raised a glass of water to Beth. 'Here's to our newest member of the Happy to Help Hub team, Beth Horton.'

Everyone raised their glass, and Beth blushed. She'd been in many meetings during her time as a teacher but none that made her cheeks flush.

Wow! They've really made me part of their community.

She felt a tad overwhelmed and told her eyes not to water. She wasn't going to be emotional because she had so many people around her showing support. No, sir! Old Beth was in there somewhere, and she could blimming well come out and act normal. Glancing at each person in turn as they tucked into their Sunday roast, she pretended she was at a PTA, and just like that, she relaxed.

CHAPTER 17

Spencer

The beginning of March seemed to come out of nowhere. What with everything going on, Spencer hadn't thought much about his birthday, not that he did much. Normally he would shrug off any attempts Lottie made to make a fuss and go off on his own to get drunk.

He looked in the mirror at the back of the flower shop, wondering how he'd managed to make it to thirty-six. There was a time he was sure he wouldn't make it to ten.

Being alone in Berry Blooms all morning was relaxing. Lottie was out delivering her homegrown vegetables to some neighbours, and Beth was at her first parent and baby gathering. He was set to go with her the week before, but it got cancelled the last minute due to a bout of flu going around.

He hadn't told her it was his birthday and hoped his sister hadn't either. It wasn't a big deal, so there was no point bringing it to anyone's attention. Best just to crack on with work, especially as his staff were off sick too. Luckily, he'd had a quiet morning so could get on with creating a guitar wreath for a funeral without too many interruptions.

Staring at the flower he held, he wondered what kind of wreath someone would make for his funeral. Maybe a Sunshine Superhero badge could represent him.

His mind drifted to the boys, hoping they were having a good day. He couldn't wait to start getting organized with them for camping at the end of the month. He was looking forward to going himself and was grateful Will would be attending as a helper.

The shop bell jingled, announcing someone's entrance, so Spencer went to the counter to see who he could assist.

'Happy birthday, Spence,' said Luna, handing over a card. 'If it's a soppy one, don't blame me. Our Alice picked it.'

'Thanks.' He opened the envelope to see a big smiley teddy bear on the front.

The door opened again, and in walked Robson, greeting card in hand. 'Oh, snap,' he said, laughing at the one Spencer held.

Spencer opened his card. 'Thanks, mate, but you lot don't need to buy me cards.'

Luna huffed. 'Oh, hush. It's your birthday.'

'And we're having dinner at mine tonight,' said Robson, thumbing towards the door. 'Lottie's arranged a small buffet for you, so no fuss.' He showed his palms as he grinned.

Spencer shook his head. 'She knows I don't really celebrate today.'

'It's different once you become a family man,' said Luna, nudging Robson's elbow. 'Archie will expect you to blow out candles and everything.'

'I doubt that.' Spencer propped his cards up by the till.

Robson turned to Luna. 'Can you believe it, our Spencer all grown up and a dad? Didn't see that coming.' He winked, and Spencer rolled his eyes.

'It's not that hard to believe I can be a dad.'

Robson chuckled. 'No, I meant it's hard to believe you've grown up.'

'Oh, ha ha!'

'Right,' said Robson, tapping the counter. 'I'm off, got a pub to run. I'll see you two later.'

Spencer was in no mood to go to the pub later, but he smiled anyway and nodded as his friend darted off.

'Hey,' said Luna. 'Enjoy this new chapter of your life. It's nice having your family around you.'

'Well, it's only Archie. Beth's not really . . . What I mean is, erm . . .' He had no idea what he was trying to say or why he felt the need to explain anything in the first place, so he shut up.

'She's still living with you, isn't she?'

She was, and no more had been said about it until now. He simply bobbed his head, then started faffing about with his birthday cards as though they needed moving.

'Like I said, it's nice having family around. Make the most of it, son.' Luna waved on her way to the door, and Spencer followed her outside.

There were a few people walking along, some looking out at the boats, others stopping to natter by the large wooden flower tubs on the pavement. The contents looked a bit dismal, which gave him an idea.

Communal gardening badge.

That would cheer the street up and give the boys something else to do. It wouldn't be the first time Spencer and Lottie had supplied the flowers for Harbour End Road, so he knew he didn't need permission. In fact, he was quite sure Councillor Seabridge now expected it from Berry Blooms.

Sophie came out of her fishmongers, Sea Shanty Shack, all smiles and a skip in her step as she approached. 'Happy birthday,' she half sang, then pulled him in for a hug.

'Thanks.' He stepped back and grinned. 'What, nothing from your shop for my birthday tea?'

She shoved his arm. 'Lottie said we're meeting in the pub for dinner.'

'Yes, it seems that way.'

'You're like me. I'm not much of a birthday fan. Well, not my own, that is.'

'It's just weird, isn't it? I know it was the day I was born, but it really belongs to your parents. They're the ones who . . . Oh, ignore me. Obviously I'm not talking about my own parents. I don't think they knew when my birthday was. Mind you, half the time they didn't know what day of the year they were in let alone anything else.'

Sophie stared across the road at the sea. 'I started to feel differently about my birthday after my parents died, so, yeah, I guess you're right. It is more their day.'

'You don't do much on yours.'

'No, I like a peaceful day. It helps me.'

He nodded. 'Me too, but my aunt liked to make a fuss, so that's where Lottie gets it from, and now I've got Luna telling me I have to celebrate because I have a kid, like Archie's going to know.'

'We'll have to make a fuss when it's his first birthday. When is that?'

He remembered asking Beth, and how strange the question felt rolling off his tongue. 'November tenth.'

'Ooh, something else to look forward to at the end of the year.'

He chuckled at her beaming out to sea. 'That and your wedding, eh, Soph?'

She playfully bumped his shoulder with her own. 'Be yours next.'

'Oh no. We're just friends.' Was that even the right word to use? He had no idea how to label their relationship. Beth needed a hand, and he had two to offer.

'You just seem lighter,' said Sophie, pointing at his cheek, which Spencer then touched.

'Lighter?'

'Yeah, you know, when a person has a certain look about their face. As though they have no worries.'

Spencer burst out laughing. 'I don't think I've ever had that face.'

'I can see a difference. A glow.' She leaned forward and kissed his cheek. 'Now, get back to work. Just because it's your birthday doesn't mean you get to skive.'

He watched her jog back to her shop, then turned to take in the clear blue sky. Did he really have a glow? He had to laugh. Archie had him up in the night, crying from trapped wind. Bloodshot eyes were all he could see when he peered at himself first thing, but perhaps life did feel a tad lighter since he started his new job. It was, after all, something he had worked towards. Beth and Archie weren't part of the plan.

I wonder how she's getting on.

He stood in his doorway, staring at the spot he had first met his son. It didn't feel as though a couple of weeks had passed. More like months. It was as though they had always been in his life, and yet, they hardly knew each other.

Wishing he was part of the parent and baby group over in the church hall, he contemplated shutting up shop for a few hours. It was no good. He had work to do, and he was sure Beth would call if she couldn't cope. They had agreed to ask each other for help if needed. He had to trust everything was fine.

His phone vibrated on the counter, making him dash that way in case he had somehow manifested trouble. 'Hello, Deb. Everything okay with the boys?'

Debra's laugh crackled the phone. 'Will you stop asking that every time I call. I just wanted to wish you a happy birthday.'

Spencer slumped into the chair behind the till. He was already fed up hearing birthday greetings, and it wasn't even midday.

'And to let you know we have Anchorage Park on the second Saturday in April. Our kindness awareness festival is officially on the map.'

That perked him up. He went out the back to finish his flower arrangement. With more good news to tell the boys, no word from Beth, which he was taking as a good sign, and a free feed at the pub later, courtesy of Lottie, there wasn't really that much to grumble about. In fact, he mentally patted himself on the back for making it to another year.

Still, a smidge of negativity knocked on his brain, out of habit, as he wasn't used to this glowing malarkey, which was annoying. It wasn't as if he hadn't had a good life once Rebecca took him on.

Taking a deep breath, he tried to ignore the fact his childhood, pre-aunt, still had the ability to rattle him. It had taught him from an early age to expect doom and gloom. Rebecca had taught him life was what you make it. And even after so many years, the two mindsets fought.

Quietly sighing, he carried on making a guitar out of flowers because that was easy and relaxing.

CHAPTER 18

Beth

Beth had never felt so nervous before. She kept telling herself off for being ridiculous. All she was doing was mixing with other parents. Nothing new considering her job. So why on earth was she feeling so worried? It wasn't as if they knew about her doorstep incident. At least, she hoped not.

A young woman greeted her at the doorway to the church hall, not giving her the time to turn on her heels and run away. Oh well, she was there now. Might as well check it out. Besides, she really wanted to talk baby banks with anyone who would listen.

The hall held a light scent of Archie's baby lotion, which had Beth raise her nose to the high ceiling for a second sniff.

'Just park your pram over there, please,' said the woman who seemed to be the host.

Beth turned to the small windows lining one wall and pressed on the brake. Archie was staring up at her, eyes wide and alert. She picked him up, letting his blanket slide down to the mattress.

'Morning,' said a man around her age. 'Lovely day today.'

'Yes, nice and mild.' She watched him lift a baby dressed in a blue tracksuit from his own pram.

'I'm Edward.' He turned his child to face her. 'And this little chap is Lester. First day?'

Beth nodded as she smiled at his baby. 'Yes. I'm Beth, and this is my son, Archie.'

'Pleased to meet you, Archie,' said Edward, waggling a teething ring in his face.

'So what exactly do we do here?' she asked quietly.

'Different things each week.' He gestured to the host laying colourful soft playmats over the hard floor. 'Shelby has us sing songs, do baby yoga, talk about how we're coping, baby troubleshooting.' He snorted as he laughed.

'Hey, guys,' said a woman around Beth's age. 'I hope we're not doing stretching today. My back's gone again.'

Edward introduced Lola to Beth, then two more mums who came along.

Soon enough, Beth found herself sitting in a circle, introducing herself and Archie, as they were the only newbies in the group.

The parents were friendly and quite pleased she was a teacher, thinking she should know more than them, even after she told them she normally worked with six-year-olds.

Shelby was quick to warm up her group, having them sing something upbeat while clapping their babies' hands.

Archie appeared to be the youngest, but it didn't seem to bother him. He broke out his smile a few times, burped twice during the song, and stretched an arm, which made Beth laugh, as it looked as though he was about to dance.

'As Lola's back is hurting,' said Shelby, 'why don't we spend some time talking about how we can adjust our posture to reduce injury.'

Lola chuckled. 'All I need adjusting is the lift in my block of flats. If I didn't have to lug that big thing up and down ten flights, I might not have a bad back.' She motioned towards her pram.

Beth listened as another mum spoke of sleeping a lot in a rocking chair, as it was the only time her baby got a good sleep. Someone else said their baby would sleep well if it wasn't for her other two kids screaming the house down every night because they refused to go to bed.

The stories continued, and it was surprising to hear so many complaints. Edward said he felt lonely on the days he didn't have the energy to get out, which gained him lots of sympathy smiles. Beth wondered where his partner was but didn't like to ask. No one had asked her, so she figured it wasn't a topic unless the person brought it up.

Shelby turned to Beth. 'Would you like to talk about anything? Everything goes here.'

It would appear, seeing how a lady called Moira spoke of her haemorrhoids that hadn't gone down since giving birth over six months ago.

Beth didn't know what to say. She didn't want to go over her hospital story. It was hard enough talking about it to Jan, Pearl, and Spencer. She just wanted it gone from her mind. 'Erm, I'm not sure.'

Lola placed her daughter on the mat in front of her as she glanced at Beth. 'Aww, bad birth story, babe? There has been a couple in here the last few months.'

Beth wondered just how much her expression had given away for Lola to say that. Was trauma written all over her face? 'It wasn't what I expected,' was all she cared to add.

Moira chuckled. 'Never is, love.'

The woman who had three kids chimed in. 'My first was a bloody nightmare. Second, no problem, but this one—' she pointed at the eleven-month-old trying to crawl away — 'everything went wrong at the hospital. Don't know if it was the midwife's first day or what, but she didn't have a clue. Mind, she was on her own and looked dead on her feet.' She shook her head, her dark curls bouncing. 'Little man got distressed. I ended up being rushed off for a caesarean, my old man was in bits.'

'It happens,' said Lola. 'It's not all storks with neatly wrapped packages.'

Beth shook her head. 'No, definitely not. Although, my birth was okay. I just had problems leading up to that day.' She stopped herself, not wanting to continue. They seemed a nice enough bunch, and she was sure they would understand, but the story was exhausting, so she left it at that and hoped nobody probed.

Another woman started talking about her birth story while she sat breastfeeding, and she went on for quite some time, which seemed to bore Lola, judging by her dramatic yawn, but Beth found the birthing pool information quite interesting. Not that she would ever use one. She wouldn't be using any labour wards or tranquil birthing rooms. Just the thought of falling pregnant again brought about a cold sweat.

Just as Shelby went to change the subject to vitamin drops, Beth raised her free arm.

'Oh, you can just pop to the loo,' said Shelby, gesturing to the end of the room over by the small stage. 'You don't need to ask.'

Beth shook her head. 'No, it's not that. I just wondered if I could pick your brains while you're here.' She looked at each person in turn. 'I'm doing some voluntary work at the Happy to Help Hub. I'm sure you've all heard of it.'

They nodded, and Lola mentioned she used the food bank one time.

'Well,' added Beth, 'I want the food bank to also be a baby bank. It won't be huge or anything, as there isn't the room, but if I can get people to donate some nappies, perhaps old clothes, blankets, small bits and bobs. That sort of thing. What do you think?'

Moira raised her finger. 'I can donate to the baby bank. I'm not having any more kids, so any baby bits I no longer need can go to the Hub.'

'I can buy some nappies,' said Edward. 'I have some brand-new babygrows as well that Lester never got around to wearing.'

Lola widened her eyes at him. 'I told you before about wasting money, Ed. Doesn't matter if you're loaded. You don't have to buy everything you see.'

He bobbed his head at Beth. 'It's true. I buy far more than what's needed. Lester has a whole stack of bath robes he's never used. You can have those too.'

'You want to see if you can get anyone to donate baby milk,' said Moira. 'Costs a small fortune.'

Everyone murmured their agreement on that.

Beth felt so pleased she'd drummed up support on her first day, and that she felt relaxed at last. It was good hearing all the different birth stories, how tired everyone was, and the reassurance the group gave to each other whenever someone spoke of getting things wrong. She no longer felt alone, and after hearing Edward and Lola say they had no partner to help, she felt blessed she had Spencer.

'You could hire help,' Lola told Edward.

He wrinkled his nose. 'It would make me feel as though I'd failed.'

Moira scoffed. 'Don't be daft. If I could afford a nanny, I'd hire one straight away.' She leaned back on her hands. 'Oh, how lovely it would be to let someone else take over. My other half doesn't know one end of a baby bottle from the other. He thinks going out to work every day is hard. He should try stopping home.'

As much as Beth wanted to say something wonderful about Spencer, she held back. He wasn't her partner, so she wasn't quite sure how to explain their living arrangements. Perhaps she should talk to him, seeing how she'd been there a couple of weeks. It was nice in his flat, and she was sure if he wanted her to move out, he would say.

The rest of the morning was enjoyable. Beth even stayed for the free cup of tea and biscuits on offer. It was nice to make new friends, especially ones in a similar boat to her.

After tucking Archie up in his pram, she headed for the shops. Her son had a birthday card to buy for his father, thanks to Lottie letting her know. She needed to think of a suitable present for someone she hardly knew.

As soon as she saw the *Dad* coffee mug in the card shop, it was a done deal. Pleased with her purchase, she headed to Berry Blooms to see the man who she was growing attached to more and more each day.

Spencer beamed as she entered the shop, rushing forward to help with the door. 'How did it go?'

'Really well. I'm definitely going back. The group was so nice, and Archie had fun. We're doing baby yoga next week.'

Spencer lifted him from the pram. 'Oh, is that right?'

Archie grumbled.

'He's due a bottle.'

'I'll sort that,' said Spencer, grabbing the baby bag and heading for the back room.

'Have you had any lunch yet?'

'No. I'm still waiting for Lottie to come to work.'

'I can get us something from the café if you like.'

Spencer glanced over his shoulder at his coat. 'My wallet's in there.'

'No need. My treat.' And before he could argue, she left.

Seagulls cried above, gaining attention, and Beth watched them swoop low to the tips of the calm sea. She stopped outside Harbour Light Café, gazing at the scenery. Was it fate that brought her to Port Berry? She didn't care. All she knew was ever since meeting Jan and Spencer, life had eased.

'Gets you like that,' said Jed, appearing at her side.

Beth snapped out of her trance with the harbour. 'Oh. Yes, I guess it does.'

'Magical place,' he said, grinning.

'Magical?'

'Sure. She knows things does Port Berry.'

'Like what?'

'Like who is meant to be here.'

Beth giggled. 'What if they're not? Do they get swept out to sea?'

'Nah, they just leave.' He raised a finger before she could speak. 'However, they think that was their choice, but it was Port Berry at work. See, magical.' He tapped the side of his nose, then went over to the café door, holding it open for her.

Beth entered the nautical-themed eatery, smiling at the trawler net above her head.

'Don't you worry about Port Berry chucking you overboard, my girl. You're one of us. She knows it, and so do I.'

Beth went to say something, but the elderly man started singing a sea shanty, gaining the customers' attention, and she could do no more but smile. It was a nice feeling being part of the community. Even better feeling her smile reaching her heart.

CHAPTER 19

Spencer

The noise in the pub was down to a dull roar by the time Spencer and his friends and family had eaten most of the buffet Robson had laid out. The birthday song was sung, candles blown, and Spencer smiled into every photo taken of him. It made him realize they were his first pictures with Archie, and Lottie was making sure she snapped loads.

All in all, it wasn't a bad evening. In fact, he enjoyed the fuss more than he'd expected, even the balloon with his face on it made him smile. It was the first photo Rebecca had taken of him when he went to live with her. Why his sister had it placed on a balloon was beyond him, but there it was, swaying from time to time at the back of the buffet table.

Spencer took a moment where he wished he could go back in time and let that little boy know things were going to be okay. He lowered his head, picking up a sliver of cake from one of the plates laid out. He was always partial to chocolate fudge cake, so thanked Ginny for making it by raising it above his head in a toast her way.

She waved back from the bar, then snuggled into Will's side.

The last time Spencer had snuggled with someone was when he'd shared a bed with Beth for an hour or so during their one-night stand. Hardly a snuggle, but that was the last time he'd held a woman.

He glanced her way to see her chatting happily to Sophie and Alice. She looked so different to the woman who had told him he was a dad. It was great she was doing so well.

Lottie was in the corner with Samuel and his little sister, Hannah, all cooing over Archie, and everyone else seemed to be huddled into groups, so he took the opportunity to sneak out to the front beer garden for some fresh air and a bit of peace.

He tugged on his coat, then leaned against one of the brick pillars that made the grill shelter, listening to the faint murmur of the people in the pub for a moment before making his way across the road to the short pier, soft lighting guiding his way.

Sitting along one side, he dangled his legs down towards the dark sea lapping at the base, wondering what lurked beneath.

He'd never been one for monsters in the dark scaring him. The only baddies in his story had been real people.

The gentle whooshing sound was so soothing, Spencer closed his eyes for a second as he slowly inhaled the salty air. With no noise from the pub, and the seagulls asleep, he flopped backwards and gazed up at the stars.

'Room for a little one?' asked Beth, coming into view.

Spencer smiled warmly. 'Pull up a pew.'

Beth matched his position and pointed at the sky. 'Wow! There are so many stars.'

He felt the lightest of brushes against his hand as she lowered hers. A small wave rolled through his stomach. He chose to ignore the feeling he'd just encountered. 'They always make me feel peaceful.'

'It's peaceful out here. I saw you head this way and debated whether to join you.'

'You can always join me,' he said quietly.

'I wasn't sure if you wanted time alone.'

Spencer breathed out a quiet laugh. 'I don't mind your company.' He shifted his head slightly so he could see half her face. She was staring at the sky, with a softness about her that told him she was just as soothed as him. 'Are you much of a people person?'

The corner of her mouth curled. 'I used to think so. I've been a bit in myself since my stay in hospital.'

'How's it going with Jan?'

Her smile lifted. 'Really good.' As she turned to face him, the side of her hand touched his again. 'You've helped too,' she added softly.

Spencer studied her big chocolate eyes, almost drowning in them for a second. He blinked hard as he looked back at the sky.

'Do you think it's time I went home?' she added quietly.

Another wave hit his stomach. 'Do you feel ready for that now?'

'No. Yes. I mean, I don't know.' Her hand moved away from his, but he could still feel its presence close, so he slid his that way until he could feel her cool skin once more. 'I just don't want to outstay my welcome. You know how it is.'

He tried not to focus on the fact they were touching again. 'You're welcome to stay at mine for as long as you want, Beth. I just want you to be well.'

'I don't like being a burden though.'

He glanced her way. 'You're not. Don't think that. I like having you around. You and Archie.'

'It has been nice.'

'So, you want to stay a while longer?' He held her gaze.

'Yes,' she whispered.

'It feels like you've always been at mine.'

'It does, doesn't it? It'll be weird going home, but I'm sure we'll still see each other as much as possible.'

'Yep.' He couldn't stay staring at her, so he turned back to the stars. A few moments of listening only to the sound of the sea below helped calm the charged atmosphere he could feel building each time he met her eyes. He took some silent deep breaths, relaxing himself.

'Have you enjoyed your birthday?' came her soft voice, breaking into his meditative state.

'It's been nice.' His focus went back to their hands still touching. 'Thanks for my coffee mug. Best present ever.'

Beth's laugh was hushed, filling him with warmth. 'Archie says you're welcome.'

'Is he still with Lottie?'

'Yeah. I think she loves him more than we do.'

Spencer laughed. 'I think you're right. In fact, I do believe our little man has half of Port Berry wrapped around his finger.'

'It'll be nice for him growing up here.'

A fizz of delight took over from any churning. 'Would you stick around then?'

'Don't see why not. I've only just moved here, where I work isn't far, and Archie will have both his parents close if I stay.'

'Definitely. What are your plans for Archie when you're back at work?'

'Day care.'

'I can help with that. Perhaps be the one to pick him up at home time.'

'Yes, a shared schedule would be great.'

He leaned up on one elbow. 'I'm glad you found me.' There was a definite smile in her eyes as she gazed up at him, which he felt settle directly in the middle of his heart.

'I'm glad too,' she whispered, placing her hands behind her head.

Spencer scanned her long neck, then moved up to her mouth, before resting back on her eyes.

Don't you kiss her.

She wasn't looking away, and he wondered if she would approve of him lowering his lips to hers.

Get a grip, Spence.

He flopped back to her side, inhaling the late evening air in a steady and controlled manner.

'I could sleep here,' she said quietly, as though any louder would remove the tranquillity. 'If there wasn't that nip in the air,' she added, giggling.

It was then he noticed she wasn't wearing her coat. Quickly, he sat up and removed his. 'Here. This will help.'

Beth took a sleeve. 'Won't help you though.'

'I'm good,' he told her, lying back down. He smiled as he felt his coat drape over half his body.

'We can share.'

There was more warmth entering him than from the coat. Beth was snug at his side, and when he stole a glance, he could see her eyes were closed and her smile slight. Every ounce of willpower he had stopped him from turning to cradle her into his arms. It was just the beauty of the night playing havoc with him. The stars, the sea, being snuggled beneath the coat together.

'Five more minutes,' she muttered. 'Then we can go home and have some hot chocolate. You can use your new mug.'

The thought made him smile and turn to watch her once more. 'I'd like to go home now.'

Her eyes opened to stare his way. 'Are you cold?'

'No, just rather get Archie settled for the night before I get too tired.'

'I can do that tonight.'

'You can make the hot chocolate.'

They shared a soft smile that made Spencer rise to his feet. He wasn't tired or cold. It was just too much lying with her under the stars while wanting to kiss her mouth, cheek, all along her neck.

'Right!' he said louder than intended. 'Let's get a wriggle on.' He held out his hand, which he regretted as soon as her slim fingers entwined with his. His stomach really could take no more disturbance.

Beth went to hand back his coat, but he shook his head, wrapping it around her before they walked back to the pub in companionable silence.

CHAPTER 20

Beth

Ryan and Leo were planting flowers in one of the large tubs along Harbour End Road, and Beth was helping Jax tidy up another one. The sun had poked its head out for the morning, bringing some springtime warmth, which helped relax her soul no end.

It was nice doing some gardening with the kids, and it seemed they were enjoying earning another badge. Spencer was pulling a bag of soil from his van, and Beth was trying not to ogle his biceps each time they flexed.

'Shall we go shop and get some crisps?' she asked Jax.

He pulled off his green gardening gloves as he nodded.

Beth glanced at him as they headed to the Treasure Chest. 'Would you like to pay at the counter?'

Jax froze for a second, then moved closer to her side as they approached the door. 'No,' he replied quietly.

'That's okay. Perhaps another time.' She opened the door, letting him go first. 'You pick something for the others, and I'll do the talking.'

His face relaxed a touch, so Beth headed to the counter to say hello to Alice's mum, Lizzie.

Beady blue eyes held a glint Beth normally saw in Luna. 'Your mum not helping you out today?'

Lizzie thumbed behind her. 'She's upstairs, crafting.'

As Luna seemed very much the resident witch, Beth wasn't quite sure which kind of crafting was meant. Not wishing to ask, she simply gestured at Jax, pointing out they were just grabbing some snacks.

'Mum says little Archie is getting big.'

'He's four months now.'

'Aww, I miss my grandson being that young. Teenager now. It soon goes.'

Beth happened to think raising a child went slowly. It felt as though Archie had been around forever. His first birthday seemed such a long way off.

Jax approached the counter and placed some crisps on top, avoiding eye contact with Lizzie.

The middle-aged woman smiled over at him. 'Jax, right? I know your dad, Chris.'

Beth watched the boy's dark eyes slowly roll up to the lady speaking to him.

'Those all you want?' asked Lizzie.

Jax looked to Beth.

'Yes,' said Beth, then pulled out her purse and paid. She handed the crisps back to Jax and motioned towards the door. 'Come on. Let's get back to gardening.' She waved goodbye to Lizzie, then widened her smile when she noticed Jax give the slightest of waves to the newsagent.

Was that a good sign? She had no idea. Perhaps Jax was okay with waving or smiling at shop staff. She needed to ask Spencer because she was a tad excited at the possibility Jax had made some progress.

Leaning in the back of his van with him, she nudged his elbow, making him laugh.

'What's up with you?'

Beth squealed quietly. 'Jax just went into the sweet shop with me. He didn't speak to Lizzie, but he did wave to her on our way out. Is that a step? I wasn't sure.'

Spencer almost banged his head as he straightened quickly. 'Yes, that's a step. Normally he doesn't even make eye contact.'

Beth quietly clapped her hands before flinging her arms around him. It reached a point where their celebratory embrace was going on a bit longer than necessary, so she reluctantly pulled back. 'It was good to see, Spence. You're doing wonders with those boys. Getting them out and about has really built their confidence.'

'Hmm, a little, but Ryan's mum is still on my back about his progress.' He shook his head as he closed in on her face. 'I honestly don't know how to get him to race again. I don't think it's his nerves. I just don't think he wants to be a swimmer.'

'Have you asked him?'

'No. When he's with me and the boys, he's happy getting stuck in to whatever task we've got going. I don't want to bring up their problems. This is their respite from all that.'

Beth gently swiped a piece of dirt from his neck. 'Perhaps the boys will talk if they feel the need. I know they trust you.'

His blue eyes were smiling right at her. 'Thanks for joining in today.'

'Truth be told, it helps me too.' She glanced over at the lads eating their crisps. 'It's quite therapeutic.'

Spencer glanced at the clear sky. 'That's what I think about springtime.'

Beth giggled. 'Probably because you're a florist.'

Samuel approached, pushing Archie in his pram. 'He's asleep, so I'll just pop him out back with Lottie.'

'Thanks, Sam.' Beth jogged over to Berry Blooms to open the door for him. She waved to Lottie inside, then headed back to help Spencer.

'Are you coming camping with us, Miss Horton?' asked Leo.

'Oh no. I'll be home with Archie.'

'He can come,' said Ryan.

Leo agreed. 'He's a Sunshine Superhero as well.'

It did seem they were part of the team now, but camping was Spencer's time to bond more with the boys, so she declined.

'Anyway, you'll have Will with you, and from what I hear, he's going to take you rock climbing while you're there. How exciting is that?'

The children seemed pleased with their upcoming adventure. Spencer even more so. Beth felt she already missed him, which was silly. How on earth would she be when she finally went home if she was lost without him for a couple of nights?

Getting too dependent on him needed to stop. She'd always been the independent type, so this wasn't good enough at all.

'Well, good luck to you all, because Spencer snores,' she added.

The boys started laughing while Spencer playfully frowned. 'I do not,' he told them.

Leo pulled his red cape up to his face. 'We can hide under my shield if it gets too bad. It blocks out noise.'

'Good to know,' said Ryan, putting his empty crisp packet into a nearby mesh bin.

Beth went back to the flower tub she was working on, smiling at Spencer and the children talking anti-snoring remedies. It was obvious he was a caring person. He'd certainly stepped up for her.

I need to start pulling my weight around the house. I'm sleeping better, I have more strength, and I feel relaxed. Come on, Horton. Time to pull your sleeves up.

Thinking back to life with her dad, she had done most of the housework, worked or gone to school, and organized her dad's diary.

Archie was an easy baby. As long as he was fed, had a decent sleep, and a clean nappy, he was happy enough. There wasn't much getting in her way except her mind, and that was improving, thanks to Jan.

She glanced back at Spencer, who was getting the boys to put their gloves back on. Each time she looked his way she felt blessed, but how did he really feel about her? So many times she wanted to delve into the subject but half of her wasn't prepared for a rejection, so she daren't step foot in the subject.

A heavily pregnant woman huffed as she walked past Beth on the pavement, rubbing her back.

'Are you okay?' Beth asked, approaching her.

The young woman glanced up, revealing a sheen upon her forehead. 'Just wish I could blimming relax.'

Beth pointed over the road at a bench. 'Sit there. Take the weight off.' She accompanied her to the seat.

'I've got another month yet,' said the woman. 'I feel fit to burst now.'

'I remember how uncomfortable I felt towards the end, especially when trying to sleep.'

'How many kids you got?'

Beth thumbed in the direction of the flower shop. 'Just the one. He's four months.'

'This is my first. Probably last too, going by this pregnancy.'

'Oh, has it been bad?'

'I don't know. I just feel down a lot.'

Beth smiled. 'I was the same. I thought it was going to be all about glowing and nesting.'

The woman scoffed. 'Try constant sickness and backache.'

'I used to see some pregnant women who looked happy and healthy and wonder what was wrong with me.'

'I know what you mean. If I'm honest, I get a bit upset when I see couples with their kids. It's just me, you see. I don't have anyone rubbing my feet or holding my hand, asking all the right questions in the clinic because my mind has gone blank.' The woman sighed. 'Would be nice.'

Beth glanced at Spencer, busy planting. 'Just being able to relax was all I wanted.'

'Ooh, I'm visualizing water features, palm trees, comfy chairs.'

The room at the Sunshine Centre sprang to mind. 'I know a place like that. It's a respite centre. Here, let me give you the details.' Beth pulled up the website on her phone and showed the young woman, who happily made a note on her own phone.

'Thanks. I'll definitely check that place out.'

Beth gave the woman the details for the parent and baby group as well, letting her know she'd be welcome.

Once the lady had caught her breath and left, Beth went over to tell Spencer about her chat with the woman.

His arm curled around her shoulder as he grinned. 'Beth Horton, you are officially one of life's helpers.'

'I've been hanging out with you too long.'

His hold on her tightened a touch, and much to her delight, he kissed her head. 'Best place to be.'

She laughed, nudging his ribs, then went over to help Jax with the planting. It wasn't just spring in the air, it was in her step too.

CHAPTER 21

Spencer

A local club had let the Sunshine Centre use their camping grounds, and Spencer was over the moon to have all the facilities they needed at hand.

The tents needed to go up first, and Will was teaching the boys what to do while Spencer continued to unload the centre's minibus.

He glanced at the sky. Weather was due to stay mild and dry, which was a blessing. He could just imagine waking in the night to find their tents washed away. At least the children would find it funny.

'Can we fry some bacon yet?' asked Leo.

Ryan frowned at him. 'Why bacon?'

Leo shrugged. 'Isn't that what campers do?'

'I think they eat beans,' said Jax, picking up a tent pole to hand to Will, who was doing most of the work.

'I'd rather have a bacon sandwich,' said Leo.

Will laughed. 'And I'd rather you lot mucked in. Come on.'

The boys started to help build the three tents the centre had provided.

'How many badges will we earn this weekend?' asked Leo, perusing the ones stitched to his lanyard.

Spencer glanced up, frowning, while making a start on the firepit. 'One. A camping badge.'

Ryan chuckled as Leo scoffed.

'What?' asked Spencer.

Leo pointed at the dugout. 'One for lighting a fire without matches.' He turned to Jax. 'I've seen it done on the telly.' He looked over at Will. 'Rock climbing tomorrow.'

Will held up his thumb.

'Anything else?' asked Spencer, trying not to laugh.

Leo's gaze fell to his friends as though asking for help.

'Cooking,' said Ryan. 'Bacon, of course.' He nudged Leo's arm.

'Ghost stories,' said Jax.

Will hammered a tent peg. 'Ooh, I love a good spooky tale.'

Leo huffed. 'Not too scary.'

'Think of the badge, Leo,' said Jax.

Spencer stood to help Ryan, who had got himself in a tangle with some rope. 'In that case, it had better be a good ghost story.'

'Does it have to be about ghosts?' Leo asked Jax.

Jax nodded. 'It's campfire law. My dad said.'

Spencer looked at Will and shared a grin.

It wasn't long before they were set up and looking mighty pleased with their efforts, even the grown-ups, and Spencer had them all trying to create a spark, blowing gently into tinder. Squeals of excitement erupted as small flames appeared, then Will added some fire-starter cubes to keep the fire alight, swiftly followed by a small log.

The boys ran off to find long sticks they could use to toast marshmallows, and Spencer went over to the kitchen area they'd set up, lighting a camping stove, ready to cook some bacon and make hot chocolate. His mind drifted to Beth and Archie, wondering what they were up to. It was his first night away from his son since meeting him.

'This is a good little camp we've got here,' said Will, washing his hands with a bottle of water over a plastic bowl. 'And good reception too.'

Spencer laughed. 'Have you been on your phone already?'

'I just checked to make sure I've got no messages from Ginny.'

'She'll be fine.'

'She's pregnant.'

'She'll still be fine.'

Will dried his hands on a blue tea towel. 'I know, but I still worry about her. She's my life, you know?'

No, he didn't know. He'd never felt that way about a partner before. Beth came to mind again. 'Did you know you liked her straight away?' he asked, pulling a frying pan out of a box.

Will looked deep in thought. 'I'm not sure what I thought of her when we first met. I guess there was some sort of weird pull of energy between us.' He shrugged. 'It was more the second time I saw her that had an effect on me. I didn't want to walk away. That's a good clue. When you want to spend time with them.' He smiled a smile that seemed to be just for him. 'I love hanging out with Ginny. She's my best friend.'

Spencer had no words so carried on with his chore, appreciating the smell of the bacon cooking, knowing that was sure to bring the kids back in a hurry.

'You like her, don't you?' Will had a soppy grin on his face.

'If you're talking about Beth, we're just friends.'

Will waggled a slice of bread at his head. 'Sure.'

Spencer's laugh abruptly stopped when he heard a yell, which sounded a lot like Leo.

'It's all right,' said Jax, appearing through some trees. 'Leo just tripped over himself.'

'It was a log,' corrected Leo, limping towards a camp chair.

Ryan appeared next, shaking his head. 'I didn't see a log.'

Leo plopped onto the chair and rolled up his tracksuit bottoms to reveal a grazed knee. 'Ouch, it's sore.'

Will brought the first aid kit over. 'Right, who wants to earn a nursing badge?'

Jax grimaced. 'What do we have to do?'

'Just a clean-up. He doesn't even need a plaster.' Will pulled out an antiseptic wipe.

'I'm not touching it,' said Ryan, taking a step back.

'Nor me,' said Jax.

Leo huffed. 'Oh, thanks!'

Will gently wiped over the graze, then told the boy to keep his trouser leg rolled up for a bit to let the air get to the sore.

'Are you sure I don't need a plaster?' asked Leo, assessing the damage.

Jax chuckled. 'Your mum packed superhero plasters for you, didn't she?'

Leo remained engaged with his wound. 'They're Mr Men ones, actually.'

Ryan scoffed. 'What are we, five?'

'Hey, I like the Mr Men,' said Leo.

Spencer wondered if he should start buying Archie books. There was the plastic one he had for the bath, and he seemed to like that. Perhaps bedtime stories could be introduced.

'Bacon's burning,' called Jax, standing over by the make-shift kitchen.

Spencer sprinted to the stove to save the rasher just in time. 'I'll have this one. It's only a little charred.'

Jax shook his head while laughing. 'I'll have the next one.'

Leo groaned. 'I should be fed first. I'm injured.'

Ryan patted his shoulder. 'You grazed your knee, mate. You're not dying.'

'Ooh, you won't be able to go rock climbing now,' said Jax.

Leo frowned. 'Yes, I will. Look.' He started bending and straightening his joint. 'See, all good.'

'Proper superhero, you are,' said Will, putting the first aid kit away. 'Healed so fast, it's almost a miracle.'

'My mum says healing takes as long as it takes.' Leo pulled a cereal bar from his pocket and broke it into pieces to share.

His words made Spencer wonder how long it would take for Beth to feel healed enough to go home. She'd be back at work at some point, and life would change for them all. The thought of not seeing her each day saddened him, so he focused on his present moment, making sure no more bacon got burned.

The boys sat around the fire with their drawing pads, designing their own badges to show Luna, and Will was cleaning the kitchen area while quietly singing a sea shanty.

Spencer could feel his phone in his jacket pocket tormenting him. Normally, he wouldn't feel the need to call anyone. He went over to Will for a chat to clear his head, but it was as though the man could read his mind.

'Itching to call home, eh, Spence?'

'What makes you think that?'

'Your face.'

Spencer rubbed his jaw. 'It's all a bit weird, if I'm honest. I'm not used to worrying about anyone except Lottie. Now I've got this lot always on my mind and Beth and Archie.'

'Ah, the joys of caring.'

Spencer breathed out a quiet laugh.

Will put a stack of plastic mugs away. 'I never had a family before, what with being raised in care. Ginny's the only person I've met in all my life who feels like home, and now we've a nipper on the way. I won't lie to you, Spence, I have my moments where it scares the hell out of me, but the good stuff we have is stronger than the fear, and just one look at my Ginny grounds me.'

'Spencer, what do you think?' called out Ryan, holding up his drawing.

'I still think Captain Spencer sounds better,' said Leo.

Spencer shook his head. 'Spencer is just fine. Now, let's see what you've created.' He sat between Ryan and Leo, and

Leo placed one part of his cape over Spencer's knee. 'What's that for?'

'In case you're missing Archie and Miss Horton.'

It was quite possible Spencer's heart melted a touch, but he sniffed, straightened his back, and paid attention to the lad's drawing.

'My dad misses me whenever I go anywhere,' said Jax, shading his picture.

'I don't think my mum cares about me,' mumbled Ryan, but everyone heard.

'Of course she does,' said Spencer. 'She's your mum. All mums care about their kids.' Why he said that was anyone's guess, as he knew full well it wasn't true. He was sure his own mother had hated his mere existence most days. Shaking off the memory, he offered Ryan a reassuring smile.

'Can we toast our marshmallows now?' asked Leo, and Spencer thought it the best plan, seeing how the mood had dropped.

Before long, more hot chocolate was poured, marshmallows eaten, and ghost stories told. Spencer was sure Leo wouldn't sleep after Jax told a tale of a severed hand in a school library murdering children on detention, and it took a while to get them settled into their sleeping bags. Will sang to them while Spencer sat by the fire, staring absentmindedly into the flickering flames.

It was soothing sitting in the dark, with not much going on. He closed his eyes for a moment, absorbing his surroundings.

Goodnight, Beth. Sleep well.

A high-pitched scream shot through the air, rattling his eardrums and bringing him to an immediate stand.

'It's a spider!' yelled Leo.

Ryan and Jax laughed as Will got rid of the offending creature that had dared to crawl along the child's head.

'Blimming heck, Leo. You scared the living daylights out of me.' Spencer was still clutching his chest.

Leo sat up, pointing at his mousey hair. 'How do you think I feel!'

Everyone burst out laughing while Leo went on to tell everyone he would never sleep a wink ever again.

It took a while, but the two men finally got the boys to settle down, even though it meant leaving the battery-operated lamps on all night.

Spencer clambered into his own tent, wide awake and on full alert in case anything else happened. He wasn't that vigilant with Archie. He propped his pillow up and decided to read a book on his phone. But holding the mobile only made him think of Beth again. It was late, so he shouldn't call, but maybe one short text would be acceptable. He wasn't even sure if she switched her phone off at night.

Erm, hope this doesn't wake you. Just hoping you had a good day. He shook his head and deleted the message. 'Nah, sounds like I'm thinking she can't cope without me.' He tapped out something else, mumbling the words as he went. *'In case you're still awake, thought I'd say goodnight.'* That seemed normal enough, so he sent the text.

There was some rustling in the boys' tent, but it soon went quiet again, so Spencer settled back down, ready for his book, but the screen flashed up, revealing Beth calling.

'Beth, everything okay?' he whispered.

'Yes,' she whispered back. 'Is it okay for you to talk?'

He nodded into his pillow. 'The boys are asleep now, and I think Will's about to crash, so I can talk. Are you all right?'

'Yes, I've had a good day. Just wanted to say hello.'

Spencer smiled. 'Hello.'

Her giggle warmed him.

'Is little man sleeping?'

'Yes, we're both in bed.'

He could see her there in his spare room, snuggled beneath the quilt, safe and cosy. 'What you up to tomorrow?'

'Ginny's invited me to her farm for a morning of decorating. Sophie, Lottie, and Alice are coming too. Hopefully we can help get another room sorted for her. Also, she's got chickens, so I'm going to show Archie. See what he thinks.'

'Sounds great. Has Ginny been okay? Will worries about her.'

Beth laughed. 'She's fine. I was with her earlier in her tea-room. It's ready for the grand opening as soon as you two get back.'

'I'm looking forward to it.'

To seeing you.

He swallowed hard, frowning. 'Are you tired?'

'A little. It feels strange you not being here. I think that's why I'm still awake.'

'Settle down, Beth,' he said softly. 'I'll leave the phone on till you fall asleep if you like.'

'But you need your battery.'

'I can charge it in the minibus when we drive to the rock-climbing place in the morning. Close your eyes.'

'You don't mind?' she whispered.

Spencer smiled, wishing she could see his expression. 'Close your eyes,' he repeated even quieter.

'Closed.'

'Goodnight, Beth.'

'Sweet dreams, Spencer.'

He snuggled further into his sleeping bag, placing his phone to the side of his face, and waited a good while before he closed his eyes and drifted off.

CHAPTER 22

Beth

As soon as Beth laid eyes on Ginny's rustic farmhouse, she fell in love. How wonderful to have such a home. A wood-burned sign at the entrance to the driveway announced *Happy Farm*, and that was the exact vibe it offered.

Ginny showed her inside. 'Haven't been here long, and I know I was supposed to have a housewarming party, or as I told everyone, more of a decorating party, but what with the tea shop and everything, I've had to keep putting things off.'

Beth perused the wide stairway. Even without a carpet or a polish it looked charming.

'Good thing we're helping today,' said Sophie, entering the hallway, a clean paintbrush aloft.

'I wasn't sure what to wear,' said Beth, glancing down at her jeans and shirt, thinking overalls could be needed.

Ginny waggled a hand around. 'You don't have to do much.'

Sophie scoffed. 'You didn't say that to me.' She grinned at Beth. 'Best make the most of Ginny making a fuss because you're new.'

'Please don't give me any special treatment. I'm looking forward to joining in.' Beth checked on Archie, happily gazing up at his pram mobile.

Lottie called out from the kitchen, 'You can make the tea, Beth.'

'Or just hang out with the chickens,' said Ginny, leading her towards Lottie. 'I'm sure Archie will love seeing them.'

Beth entered the country style kitchen to see Alice was also there.

'We're just having pastries before we start,' she told Beth, offering a chair.

Beth questioned them making a fuss. 'Have you all been told I'm taking things easy and getting help for my mental health?'

Sophie shook her head. 'I haven't been told much about you at all, and I didn't like to ask. We all know Archie came as a surprise to Spencer, and that you're co-parenting, but that's about it.'

Beth glanced at Lottie before turning to Sophie. 'I guess I assumed Lottie would have told Spencer's friends.'

'Not my story to tell,' said Lottie.

'No one's business but your own,' said Alice.

Beth looked at them each in turn, deciding to tell her new friends some of her story, leaving out the doorstep situation.

Lottie nodded. 'I'm glad Jan's helping.'

'Ooh, you're seeing January Riley? She's so good,' said Alice. 'It's like she's made of magic.'

Ginny laughed. 'Magic?'

Alice nibbled on some pastry. 'There's something about her that makes you feel better when you're in her presence. She has a calming effect.'

Beth agreed, feeling grateful once again to have met such a person. If only she could have met Jan sooner. What a difference it would have made. There was no point making those wishes. Future thinking was key, not past dwelling.

'How are you getting on now?' Sophie asked Beth.

'Much better. It really does make such a difference when you have a strong support team around you. For a long time, I only had my cousin, and as lovely as she is, she's always busy with her own life. Having Jan, Spencer, Lottie, and Sam helping has been brilliant. I can't thank them enough.'

'Hey, we're your family now,' said Lottie. 'No thanks needed.'

'And you have us too, should you need anything,' said Sophie, glancing at Ginny and Alice, who both nodded.

'Thank you. That's very kind. One thing I've learned lately is, it's better for me if I reach out when in need.'

'Definitely,' said Sophie. 'We all need a hand from time to time. No shame in that.'

Beth gazed at the table for a moment, not wanting to meet anyone's eyes. 'I did feel ashamed for a while.'

Ginny tutted. 'That's because there's too much stigma still attached to mental illness.' She lightly rubbed Beth's shoulder. 'You have nothing to feel ashamed of.'

Even though Beth now realised that to be true and was confident enough to speak openly about her mental health, she still felt the shame of leaving Archie on Spencer's doorstep. It was quite possible that act would haunt her forever. She understood about her state of mind at the time, and she had made sure to keep an eye on the pram until Spencer opened the door, but it didn't seem to make much of a difference.

'We speak a lot about mental health at the parent and baby club,' she told them. 'It helps when others tell you their stories. You stop feeling so abnormal.'

Ginny scoffed. 'There's no such thing as normal.'

Everyone agreed.

'So,' said Beth. 'Now you know a little more about me, how about we get started on this place?' She didn't want to sit around talking about herself, so tried for a subject change.

Ginny's smile was filled with appreciation. 'It would be good to get more of the house sorted. Will's going to decorate another bedroom as soon as he's back from camping, then we've got the tearoom opening. Hope you'll all be there. Free cupcakes will be on offer.'

'We'll be there anyway,' said Alice. 'But good to know.'

'I'm looking forward to it, Gin,' said Sophie, placing the paintbrush on the table. 'I'm so glad your dreams have all come true.' She turned to Beth. 'She's wanted a tearoom for ages now.'

'You do have a lot going on,' said Beth to Ginny. 'Perhaps you should be taking it easy as well.'

Ginny laughed. 'I've always been busy, but I will slow down once this place is in more of a liveable state before the baby comes.' She looked at Beth. 'We won't have a lot of time to do DIY then, so best do what we can now. We don't mind doing things slowly over time, but if we can just fix up the basics, that'll be good.'

Lottie pointed at the kitchen cabinet lying on the table. 'I'm cleaning these, ready for a fresh lick of paint. What a difference to the kitchen that alone will make.'

'And I'm painting the sides of the stairs and banisters, then some carpet can go down,' said Sophie.

Alice motioned at the ceiling. 'And I'm ripping off old crusty tiles. Nobody needs a gruesome bathroom.'

Ginny folded her arms, looking deep in thought for a moment. 'We've done our bedroom and the living room, so we're good there.'

'Are you having a nursery?' asked Beth. 'I could help with that.' Not that she'd created one before. Ever since Archie was born he had slept in a cot at her bedside.

'The baby will probably be in with us for a while,' said Ginny. 'But it would still be nice to have a clean room for all their bits. So, yeah, Beth, that would be great. The old wallpaper needs to come down. Most of it has peeled off anyway, but the steamer should make light work of the rest. We can do that together.'

Alice slid the plate of pastries across the empty part of the large table. 'Here, eat something first, Beth. A morning snack will give us all a boost.'

Lottie sipped some pineapple juice. 'And you can tell us if we're needed for anything for the festival.' She turned to Sophie. 'Debra has managed to get the pop-up stalls hire company to donate the stands for the day, and we've got a large tent for the centre's arts and crafts display.'

'Are you selling any of your paintings, Lott?' asked Alice.

'Yep, but just the one. I haven't had much time to paint lately. Hannah's got about three, then there are the other members' artworks too.'

Beth nodded. 'And the boys have organized a section for children to draw and make bead bracelets. They really want to showcase the things kids can do at the Sunshine Centre.'

'I'm staffing a stall,' said Alice. She smiled softly at Beth. 'Info on how to help care for cancer patients at home who are going through treatments. My sister died of cervical cancer, so I'm used to going to universities and colleges to give talks on the importance of screening, but seeing how the festival is all about kindness, I thought I could offer some helpful handy hints and tips on care I picked up along the way.'

Beth's heart went out to her. 'I'm sorry about your sister. It's great that you go into schools to raise awareness. There will be lots of information stalls at the festival. Perhaps you could add some info about screening.'

Alice nodded her agreement.

'I'll be on the Hub's stall with Will and Matt,' said Sophie.'

Lottie raised a finger. 'And I'm helping Sam showcase what the Les Powell Trust is all about.'

'I'll be advertising the baby bank, mostly, and I think Spencer is going to lend a hand all over,' said Beth, wondering if he was at the rock-climbing place yet. The grin from Sophie aimed her way didn't go unnoticed.

'How are things with him?' asked Sophie, nibbling on a croissant.

Beth tried to force away the heat building in her neck. 'He seems fine.'

Alice chuckled. 'She meant between you and Spence.'

Oh, she knew exactly what Sophie meant. She was just trying to play it down for fear of them noticing her eyes beam with delight when saying his name.

'They're just friends,' said Lottie, glancing her way as though searching for confirmation.

Beth nodded, then pretended to be interested in a cinnamon swirl.

'So leave them alone,' added Lottie.

Sophie shrugged. 'Just asking.' She smiled at Beth. 'You always look so happy together whenever I see you out and about.'

'Ignore her,' said Lottie. 'Ever since she fell in love with Matt, she sees unicorns and rainbows everywhere.'

Sophie burst out laughing. 'You can talk. I've seen the way you look at Sam.'

Lottie frowned, showing amusement. 'And how exactly is that?'

Sophie mocked a swoon. 'All fluttering eyelashes and soppy grin.'

Lottie gestured at Ginny. 'Sounds more like Will.'

Ginny laughed. 'Ah, it does. Big goof.'

It was nice seeing the women come alive while talking about their partners, and Beth wished she had that kind of love in her life. It wasn't something she'd considered much after falling pregnant, then when her mind started messing with her, she gave up all hope of ever being her old self, let alone having a decent relationship. Would anyone even want her?

'Spencer,' said Alice, pulling Beth from her thoughts.

'Hmm?' she asked, sure she'd missed some of the sentence.

'Even if you are just mates, at least you can rest easy knowing your son has a good dad.' Alice smiled. 'Makes a difference.'

Beth nodded. 'Spencer's brilliant with Archie.'

'Did you go to any parenting classes?' asked Ginny. 'My clinic is offering them, but I'm not sure yet.'

'No. I didn't feel it was for me.'

'I read one book on parenting when I took over guardianship of Benny,' said Alice. 'I found it too technical. Mum said I was being daft, and just to get on with it. I guess it was easier for me because I was living with Mum and Nan. They weren't worried about how to raise him. I just didn't want to mess him up by getting things wrong.'

Sophie moved to Alice, swinging an arm around her shoulder. 'You've done a brilliant job with Benny. He's a great kid.'

Beth glanced at Archie's pram, wondering if he would grow up being a problem child because of her mistakes. 'It is a worry,' she mumbled, not meaning to speak aloud.

'Don't worry about him,' said Lottie. 'He's got all the love in the world around him, and my aunt used to say that's all kids need.' She manoeuvred her electric wheelchair over to Archie. 'Maybe we should put him in the living room, out of the way while we decorate,' she whispered. 'He's asleep.'

'I'll do it,' said Alice, looking at Beth for approval.

Beth nodded, and Alice wheeled the pram off to the cosy living room, leaving the door ajar.

Everyone made a start on their tasks, but Ginny took Beth's arm and guided her to the back door. 'Here, let me show you the chicken coop first. I'm going to get more rescue animals once the baby's here. It was always the plan.'

Beth inhaled the fresh day as she headed over to the pen. 'It's beautiful here.' The green fields stretched far and wide, drawing her in even more. Oh, how she would love to flick off her shoes and run through the grass, spin in circles, and jump for joy. 'It makes me feel free.' She frowned at herself, then glanced at Ginny. 'Does that even make sense?'

Ginny smiled, gazing out at the view. 'Yep. Gets me every time, and I used to have a sea view. Wouldn't get me moving from here. Not now. I'm looking forward to it being more of a rescue farm.' She pointed to one side. 'Got a large outhouse over there, and a smaller one just behind. We've not figured out what to do with those yet, but whatever comes of this place, it will be farm vibes only.'

'It's relaxing just standing here.'

'Will says that. He loves our home just as much as me.'

Beth turned to smile. 'I'm glad you're happy.'

Ginny nudged her elbow. 'Wasn't always that way, so don't feel too bad if you find yourself treading water for a while. We've all been there at some point.'

Apart from the pregnancy problem, Beth realized she hadn't had much in the way of treading water during her life. Perhaps Ginny was right, and everyone had to have a turn of doom and gloom. She gazed once more at the acres before her. Jan did tell her to simply look at the bad times as chapters, rather than the whole story.

'It's not always easy turning the page, is it?' she found herself saying out loud.

Ginny smiled warmly. 'No, but look what can happen if you do.' Her arms splayed to the scene before them. 'I never thought I'd find such peace in my life, Beth, but I did. You have to look at people who go from doom and gloom to their own happy farm and know it's doable. The ones that walk before you, show you the way.'

Beth raised her chin. It was time she started building a life she wanted. Happy Farm had inspired her no end. 'Thanks, Gin.'

'That's what friends are for, chick.'

A wave of warmth filled Beth. She hadn't just found Spencer, she'd discovered a whole village of friendship, and for that she was grateful.

CHAPTER 23

Spencer

The six-metre rock face only seemed to intimidate Jax, as Ryan and Leo were raring to go.

'This is the beginners' route,' said Will, standing at the bottom, holding his rope with the guide, Graham.

'How do I know where to climb?' Jax asked Will, gazing up.

Graham guided him to a large boulder and pointed at a crevasse. 'You have to figure it out as you go. Give it a try, and don't worry about falling. You're secure.'

Spencer motioned towards a wide crack. 'Step in that, Jax. Looks like a good start.'

Jax did as he was instructed, and everyone watched as the boy quietly navigated his journey, with the odd tip called out from Graham.

Spencer turned to Leo and Ryan. 'Hear that? Push up with your legs.'

Leo was concentrating on Jax. 'I'm just going to follow him.'

Will chuckled. 'And are you going to abseil back down if Jax doesn't?'

Leo shrugged, trying to place a piece of his cape in his mouth, which was proving a task, seeing how his clothing had been secured so nothing would obstruct him during his climb. 'I'm going to do it.'

'Don't worry if you change your mind once up top,' said Will. 'It looks different from that angle.'

Spencer double-checked Leo's cape was tucked in. There was no way the kid was removing his emotional support item of clothing, so stopping it from flapping was the next best thing.

Jax came to a halt close to the top. 'I don't know where to go, Spencer,' he called.

Graham spoke first. 'Take a moment, Jax. Think of it like a puzzle. There's a pathway, and you've just got to find the right track.'

Will nudged Spencer. 'Breathe. He's perfectly safe.'

As much as Spencer could see the boys were filled with excitement, he was still slightly apprehensive about the activity now they were faced with the large rock.

Jax started climbing again, and it wasn't long before he was up top with Graham's team.

'Ready, Leo?' asked Spencer, checking him over with Graham.

Leo was eager to get started and climbed a lot faster than Jax had.

Will turned to Ryan. 'It's a lot easier when you go last.'

Ryan smiled. 'I'm okay. I'm looking forward to my turn.'

'Good,' said Spencer, his eyes on Leo's small hands roaming across the rough surface.

'Pay close attention to the details of the rock,' Will told Ryan. 'With climbing, you're part of the landscape, you're in each gap, each step. Fully alert to the structure around you.'

Spencer could see Ryan was paying close attention, and it was good to see the boy having fun.

Leo's squeal echoed down the precipice. 'I did it,' he cheered.

Spencer started clapping as Graham got Ryan ready for the climb. He turned to Will and grinned. 'I reckon they'll want to climb again if they get back down here.'

Will nodded. 'Gets you like that. At first, it's daunting, but once you've showed yourself what you're capable of, you get a rush of excitement, and it frees your soul.'

A gentle breeze rustled the trees around them, and Spencer closed his eyes for a second while inhaling the woodland scent. How free he already felt just being surrounded by Mother Nature. One day he hoped to stand in the same spot and watch his son climb to the sky. He would raise Archie to be active and to enjoy the beauty of nature. He opened his eyes and watched Ryan begin his ascent.

'You going up next, Spence?' asked Will.

'I'll see if they abseil. If so, I'll climb after they go back up.'

'Yeah, I want to be down here for that too.'

Graham was telling Ryan not to use his knees on the ledges, and the boy huffed before using his arms to pull himself higher. Everyone knew Ryan was as fit as a butcher's dog, so why he was on the go-slow was surprising. Perhaps he was absorbing every moment because of what Will had told him.

'He's been quiet this morning,' said Will.

Spencer was watching Ryan carefully. 'Maybe the thought of rock climbing made him nervous.'

'I wish he would say if something was on his mind.'

'He keeps everything close to his chest.'

Will pointed up. 'They're good kids you've got there, Spence. I reckon all you've been doing with them will help open them up soon enough.'

'Their confidence is growing, but I'm not sure how much will change for them.'

'Confidence changes a lot, mate.'

Spencer nodded, mainly to himself. He'd give anything to see Leo live life without triggers, hear Jax's idle chit-chat with those he encountered, and have Ryan use his voice to tell all what his heart really desired.

'And he's done it,' said Will, interrupting Spencer's thoughts.

One of Graham's team called out to let them know the boys were coming back down. So Spencer, Will, and Graham moved over to a different part of the rock face to watch the lads abseil.

Leo was the first to descend, slowly pushing his feet from the rock, and Spencer was sure he could hear the boy humming.

The sun peeked through the trees, creating sparkles of light on the boulders down below for a moment, and some birds nestled in branches seemed to join in with Leo's song.

'I was flying,' said Leo, landing at the bottom. His cheeks were flushed, and eyes wide with jubilation.

'You enjoyed that then?' asked Spencer, grinning.

Leo spun in a circle as soon as his harness was unclipped. 'I want to do it again, and again, and again.'

'Ah,' said Graham, getting ready for the next child to abseil. 'I see you have learned rock language.'

Leo giggled. 'What did I say?'

'It's not the words,' said Graham, adding a smile. 'It's how this makes you feel. That is the language.'

Jax was the next one down, and unlike Leo, he wasn't keen to do a repeat performance, stating he much preferred going up to coming down. Leo tried to tell him about the rock language, but Jax felt he'd chatted enough with the precipice to last a lifetime. He'd earned his badge, and that was good enough.

Once Ryan was down, Graham had everyone sit down for a while and sip some water before they would climb again to head back to camp. He explained how much exercise their bodies were receiving and that a little rest would be beneficial.

The boys started to get restless within minutes and went off to mooch around by the trees while Spencer and Will questioned Graham on harder routes and all the places he had scaled.

It wasn't long before Graham had Jax back on the rock face, and this time Jax figured out his pathway a lot quicker.

'They'll eat well this lunchtime,' said Will, nudging Spencer's arm. 'I'm hungry already.'

'We'll cook the burgers as soon as we're back in camp,' said Spencer. 'Then get ready to head home.' He laughed. 'Not sure how I'm going to beat this.'

'What about horse riding? They might like to give that a go.'

Spencer nodded. He'd speak to Debra. After the morning they'd had, he felt anything was possible for the boys.

'I saw a fella flying a kite over the park the other day,' said Will. 'You could look into that. How to make them and so on.'

'I like that idea,' said Spencer, turning to see Leo and Ryan balancing on some small boulders low to the ground, Leo posing like a superhero. 'Get off those before one of you slips.'

Leo stepped down, apologizing. 'I was being a statue.'

Ryan decided to jump. His foot skidded, causing him to tip to one side and land on his arm. 'Ouch!' he groaned, getting up.

Leo's mouth was gaping. 'You okay?'

Spencer darted to Ryan's side. 'What hurts?'

Ryan raised his elbow. 'My arm.'

Will quickly assessed the damage. 'Can't see any major problems. Just bruised.'

'All okay over there?' asked Graham, signalling up to his team, who already had Jax in their care.

Spencer gave him the thumbs up.

One of Graham's team raced through the trees quickly to check Ryan over. His arm was indeed bruised but okay, which was a relief for everyone.

Spencer told Will he would go with the team member the long way round to the top and meet him at the minibus, as he didn't want Ryan to climb again now his arm was bruised.

'Oh, but I want to climb,' said Ryan.

'Graham won't let anyone with an injury climb,' Spencer told him as they walked away.

'It's just a bruise. Look.' Ryan waggled his arm to prove his point.

'All the same. It's the rules.'

They met the others back at the minibus, Spencer thanking the rock-climbing team for a great day and for being so efficient when it came to Ryan's tumble.

The boys were in good spirits on the drive back to camp for lunch, even if Ryan was a tad fed up he had missed out on climbing again.

Back at the camp, Spencer filled out the incident report, then checked in with Debra to let her know they were heading back to the centre soon.

Will got the lads to help pack up, and it wasn't long before they were on the road.

The children chatted excitedly about their adventure, the spider that crawled on Leo, the marshmallows they'd roasted, sleeping in a tent, and how they had survived knee grazes and bruised arms.

Leo said it was his idea to try to balance on the small boulder, and that he had paid attention to the health and safety chat back at the rock-climbing centre, but he didn't think standing on a low piece of rock would be dangerous.

'At least I can tell my mum my arm is too bruised to swim now,' said Ryan, staring out the minibus window.

Spencer held back a frown but found he couldn't bite back his thoughts any longer. 'Ryan, it sounds like you don't want to swim at all.'

Leo placed a piece of his cape over Ryan's leg. 'I thought it was just your anxiety about racing.'

Ryan shook his head. 'It's stressful, not fun, but my mum wants me to be an Olympic swimmer one day.' He sounded deflated.

'And what do you want?' asked Spencer.

The boy sighed quietly. 'Not to swim again.'

Spencer knew he couldn't get involved in the boy's life outside of the centre, but he figured it wouldn't hurt to give one piece of advice. 'Have you spoken to your mum about this, Ryan?'

'She's not easy to talk to.'

'Perhaps you could try again.'

Ryan gave a small head bob, then turned to his friends to talk about the kindness festival, showing Spencer he wanted a subject change.

It quietened down a bit as they neared the centre, with the exception of the odd rustle of crisp packets.

'Sorry,' said Ryan suddenly, gaining everyone's attention. 'My mum will probably shout when she finds out I bruised my arm.'

Spencer shook his head. 'It was just an accident, that's all. I'm sure she'll understand. She'll just be pleased to see you're fine.'

'It's all right,' said Leo.

'No, it's not,' said Ryan quietly, turning to the window, steaming the pane with his breath. He didn't need to say another word. Spencer already got the memo: Ryan's swimming was the most important thing in the world.

Debra was standing in the main entrance of the Sunshine Centre when they pulled up, giving them a welcome wave.

Spencer said a warm hello as they all headed inside where the parents were waiting to take their children home.

Leo's mum was the first to cradle her child. 'How was your adventure, my little lion?'

Leo beamed. 'A huge spider walked over my face, and we told ghost stories, and I climbed the tallest mountain, and Ryan bruised his arm, and—'

Annette gasped. 'What?' She scanned Ryan's arm, not rushing to comfort him or ask after his wellbeing. Her icy glare chilled the room. 'How did he bruise his arm? Have you any idea how important his next race is?'

Bonnie bent to Ryan's eye level and lightly stroked back his blond locks. 'You poor thing. How are you feeling?'

Ryan went to say that he was fine, but his mother cut across him.

'Never mind that,' snapped Annette. 'I want an explanation.'

Spencer faced Ryan's mum and told her what had happened, including how Graham's medical team had double-checked Ryan's arm to confirm it was just bruised, and that it had been filed in the incident book, not that it helped anything simmer down.

'I've a good mind to sue the lot of you, and get this centre and the stupid rock-climbing place shut down.' Annette paced by the office door.

Chris gave Jax a cuddle as his child leaned into his side. 'A bit dramatic, don't you think, Annette?'

If the woman's eyes could turn red and shoot laser beams, Spencer was sure Chris would be toast by now.

'Perhaps if your son was set to become an Olympian, you'd have something sensible to add,' she growled.

Chris shook his head. 'He slipped. And more importantly, he's all right. It's just a bruise.'

Annette pointed a finger at Spencer. 'He should have been keeping an eye on the children, not letting them wander off to do whatever they wanted. I put my trust in this centre, and now look.' Her finger moved to Ryan, who started crying.

'Hey, it's okay,' said Spencer, about to squat to comfort Ryan.

'Don't you touch him,' snapped Annette. 'You've done enough damage.'

Bonnie gave Ryan a hug instead, seeing how Annette didn't bother. She whispered soothing words while his mother continued to rant.

Debra tried to calm Annette. 'If you'd like to wait, I can give you a copy of the incident report. The rock-climbing centre will email me one as well. I can fetch you some tea and—'

'Tea!' yelled Annette. 'I don't want your bloody tea.' She whipped around to face Ryan. 'You can still race, right? Bruised, they said.'

Ryan sniffed. 'I don't want to swim.'

'Of course you do. It's just a bit of stage fright at the start, that's all, you know, like those actors get.'

Ryan shook his head. 'I don't want to swim,' he repeated quietly. 'Spencer said I should tell you.'

Annette glared at Spencer. 'Oh, so you put this in his head, did you?'

Spencer found his mouth gaping.

'Perhaps we could discuss this further at the children's progress meeting next week,' suggested Debra.

'Yes, we will,' snapped Annette. 'My husband is home from work then and will want to attend.'

Ryan's sniffles caused Bonnie to give him another hug. She glared over at Annette. 'Could you calm down, please?'

Annette moved her son away. 'Why should I? Look at what bringing Ryan here has achieved. All I wanted was for you lot to bring back the confidence he lost. He needs to swim.'

'He doesn't want to,' said Bonnie.

Annette swung open the main door with such force, it was a surprise it didn't come off its hinges. 'Of course he does, you stupid woman.'

'Hey!' snapped Chris, but Annette stormed off.

Jax looked up at his dad. 'Is she really going to close the centre?'

Chris shook his head. 'No. She's just upset right now, that's all.'

'Everything will get sorted at the meeting,' said Debra, looking more hopeful than Spencer felt.

No one had met Ryan's dad yet, so Spencer didn't know if they would have two irate parents on their hands wanting to shut them down. He only hoped the man was reasonable enough.

With a banging headache, a need for dinner, and his heart in pieces for Ryan, Spencer went off to Debra's office to talk about the trip, when all he really wanted was to go home. He was looking forward to seeing Beth and Archie, but he wasn't sure how much joy he could bring to their evening while feeling utterly exhausted on every level.

CHAPTER 24

Beth

Beth wasn't sure what time Spencer would be home from camping, and as she hadn't heard from him all day, she decided to make a cold dinner of hard-boiled eggs, ham, salad, and potato salad. At least if he'd already eaten, it would keep in the fridge for the next night.

Archie was settled on a spongey mat in a small round playpen, staring up at a musical mobile. He'd been fed and bathed, and Beth hadn't once felt stressed or pressured to meet any deadlines she'd created. In fact, since living with Spencer, she'd stopped trying to make Archie fit into routines, finding working around him instead slightly easier.

Beth started to hum along to the baby music as she chopped lettuce. It was nice to have a proper appetite back, and her energy. She was enjoying cooking again, pottering around Spencer's small kitchen.

She'd had a good day spending time at Ginny's, then seeing Jan for a chat. She'd popped back to her flat to pick up some more clothes, and while there contemplated doing her own decorating. After seeing the farmhouse, and dreaming of such a cosy home, inspiration had hit. If she just poured some love into her own place, she was sure she'd feel better about living there.

'I think it's because we haven't been there long,' she told Archie, peering his way. 'I'll speak to your dad about helping make the place homely.'

She put the chopping knife down and went over to the playpen. If only Archie could tell her what would make him happy. He seemed happy. His eyes shifted from the mobile to her, and all she saw was Spencer for a moment.

'Do you prefer living here?' she asked quietly, as though someone might overhear.

Archie went back to staring at the dangling teddy bears.

Beth glanced around the room. It was silly to think she could stay with Spencer forever. Maybe she was just nervous about being on her own again. She decided to bring up the subject with Jan at their next session.

Feeling proud about having coped quite well while Spencer was away, Beth practically skipped back to the kitchen to finish preparing dinner. It was so nice to feel alive again. Wow, what a difference the last few weeks had made. She was starting to believe going back to work after maternity leave was doable, as she was sure at one point she would quit her job and spend the rest of her life curled up in a ball in the corner of the bedroom.

Beth smiled at the pastel-blue jug filled with pink tulips on the windowsill in front of her. She couldn't look at a flower now without thinking of Spencer. Speaking of which . . . She turned to the door on hearing it open.

Spencer entered, dropping his holdall on the spot while kicking off his boots. He smiled, but it looked as tired as the rest of his pale face.

'You okay?' Beth stepped closer, inspecting him from head to toe.

His shoulders hunched as he sighed. 'I'm whacked.'

'Long drive, was it? Traffic bad?'

'No. We actually came back earlier than expected, but I've been at the centre . . . forever.' He flopped onto a kitchen chair, and Beth went to the fridge to fetch some orange juice, thinking he needed a boost.

'You don't look very well, Spence.' She placed the glass in front of him, then put one hand on his forehead.

Spencer's head dipped slightly as he closed his eyes. 'I'm okay,' he mumbled.

Beth removed her hand and sat to his side. 'Drink your juice.'

He sat up a bit and took a sip. 'Ryan bruised his arm.'

'Oh no. How did he manage that?'

'Slipped.'

Beth sat in silence while Spencer explained what had happened at rock climbing. She was relieved Ryan was okay. Spencer, not so much.

'Let's get some dinner in you,' she told him, moving to the worktop to plate up some food. 'Put some energy back.'

'Thanks,' came a feeble reply.

Beth quickly sorted their food while Spencer went over to say hello to Archie.

'Oh, he's asleep.' Spencer sat on the sofa and pressed his head back, closing his eyes. 'Seems like a good plan.'

Without trying to disturb him too much, Beth draped a blanket over his legs, then went to fetch their food. She sat by his side, plate on lap, and placed his to her side.

'I smell food.'

She grinned at his half-smile. 'I can feed you if you're that tired. Even do aeroplane noises like you do for Archie with his bottle.'

His grin widened. 'Don't tempt me.'

Beth averted her eyes as his opened. She raised her fork to her mouth as he shifted and took his plate.

'Thanks for dinner,' he said softly. It seemed as though he was going to say something else, but his head lowered as his hand lifted to support his chin.

Immediately, Beth placed both their plates on the floor and shuffled closer to his side. 'Hey, it's okay.'

'It's just . . . It was so . . . Annette was . . .' He sighed slowly and heavily.

Beth started to rub circles on the top of his back, hoping to soothe his weary soul. It was obvious Ryan's accident was affecting him more than he had said. 'It'll be okay.'

'I don't want the centre getting negative reviews because Ryan bruised his arm on my watch. I feel terrible, Beth.'

She pressed her head against his shoulder for a moment. 'It's not your fault. Annette will calm down and see it for the accident it was.'

'I'll find out at the meeting, but I won't hold my breath. Jeez, you should have heard her. It's like all that matters in her life is Ryan being in the Olympics one day.' He raked a hand through his copper locks, then turned his head to gaze her way.

Beth stopped stroking his back. 'I guess it's their dream.'

Spencer scoffed. 'Her dream.'

'You don't think it's Ryan's?'

Flopping back into the sofa, Spencer sighed. 'Ryan told his mum he didn't want to swim, all because I told him he should let his mum know how he feels. Annette didn't listen. She just blamed me for putting the idea in his head.' He groaned quietly. 'I feel absolutely shattered.'

Beth lifted a plate to his lap. 'Eat something, and I'll run you a bath.'

Spencer sniffed his armpit. 'Trying to tell me something?'

It was good to see his humour was still in there. 'Trying to help you relax.'

He glanced at his dinner. 'I'm too wound up.'

'Do you want me to show you one of the techniques I learned?'

A droopy smile appeared just before he nodded. 'Go on then.'

Beth removed his plate again and told him to lie flat as she slid to the floor at his side.

'I feel better already.'

She nudged his foot. 'Close your eyes and follow the instructions.'

'Yes, Miss Horton,' he whispered.

'We're going to start with your feet, then work our way up to your head.'

'Are you going to massage me?'

Beth smiled to herself, then thought it best not to think about her hands all over him. 'Sort of.'

Spencer yawned, stretching his limbs. 'Okay, I'm ready.'

'I want you to scrunch your toes, then release, then take a moment to think about the difference between tension and relaxation.'

He did as he was told.

'Now, stiffen your legs and release. Think about the difference.' She waited a beat, then tried not to giggle as she told him to clench his bum. 'Now tighten your stomach . . . And relax. Note the way your body feels when relaxed.'

Spencer's chest lifted and fell steadily as he continued to tighten parts of his body and then relax them.

'Clench your fists,' she said quietly, trying to make her voice sound soothing. 'Now, your shoulders.'

He rolled his neck from side to side before stretching his mouth and scrunching his eyes, as instructed.

Beth continued to say the same thing over and over, reminding him to take note of the difference in tension and relaxation. There was something else she wanted to try while he was settled. It was something Lola had taught her at the parent and baby club. 'Spencer, is it okay if I touch your face now?' she asked quietly.

A slow smile appeared along with a consenting groan.

Beth crawled over to his head so she was looking down at him from behind. She placed her fingertips on his eyebrows and lightly massaged around the area before moving to his temples.

Spencer grumbled his approval.

Part of her wanted to lean over and kiss his head, but she told herself off for the thought and carried on massaging his cheekbones.

'Beth,' he mumbled. 'I feel better, thank you.'

She removed her fingers and stared at his face for a moment.

'I'm just going to rest here for a bit,' he added. 'Please, eat your dinner.'

'Okay. I'll put yours in the fridge.' She got up to do that, then went to check on Archie before turning back to Spencer. They were both sleeping, so she covered Spencer with the blanket, took Archie to his cot, then sat and had her dinner alone. Only, she didn't feel alone. She felt part of something wonderful. A family.

CHAPTER 25

Spencer

Ginny's Tearoom was officially open and half of Port Berry were in and out all day for the grand opening. Alice stood on the pavement outside with Will handing out mini cupcake samples to anyone passing by, Matt was cleaning tables with Sophie, and Robson had joined in with Ginny's staff serving hot beverages.

Spencer sat by one of the windows, Beth and Archie to his side. He smoothed over the boat print tablecloth, scooping some blueberry muffin crumbs into his palm. He hadn't had much appetite all morning, but the sweet treat was hard to resist, plus Beth seemed keen for him to eat something.

Beth bobbed a pale-blue balloon attached to the table, pulling it down so Archie could see. She was laughing at his little mouth opening every time it came close. 'I'm sure he thinks everything is food.'

Spencer rested back against the exposed brick wall and gazed out at the sea across the road from the tea shop. The pier looked empty, and the waves calm enough. All the seagulls had got wind of the cakes on offer, one of them diving in on Alice and the tray in her hands. He had to laugh as she squealed while Will waved the bird away. He gazed back at the tablecloth.

'Why don't we get your face painted?' suggested Beth, and when Spencer looked up, he realized she was talking to him.

'That's for the kids.'

'Nonsense. Matt has sparkles across his nose, and I saw a star on Will's forehead. I'm not sure about Ginny's rosy cheeks, as they look real.' She laughed, gazing around the light and airy tearoom. 'But look, Sophie's having her face painted now.'

He wasn't quite sure why Sophie wanted a zebra face, but he knew he didn't want one. 'Get yourself a rainbow or something.' He gestured at a boy who had one on each cheek.

'Ooh, no. What if I get a rash?'

Spencer frowned. 'What if *I* get a rash?'

Beth giggled. 'We'll cover it up with more face paint.' She stood, taking Archie with her. 'I'm just going to show him the seagulls.'

'Mind they don't take off with him. They're on form today.' He followed her to the opened door.

Bonnie approached with Leo. 'Oh, this place looks so quaint,' she said, staring up at the pretty cursive sign.

Leo was busy perusing what was on offer on Will's tray. 'How many am I allowed?'

Will chuckled. 'Are you trying to earn a cupcake eating badge now, lad?'

Leo's eyes widened at Spencer.

'Nope,' said Spencer. 'You'll be sick.'

Leo grinned at his mum. 'Okay, no badge for that. I'll just have one.' He picked up two. 'Maybe more.'

Bonnie spotted the lady painting Sophie's face at the other end of the shop. 'Look, Leo, let's go get our sparkle on.'

With a mouthful of vanilla frosting, he agreed, nudging Spencer in the same direction.

Normally, Spencer would be one of the first in line to have some fun, but he just couldn't shake off the gloominess he'd been feeling since Ryan hurt his arm. He told Leo to go ahead without him, then turned back to the window to see if Ryan and his mum had turned up. The odds were slim, but he had hoped they would take up the invitation. At least then he could have another chance to talk to Annette before their meeting.

Jax was outside with his dad, but no sign of Ryan. He waved at Spencer, then moved to a table to watch a man make balloon animals.

Ginny lightly placed a hand on Spencer's back. 'You okay, chick?'

He forced a smile as he nodded. 'Yeah, fine. Good turn-out, Gin. Lovely what you've done with the place.'

She smiled up at the dark wooden beams crossing the white ceiling. 'I've been visualizing this business for a good while now. It's a good feeling when you see it all come together.' She laughed, motioning towards Will, surrounded by a group of kids. 'He used to get more excited over my mood boards than I did.'

'You had mood boards?'

'It helps. Haven't you got one for anything?'

'I don't think I put that much detail into things.'

Ginny leaned into his arm. 'I've always been a dreamer. When you spend so much time doing it, you just picture everything in so much detail.'

Spencer placed an arm around her shoulder as they both stared outside. 'Did you dream up Willard Pendleton?'

Will walked towards them with an empty tray. He was grinning from ear to ear, and Spencer noticed the smile in Ginny's hazel eyes.

'I think I did,' she told Spencer, before following her partner to the counter for more cupcake samples.

Jax approached, holding a balloon dog aloft. 'What are we doing for our next badge? Leo said something about cupcakes.'

'I don't know yet. I'm not sure what's happening with the Sunshine Superheroes until next week.'

Jax tapped the leg of a nearby table with his foot. 'You mean once Ryan's mum has spoken at our progress meeting.' He looked to his dad, who was talking to Bonnie, waiting in line at the face-painting table.

Spencer poked the nose of the balloon dog. 'Hey, don't you worry about anything. Debra's been running that centre for years. She'll sort everything. All you have to do is enjoy your day. Now, how about getting your face painted? I'm thinking lion.'

Jax wrinkled his nose, then went over to Leo, who was ordering a milkshake.

Beth came back, still holding Archie, and proceeded to tell him that Jed was out front, dressed as a pirate. She was laughing while encouraging him to take a look.

It was no surprise to Spencer to see their friends helping to make Ginny's day special. Jed already had a group of people around him, listening to his tall tales of treasure maps and ferocious storms.

Lottie came whizzing along the pavement, dressed as a mermaid, telling everyone she passed that the pirates had saved her, and to celebrate they should all drink tea and eat cake.

Samuel was close behind, looking like he'd just stepped off a pirate ship. His hat was held high, then dipped low to rest upon Archie's head, hiding him immediately.

Beth laughed, removing the headwear so the baby could stare at the birds once more.

Spencer went back inside to order a couple of orange juices. One of the framed harbour paintings on the wall was lopsided, so he straightened that while he waited, then forced himself to hum along to the music playing to see if that would lift his mood.

Beth was sitting inside by the time he got their drinks. A piece of pastel floral bunting was draped over her chair, having become detached from the window. 'I was just going to put Archie in the pram and pin this back up.'

'I'll do it.' He stood on the chair to her side and fixed the garland back in place. 'I just sorted a picture that had been knocked.' He sat down and sipped his drink.

'It is so busy, which is great for Ginny. I'm so pleased for her. She's beyond happy.'

Spencer was pleased to see Beth so happy. 'Here, let me hold him for a bit. Your arms must be aching by now.'

Beth chuckled. 'He doesn't want to be in the pram.'

'Maybe he needs one where he can sit up and see the world. He loves looking around.'

'His pram came with one of those seats. I'm not sure what age babies are when they move into that type.'

Spencer whipped out his phone as he placed Archie to his chest so the baby could see over his shoulder. 'Let's have a look.'

Beth drank some juice. 'It would be nice for him to have a view when we go on walks.'

'Here we go. Says here babies should stay in the carrycot prams until they're around five to six months or can sit up unaided.' He put the phone on the table and patted Archie's padded bum. 'That counts you out, matey.'

'It won't be long. And those pushchair seat units are quite padded, so we'll see how he goes next month.'

Spencer glanced out the window. 'It'll be nice for him come summer.'

'The parent and baby group go on daytrips in the summer.'

'Do you think you'll join them?'

'Definitely, I'm looking forward to it. You can come too. We only have one dad who attends. He might be along later. I did invite them all, but I haven't spotted anyone from the group yet.'

'So, who is this dad?'

'Edward. He's really nice. A single parent. Not too sure of his story, but I think he's rich. He's always splashing out on his son. Can't say I've ever seen little Lester in the same outfit twice.' Beth glanced at the door as a man entered. 'I'll introduce you if he shows up. He's so friendly. He's asked us to come to his for a playdate.'

Spencer quirked an eyebrow.

I bet he did.

'That's nice of him.'

Beth nodded. 'I told him I haven't got time at the moment, what with the festival coming up and me trying to get the baby bank sorted. Ooh, that reminds me. Will you come to club with me next time? Everyone has agreed to donate something, and Edward has loads of new bits and pieces. I could do with a hand.'

Spencer unclenched his jaw before agreeing. 'It'll be nice to finally meet them.'

'It's been really good for me going there. Makes me feel normal.'

'You are normal.'

Beth shrugged. 'I used to think all the other parents had their lives sorted, and I was the only one doing a lousy job, but since talking with the group, I can see that's not the case. We're all in the same boat, tired and trying the best we can.'

He settled Archie across his chest and smiled down at the wide eyes peering his way. 'You're doing just fine, Beth.'

She reached over to stroke Archie's fine hair. 'Well, at least I haven't had backache in a while.'

Spencer laughed. 'That's because I'm the one who carries the pram up and down the stairs.'

Beth grinned. 'True.' She settled back, sipping her drink. 'Wouldn't it be nice to have a little house. Perhaps a garden. I would say it's something I could work towards, but I haven't even made a start on decorating my flat yet.'

'Let me know when you want to, and I can help.' He met her eyes and quickly added, 'Not that there's any rush. You know you're welcome to stay at mine for as long as you want.'

'I think Archie will spend a lot of time at yours when I go back to work. Mostly after his time at day care, as my hours are long.'

'I thought teachers finished early.'

Beth scoffed. 'No. Everyone thinks that, but we work after school ends, and you wait till you see how much I have to bring home with me. There's not enough hours in the week for my job. I work during the holidays too. Being a primary school teacher is pretty full on.'

'Oh, well, in that case, I'm sure we'll figure out a routine that suits us all. Do you find your job stressful?'

'Sometimes, that's why I was thinking of shifting my career slightly. My friend went to work in a different sector and she has a lighter load now. I guess it just depends on what you take on. I planned to take a step back before I fell pregnant. Now I'm thinking it's probably for the best. Might just take some time to sort a new role.'

'At least you have time to think during your maternity leave.'

Beth smiled. 'And having your help gives me breathing room, Spencer. I want you to know that.'

Spencer got up to place Archie in the pram. 'I'm glad you feel better, Beth. I'll always do what I can to help.' He stole a glance her way to catch her smile.

Maybe Ginny was on to something with that dreaming malarkey, because he could see himself with Beth and Archie together in a house with a garden, living happily ever after. It was a nice visualization, except for the part where some bloke called Edward was suddenly sitting on his porch swing, having a playdate with Beth.

He silently chastised himself for feeling a tad jealous, then slightly deflated at the thought of Beth having a life away from him, as he was feeling more and more attached to her each day, which went against everything he believed for himself. Could he really have a relationship? He'd never been in one before.

Beth met his gaze for a moment and smiled.

He'd never met anyone who made him want to settle down before. Perhaps he was getting ahead of himself. It was for the best if he stayed focused on helping Beth and looking after Archie.

CHAPTER 26

Beth

With a diet of finger sandwiches and cake for most of the day, Beth felt quite full, although she was sure she could squeeze something in for dinner. The tearoom opening day was drawing to a close, and had been a great success. The entertainment had left and so had most of the customers, leaving the odd straggler behind as Ginny tidied up for the day.

'What can I do?' asked Beth, keen to help.

Will plopped Ginny onto a nearby chair. 'Nothing, thanks.' He turned to his partner. 'You can both head home. We've got this covered.' He gestured at Sophie, Matt, and Alice.

Beth wondered where Spencer was. She hadn't seen him in a while but hadn't taken much notice until now. 'I don't mind helping clear up,' she told Will.

'And I should be the last one going home,' said Ginny.

Will waggled a finger at her. 'You're growing a baby, you can rest.' He turned back to Beth. 'And you've not long had one, so you can rest too.'

Ginny tapped his thigh. 'Oh, stop fussing. Although, a cup of tea would be nice. I haven't had time to have one today.'

Beth watched him bend to kiss Ginny's cheek before heading off to make her a cuppa. 'You look worn out, Gin.'

'I'm okay. It's just been a long day. I'll get into a proper routine now we're open.' Ginny yawned. 'I think I'll get a bag of chips on the way home. I honestly don't think I can handle much dinner this evening.'

It sounded like a good idea to Beth as well. 'When I find Spencer, I might get some too.' She glanced down at Archie snuggled in his pram. 'And he'll want a bottle soon.'

Ginny smiled at the baby. 'I saw Spencer head towards the pub with Robson a little while ago. He was helping take some chairs back I borrowed for outside. Perhaps he's still in there.'

'Okay, I'll check.' Beth waved goodbye to everyone, declined the offer of lemon tartlets, then made her way along the road to the Jolly Pirate.

There was a nip in the air as the sun went down, but it hadn't made the people in the front beer garden move to the warmth of the pub.

Beth scanned the area to see if Spencer was chatting outside, but he was nowhere in sight, so she pushed the pram through the small crowd to enter the premises. There seemed to be more people out front than cosying up by the bar, but there were at least two people looking rather cosy in that direction.

Spencer was sitting on a stool, facing the bar with a blonde woman to his side, practically stuck to his arm. Her full lips were close to his ear, whispering what, Beth could only imagine.

With a heavy heart and no more appetite for chips, Beth turned around and headed back into the chill. She paused for a while by a tall patio heater, remembering Spencer had the door keys. The last thing she wanted was to interrupt him getting snuggly with a woman. After all, was it her business if he started dating?

Feeling quite agitated about the fact, she marched back inside, parking the pram by his legs.

Bleary eyes rolled up her body, stopping at her mouth for a moment before meeting her glare. 'Beth. Hi.'

Beth stilled on noticing how drained his face looked, then ruby-red lips caught her attention as they moved into the frame. Ignoring the woman, she focused on Spencer. 'I'm just heading home,' she said softly. 'You have the keys.'

'Oh.' He patted his pocket. 'Right, yeah.' He went to stand, but Beth placed one hand on his shoulder.

'You can stay if you like. I don't mind.' It was such a fib, but she could hardly say she felt jealous.

'Is this your wife?' asked the woman.

Spencer gazed at her as though just realizing she was there. 'What? Oh, erm, no.'

It was the truth, but for some reason, Beth felt as though he'd just whacked her in the gut. The worst part was him not bothering to introduce her at all. She took the keys and made a quick exit, wanting some fresh air.

It took a moment before she slowed her pace, mentally shaking her head at herself for being silly. She had no claim over Spencer. They were Archie's parents, that was all. The man had every right to chat up women in pubs. She couldn't expect him to stay single forever. After all, he had told her she was the last woman he'd slept with, and that had been quite some time ago.

Beth took a calming breath as she strolled to the chip shop.

'Hey, Beth. Wait,' Spencer called.

She peered over her shoulder but carried on moving forward, still not stopping when he caught up to her.

'Oh, hi,' she said casually. 'I thought you were staying in the pub.'

With your new friend.

'No. I was helping Robson with some chairs, then got chatting and was given a drink, but I couldn't face it. I was about to head back to the tearoom.'

Beth brought the pram to a halt so she could face him. 'Are you okay?'

'Just tired. I did feel like drowning my sorrows as soon as I sat down, but the whisky put me off.' He breathed out a small laugh, then gazed down at Archie, staring back at him.

'You're really taking Ryan's accident badly, aren't you?'

He shrugged one shoulder. 'It's made me rethink my job at the centre.'

Beth shook her head. 'If you're going to work with kids, you're going to have to deal with accidents happening. Trust me, I work in a primary school.'

'I just feel really bad it happened on my watch.'

'You do feel that way, but these things happen. Spence, it's not your fault.' She watched him sigh deeply as he stared out to sea.

'If I can't handle seeing kids get hurt, I won't be able to work with them. It's not something I thought about when training, and I did first aid courses as well.' His shoulders slumped as he held the pram. 'Oh, I don't know, Beth. Annette blaming me for Ryan not swimming is rattling around as well. My head feels all over the place since it happened.'

'So you thought it best to get drunk and have a one-night stand?'

I shouldn't have said that.

She went to apologize, but Spencer got in first.

'Really? That's what you saw when you came in the pub?'

It was what she'd assumed but words were suddenly failing her. Most probably due to the hurt flashing through his eyes.

'I was talking to Robson, then he went back to work, and some lady sat next to me.'

'It's none of my business,' were the only words that seemed to blurt out from nowhere.

Spencer quirked one eyebrow. 'Well, I'm making it your business. I don't want you thinking I'm that person again. I don't want anyone thinking that of me. I spent a long time cleaning up my act, and barring the mistake I made with you, I've been doing—'

'Mistake?' Beth had a lump stuck in her throat as she gazed at her son, fluttering his eyes to a close.

'No, that's not what I meant,' said Spencer quickly. 'I love him, and I . . . That's not what I meant at all.'

'Look, Spence. We're just co-parenting, right?' He didn't reply, so she continued. 'We don't have to explain to each other if we want to date. We—'

'I wasn't dating. She just spoke to me. I can't help it.' He pointed to his head. 'It's my hair. It often attracts women. They start talking about Scotland and kilts and . . .'

Beth burst out laughing, flapping one hand in his face. 'Sorry,' she mumbled through a giggle. 'That's just so funny.'

Spencer frowned, raking his locks with one hand. 'Glad I amuse you.' A slow smile built as their eyes met. 'I don't want to date anyone, Beth,' he added quietly.

They stood for a moment in silence, then Beth swallowed hard and gestured up the road. 'Do you fancy chips now.'

His lips twisted to one side. 'Hmm.'

They walked along the harbour, Beth pushing the pram, Spencer's hands shoved into his coat pockets. The wind whipped up the sea as the streetlights came on to guide the way, and all seemed settled again until Beth opened her mouth.

'I know you said you don't want to date just yet, but one day you will, so perhaps it's best I start fixing up my flat now, ready to move back. You'll want to bring a woman home at some point, and I don't want to be in the way.'

Spencer grabbed the pram handle, stopping her in her tracks. 'Whoa! Let's just get one thing straight right here and now. You are not in my way. I'm not bringing anyone home, and women are the last thing on my mind at the moment. But if you want to go back to yours, then, yeah, sure, I'll help you decorate. I'll make sure you and Archie are settled and happy. You two are what's important in my life.'

Beth took a deep breath. 'I hate feeling like a burden.'

'You're not. I love living with you. I mean, it's nice having you both around. I just want you to be happy, Beth.'

A beat passed.

'How are you feeling?' he asked softly.

Annoyed about blondie in the pub, stupid for being jealous.

'I'm okay. I think we should be more worried about you. I want you to be happy as well.'

'I'll be all right.'

'Do you think Ryan getting hurt was triggering for you?' Beth shook her head at herself. 'I sound like Jan now.'

Spencer laughed quietly. 'Maybe I should speak to her.'

'Seriously though, Spence. It could be why it's affecting you so badly.' He didn't reply, but his expression held a thousand sad stories, and all Beth could do was reach out and pull him into her arms.

Spencer held her back, and his warmth was so soothing, but she had to stay focused. It wasn't her turn to be comforted. It was his.

Lightly, Beth stroked circles over his coat with one hand as the other found its way to the back of his neck, resting upon his upturned collar. It was heartbreaking to think of the things he'd been through as a child. How it had stayed deep within him. Perhaps it would be for the best if he spoke to a therapist, but she got the feeling he was the type who liked to figure things out for himself. At least she could help by offering a hug or two when needed, and it was obvious he needed one, especially as he was clinging to her so tightly.

Spencer's head shifted so their cheeks were touching, but Beth slowly pulled away, as the backflips the butterflies in her stomach were doing was all too much. The last thing she wanted was intimacy attached to pain.

I want to kiss you, Spencer Jordan, but not like this.

She smiled gently as he shoved his hands back in his pockets. 'Let's get some dinner and go home. I feel a blanket and film night coming on.'

He nodded slightly. 'Sounds good.'

Beth motioned to the pram. 'Do you want to push him?'

'Sure.' He placed his hands on the handle, then poked out his elbow, offering his arm.

Beth curled her arm around his and lightly tapped his shoulder with her head before they set off. How on earth was she ever going to go home when she felt she was there already with him?

Spencer glanced her way and smiled, then started chatting about the Hub as they passed it by. He had such a way of making everything feel normal again, and Beth wished she could stay by his side forever.

CHAPTER 27

Spencer

Spencer headed over to the coffee machine in Debra's office to grab a cup. The children's progress meeting was about to start, and he figured Ryan's mum was going to want to speak first.

'Ryan is still saying he doesn't want to swim,' said Annette to Debra. 'So I already know what his progress is here.'

Debra spoke next. 'The boys have so much fun here. That's good for Ryan.'

Annette frowned at her. 'I'm glad my son has a stress-free time here, when he's not having accidents, but it's not making any difference when it comes to how he is at the poolside. And Spencer shouldn't have told him he doesn't have to swim.'

Debra showed gratitude towards Spencer for handing her a coffee. 'That's not what Spencer said.'

'I told him to speak to you about what he wants,' said Spencer, sitting down.

'My Ryan has a talent,' said Annette.

Debra looked at the reports in front of her. 'And Ryan shows great strengths here. He's thoughtful and helpful, and exceeds in all group activities.'

Annette sat a little higher. 'He's very smart.'

Spencer offered a friendly smile. 'Please don't punish the centre for Ryan still not swimming.'

Annette raised her eyebrows. 'Who says I'm trying to punish anyone?'

Debra smiled softly. 'Let's talk about how Ryan is—'

Annette rolled her eyes. 'I don't expect you to understand. I have a gifted child. This is bigger than a bruise or irresponsible staff.' She gestured at Spencer.

Spencer took a calming breath. He really had given up all hope of her accepting an apology. Debra had assured everyone before Annette turned up that she wouldn't be able to close the centre. Word had got out, and some of the members were already stressed, others angry. Annette didn't have the power she thought she had, but her words the previous week were still causing quite a stir.

The door opened and in walked a tall man, who Spencer could clearly see was Ryan's dad, judging by his features.

'Sorry I'm late,' he said, rushing to a chair by his wife's side. 'I've literally just came straight from the airport.'

'About time,' snapped Annette.

Her husband kissed her head, then smiled around the room. 'I'm Harry.' He noticed the coffee machine. 'Ooh, is it okay if I—'

'I'll do it,' said Spencer, seeing Annette nudge her husband.

'Am I late for our Ryan's progress report?' asked Harry. 'Netty said coming here hasn't helped with his swimming issue.'

Annette frowned at him. 'How many times have I told you not to call me that in public,' she whispered through clenched teeth, but everyone heard.

Spencer handed a coffee to Harry. 'Do you want milk?'

'No, ta. Black is fine.'

'We were just discussing Ryan,' Annette told her husband.

Debra slid some papers Harry's way. 'These are the incident reports from here and the rock-climbing centre. As you will see, Ryan slipped on a flat rock poking out of the ground and was thoroughly checked on-site.'

Harry's hazel eyes held a gentleness as he turned to Spencer. 'Kids, eh!'

'Really, that's all you're going to say?' Annette sat back, folding her arms in a strop.

'He slipped and bruised his arm.' Harry looked to his wife.

Annette leaned towards him. 'And what about him not wanting to swim? Or is that subject too boring for you to get into? No doubt you'd rather be at one of your own meetings, happily talking about stupid lemurs or other creatures for hours, but five minutes about your son, and, well, you just don't care.'

'Of course I care, Annette. But the way you acted, I thought they'd hurt him on purpose.'

Debra sat up. 'I can assure you we would never—'

'You threatened to close down the Sunshine Centre,' said Harry, eyes still firmly on his wife.

It was quite possible Annette was going to explode. Her neck was redder than her face, and her teeth were on full display. 'You know how big the next competition is for Ryan. He has to win, but thanks to this lot, he won't compete. This centre clearly doesn't build confidence. It hasn't helped Ryan at all.'

Harry gently took her hand. 'Annette, I know you're upset, but—'

'Upset! Upset!' Annette stood, towering over him. 'We're talking about the Olympics.'

'He's ten!' said Harry.

'He's in training,' spat Annette. 'I should have never brought him here. Confidence, what a joke. All he's done is come home with stupid badges and no desire to swim.'

Spencer went to speak, but Harry turned his way.

'He told me about the Sunshine Superheroes. He loves those badges. Well done. Such a good idea.'

'Oh, now you're being stupid, Harry.' Annette fixed her glare on Spencer. 'Your superhero malarkey ends right now. I'll not have my son party to such nonsense any longer.'

'What are you talking about?' said Harry. 'He loves earning his badges, and he loves this centre.'

The door flew open, revealing Ryan in the doorway. 'And I hate swimming,' he yelled.

All eyes were on the crying lad.

'You're supposed to be waiting in the art room,' said Annette.

Ryan ran straight into his dad's arms and sobbed some more.

'Hey, hey, Ry,' said Harry, soothing his child. 'It's all right, son.'

'Please don't leave again, Dad,' were the boy's muffled words.

Spencer's heart broke in a million places, but he was so glad Ryan was using his words to communicate.

Watery eyes peered over Harry's shoulder to look at Spencer. 'I'm sorry,' Ryan told him.

'You have nothing to be sorry for,' said Spencer.

Harry pulled his child back so he could cup his face. 'Good to be able to have a hug, eh, son?'

Ryan sniffed as he nodded. 'I wish you didn't work away so much. I miss you.'

'We always video call.'

'I like it when you're here.'

Harry brushed back Ryan's blond locks. 'How about you tell me what else you like, or should we talk about what you don't?'

Spencer prayed Ryan wouldn't shy away now. 'You can speak freely. You're in a safe space.'

Annette scoffed. 'My son's always in a safe space. The only time he wasn't was when he was with you.'

Ryan shook his head as he turned to his mum. 'It wasn't Spencer's fault.'

'That's right,' said Leo, stepping through the opened doorway, leaving his mum and Chris standing behind in the hallway, peering inside at the commotion. 'Captain Spencer isn't to blame.' He flapped his cape and nodded at Ryan. 'We were playing statues on some small rocks. I stepped off okay, but Ryan slipped and landed on his arm.'

'And I was happy I bruised my arm,' said Ryan.

Annette's eyes widened.

Harry pulled his son closer. 'Ry, why would you say that?' he asked gently.

'Because I don't want to swim, and if having a bruised arm helps keep me out of the pool, then I'm glad.'

'Why didn't you tell me, Ry?' Harry slowly turned to his wife.

'I told Mum, but she won't listen to me.'

'He's being ridiculous,' said Annette, lowering her voice.

Harry looked at Ryan. 'Just so we're clear, do you or do you not want to be a swimmer?'

Ryan's head bobbed slightly from side to side. 'I hate it, Dad.' His little voice cracked, which caused Bonnie to shed a tear. 'I want to be like you when I grow up. I like wildlife and photography, and—'

'Oh, so I have you to blame for this, do I?' Annette glared at her husband. 'You've turned him against his dream just so he can grow up to travel the world with you, taking silly snapshots of animals.'

'We both know this is your dream,' said Harry calmly. 'Come on, love, it's time to let this go. You're the swimming champion in our family, and one we're proud of, without an Olympic medal. Let our son choose his own path now. You gave him the best chance, but it's clear it's not for him.'

Annette turned to her son. 'Tell the truth, Ryan. No one believes you don't want to swim.'

'He doesn't,' said Leo, standing in one of his superhero poses. 'He told me.'

'Well, I don't believe it,' snapped Annette. 'Nor do I believe my son wants to be a wildlife photographer.'

'It's true,' said Ryan, looking nervous. 'I don't want to be a swimmer, Mum.'

Spencer could feel his blood starting to boil. Poor Ryan didn't want to swim, and his mother wasn't listening. 'Why don't you listen to him? He doesn't like swimming.' His own mother flashed through his mind.

Stop making him do things he doesn't want to. Why can't you be a decent mum and look after your kid for once. He needs you, but all you think about is yourself, you selfish cow.

Debra touched his arm, bringing him out of the trance he had fallen into with Annette, or rather, his own mother.

All he wanted was to yell at Annette for being so uncaring, for not helping her child, and for holding the same smug look in her eye that his own mother used to have, but he knew he couldn't say his thoughts out loud, and he had to get a grip on the trigger that had just rattled him. Annette wasn't his mum, no matter how selfish she was acting, putting her own wants and needs first. He took a silent calming breath, releasing all memories of his mother.

Leo approached, wrapping his cape around Spencer's leg.

'I'm not listening to this anymore.' Annette got up, swiping her coat from the back of the chair.

'Wait,' said Harry. 'This gets sorted right here and now, for Ryan's sake.' He gestured at their son. 'From now on, he gets a say in his future, and if he doesn't want to train for the Olympics, then he won't.'

'But—'

'No buts,' said Harry. 'Ryan's mental health comes first, and making him do something he clearly doesn't want to do is affecting him. Jeez, Netty, he freezes at the poolside.' He held Ryan's hand. 'And if this centre is the only thing making him happy at the moment, then it's best he stays a member. He has told me all about the kindness festival, and how he's excited to take part. It seems to me the only time our Ryan is smiling is when he talks about Spencer and the centre.' He turned to his child. 'You can stay, son, and you don't have to worry about swimming anymore, and if your mother has anything to say about that, she can speak to me.' He softened his gaze at his wife. 'In private. At home. Come on, love. Like I said, it's time to let this go.'

Annette swung her handbag over her shoulder and huffed. 'Fine.' She looked at Ryan. 'If you truly don't want to swim, then you don't have to.'

Ryan's sad eyes widened in surprise. 'Really?'

Annette didn't look too happy about it, but she gave a brief nod. 'I just didn't want your talent to go to waste. But, if that's what you truly want.'

'I do.'

Annette looked to Debra. 'I'd like a copy of Ryan's progress report, please.'

Debra quickly handed it over. 'We love having him here.'

Annette scanned the paper. 'I'm sure he can stay a member.' The words seemed to bite her.

Harry smiled at Debra. 'We're going to head home. I'm sorry it got a little heated in here.'

Debra stepped forward to pat Ryan's shoulder. 'I'm just glad things are sorted.'

Annette ignored her as she headed outside.

'Ryan knows to use his voice to communicate what he wants now,' said Spencer, smiling down at the boy. 'Don't you?'

A nod and a slight murmur came from the boy before he spoke. 'I didn't mean to get you into trouble, Spencer. And I didn't know my mum would try to close the centre.'

Spencer lowered to Ryan's height. 'Hey, it's okay. It's sorted now, and your dad's home. How great is that? You can bring him to the festival. Show him what the Sunshine Superheroes achieved.' It was a relief to see Ryan looking settled.

Ryan nodded, then headed outside with his dad.

Spencer stood in the office doorway, seeing them off, then turned to Bonnie and Chris, his thoughts still with Ryan as the other parents entered the room.

Bonnie blinked hard. 'I think I need an hour in the quiet room after hearing that.' She turned to Leo. 'Go sit back with Jax while we talk about your progress.'

'Oh, he left,' said Leo, pointing towards the door.

'What do you mean he left?' asked Chris, rushing back outside, quickly followed by everyone.

'He walked out. He was worried the centre was going to close because Ryan's mum said it didn't build confidence.' He lowered his eyes. 'We were listening at the door with Ryan.'

Spencer was just as alarmed as Chris. 'Where did he go?'

Leo shrugged. 'He didn't say.'

Everyone ran out into the car park, calling out for Jax, but he was nowhere to be found. The whole centre was thoroughly searched, but the boy was gone.

CHAPTER 28

Beth

After a long chat with Jan, Beth was feeling quite refreshed as she walked down to Harbour End Road. It was a mild day, with a blue sky and fluffy white clouds. She folded her arms, then dropped them to her sides before shoving her hands in her jacket pockets. She really had no idea what to do with her hands anymore when not pushing Archie's pram.

Beth said hello to a young couple passing by who she'd once helped serve in the flower shop when she was there talking to Lottie and a wave of customers had entered. It felt nice strolling along and seeing people she knew. The Port Berry community was definitely rubbing off on her. An elderly man waved to her, stopping to let her know he had a box of cereal for the food bank at the Hub.

Helping others had lifted Beth's spirits, and the peace she had in her life had made such a difference to her anxiety levels. It was good to inhale the fresh air and have it fill her lungs.

She took the box of cereal from the man and carried on with her journey home. Just thinking about heading to Spencer's brought fizz to her stomach, even though she knew he was at the Sunshine Centre for the morning.

Archie was in Berry Blooms with Lottie and Samuel, and Beth had to wonder if her son would one day work in the shop. She was happy he had so much love surrounding him. She was sure no matter what path he chose in life, he would walk it with a smile.

Beth's smile grew as she turned the corner to meet the harbour. The seagulls seemed as settled as the small boats bobbing on the dark waves. She decided she'd drop the cereal into the Hub, fetch Archie, then send Spencer a message to let him know they were in Harbour Light Café for lunch, in case he wanted to join them.

A pink bicycle came whizzing past, bell jingling and sparkly tassels flapping, and Beth was sure Jax was the rider.

The boy almost toppled off the bike as he came to an abrupt halt outside Treasure Chest newsagents.

'Jax?' she called, seeing it was him.

He turned, face flushed and alarmed.

Beth jogged towards him to see just how out of breath he was. 'What on earth? Is that your bike? What are you doing?' She looked around for signs of Chris. 'Where's your dad?'

Jax thumbed up the road, clutched his knees, then nodded towards the shop door. 'I'm going to show her,' he spluttered.

Beth glanced around the street again. 'Show who?'

Jax straightened, revealing bloodshot eyes and a runny nose. 'Ryan's mum.'

She watched him cuff his nostrils while glaring at the shop. 'I'm sorry, Jax, but I'm really lost right now.'

'I'm not,' he said sharply. 'I knew all the quickest ways here.'

Beth glanced at the wicker basket on the front of the bicycle. 'Okay, I need you to explain what's going on. You're on your own, right?'

He nodded. 'Had to come.'

'To the sweet shop?'

'Yep. She said Spencer wasn't making progress with us, but if I show her, she can't close us down?'

Beth narrowed her eyes. 'Ryan's mum?'

Jax took a deep breath as he nodded. 'I'm doing it, Miss Horton.' And before she could utter another word, he flung the door open and marched straight to the crisps.

Beth stood in the doorway, suddenly realizing what his quest was, but she still wasn't entirely sure about its backstory.

Jax didn't waste time choosing flavours. He simply picked up the nearest bag to him and headed towards Lizzie at the counter.

Beth stretched her head for a better view, then saw him sprint her way.

'I haven't got any money,' he said, looking quite distraught about that fact.

'Oh, here.' Beth quickly rummaged in her handbag and pulled a coin from her purse.

There was a look of sheer determination that hit his dark eyes as he thanked her, and Beth held her breath as he marched back to Lizzie to pay for his snack.

'Just these, please,' he said softly, and Beth's heart went out to him.

She heard Lizzie mutter something, then Jax came back and handed her the change, looking mighty pleased with himself, if not a little bewildered as he left.

Jax plopped to the pavement and hugged the green packet to his chest.

Beth glanced down at him. 'Oh, well, in for a penny,' she muttered, then sat next to him.

'I did it, Miss Horton.'

'Yes, you did. How do you feel?'

He shrugged one shoulder. 'Not sure. Happy, but worried.'

'What's worrying you?'

'What if I can't do it again?'

Beth knew what that felt like. She too had many moments where she wondered if her contentment would be short-lived. 'We have to take our wins when they come. Just now was one, so right now, that's all we focus on.'

Jax opened the packet of pickled onion crisps and offered it her way.

Beth placed one into her mouth. 'Thank you.'

He smiled, then started to eat. 'I don't think I would have spoken to the shopkeeper if I wasn't so angry.'

'Is that what drove you?'

'Got me all the way here.'

Beth gestured at the bike. 'On that?'

'It's Olivia's. She's a girl from the centre, and she left it outside.' He quickly shook his head as he frowned. 'I didn't steal it. Just borrowed it. She won't mind.'

'Wait a minute. Did you ride all the way here from the Sunshine Centre?'

'It's not that far.'

Beth looked down the road. 'It's in Penzance.'

'It's only next door. That's what Dad always says. It did take longer than it normally does, even with the shortcuts.'

'I bet you're normally in a car, that's why.'

Jax nodded and started munching his food again.

'Does your dad know you're here?'

'Nope,' he said, mouth full. 'He wouldn't have let me.' He shifted on the ground so he was facing her. 'But I didn't have a choice. You didn't hear what Ryan's mum was saying.'

'Listen, Jax, whatever Annette said, it was just because she was upset. She has no power to close down respite centres.'

'But she said it doesn't work. But see.' He pointed at the shop. 'I showed her.'

Beth nodded. 'You certainly did, but, Jax, you can't just go off on your own and not tell anyone.'

'You know.'

'Only because I saw you.'

Jax shrugged. 'It's done now. And anyway, they're still in the meeting, so they won't know I've gone. I'm going back in a minute to tell them what I did, and I don't care about badges. This was for the centre, not me.'

'I'm going to have to call Spencer. Let him know you're here.'

'Can't we tell him when I get back?'

'You're not going anywhere, mister. You're staying right here with me until someone comes to collect you.'

Jax shrugged, tossing a crisp to an onlooking seagull.

Beth whipped out her phone, wondering if Spencer was none the wiser to the boy's disappearing act. She thought it best to speak rather than text, even if he was still in the meeting.

Spencer sounded flustered. 'Beth, I can't talk. Jax has run off, and we're all out trying to find him. He left the—'

'He's here, with me. Spencer, did you hear me?'

'He's with you? Where?'

'We're outside Lizzie's. Let Chris know, and we'll wait here till someone arrives.'

'Is he all right?'

'Yes, he's fine. I'll speak to you when you get here.'

'Okay, see you in a minute.'

Beth turned back to Jax. 'Everyone's out looking for you.'

There was an apology sitting in the lad's eyes, but he didn't say anything.

'So,' said Beth, wanting Jax to focus on his achievement, rather than the telling-off he was about to receive from his dad. 'Do you feel like talking to anyone else today? I still have this box of cereal to drop off in the Hub.'

'No. Once was enough for today.'

'That's okay. I don't have social anxiety, but I do have a different form, and I know it can be tricky to navigate at times.'

Jax's big eyes rolled her way. 'Dad doesn't think I have that. He did before, and he sent me to see a therapist once, but I wouldn't speak to her, so it didn't help.'

'Why doesn't he think you have that now?'

'Because he met Olivia at the centre, and now he thinks I might be like her.'

'And what is that exactly?'

'I don't know what's wrong with her. She just doesn't speak at all. She can. She just won't, but she will sign. Dad told me she stopped talking after she saw her mum die, and that might be why I stopped. But I'm not the same as Olivia. I talk to some people, and I didn't see my mum die. Olivia's mum was run over right in front of her.'

'Trauma does strange things to people. Maybe your mum's death did affect you more than you realize.'

Jax inhaled deeply. 'I miss her.'

'I miss mine too.'

'Did you stop talking when your mum died?'

'No, but I did have some trauma when I was pregnant, and that messed with my mind.'

Jax offered her his last crisp, which she declined. 'Are you okay now?'

'I'm getting better, just like you. And look at Olivia. She found her own way to deal with the world. I found that having people help me has made me more confident to face up to my problems.'

'Spencer helped me. I love the Sunshine Centre, that's why I got so mad. It does help people. Olivia didn't start sign language till she went there.'

Beth hugged the box of cereal. 'Sometimes we just need a place that feels like home.'

Jax nodded. 'The Sunshine Centre is my second home. Dad says that. He says I always smile there.'

'What about life at home with your dad? How's that?'

'Good. Dad's always been happy. Not when Mum died. He was sad a lot then, but he's better now. He says I help him.'

'You helped me too.'

Jax's eyes widened. 'Really?'

'Yeah. All of you Sunshine Superheroes. Letting me come out for a walk in the park with you, and when we planted flowers.' She gestured to a tub close by. 'It all helped.'

'You should start getting badges too, Miss Horton.'

Beth chuckled. 'You know, I think you're right. I'll tell Spencer.'

'We should make him one too.'

'Saying what?'

'Best captain ever.'

'I think he'd like that. Do you want me to ask Luna to make one? It could be a surprise.'

Jax sat up, crossing his legs. 'Yeah, let's give it to him at the festival.' His shoulders slumped. 'That's if Ryan's mum hasn't closed that down as well.'

'She hasn't. Debra has been working with Councillor Seabridge to make sure the day runs smoothly.'

'I hope Ryan's told his mum the truth.'

'What truth?'

'That he doesn't want to swim.'

Beth bobbed her head. 'He must really hate the water.'

'No. Just having to race. But he did tell Leo and me that he wasn't going in the water ever again.' Jax frowned. 'Is that Ryan's trauma?'

'Could be. Perhaps one day he'll swim for fun again.'

Spencer's van pulled up, and Beth and Jax stood immediately. Spencer jumped out and pointed at the bike. 'Jax, seriously!'

Beth quickly explained, leaving Spencer quite dumbfounded. 'So you see, he just wanted to prove to Annette that the centre does help people.'

'I would have come with you,' Spencer told Jax.

'I wasn't thinking. I just went.'

'At least you're safe. Jeez, Jax, you scared everyone.'

Jax dipped his head. 'I know that now, and I'm sorry.'

'Never mind,' said Spencer, but Beth could see he clearly did mind. 'You just promise not to run off again.'

'But Ryan's mum—'

'It's sorted,' said Spencer. 'The centre isn't closing, and Ryan told his mum he doesn't want to race.'

'About time,' Jax huffed, placing his empty crisp packet in the mesh bin.

'Oh, and about that,' said Spencer, gesturing at the dustbin. He raised his palm, asking the boy to give him a high five, which Jax happily did. 'Well done, mate. You must feel so proud of yourself. I'm definitely proud of you.'

Jax shrugged, but his grin was on show. 'It's just a step forward,' he said simply.

'It certainly is,' said Beth, nudging his arm.

Jax rolled back his shoulders and raised his chin. 'It's just what we Sunshine Superheroes do. Take one step at a time. Right, Miss Horton.'

Beth smiled at Spencer. 'That's right.'

Spencer quirked an eyebrow at her. 'Oh, so you're one of us now, are you?' He glanced at the box she hugged. 'You and your cereal?'

'Yes,' said Jax. 'And Miss Horton needs her own badge.'

Spencer breathed out a quiet laugh. 'Is that right? And what for exactly?'

Jax grinned at Beth. 'Finding lost children.'

Beth pointed at the bike. 'I didn't find you, you just rode out in front of me.'

Spencer picked up the pink bicycle and placed it in the back of his van. 'You owe Olivia an apology for stealing her bike.'

'I borrowed it,' said Jax. 'Ooh, I can buy her a bar of chocolate.' He patted his pockets, then frowned as though remembering he had no money.

Beth handed him the change she had shoved into her pocket. 'You ready for round two now?'

Jax glanced at the shop door. 'Least I can do.' He took a breath, then headed inside, with Beth and Spencer watching from the doorway.

'Hello again, young Jax,' said Lizzie. 'Choccy this time, eh? Good choice.'

'It's for my friend Olivia.'

Spencer gripped Beth's arm, making her grin. 'How marvellous is that?'

'It's a joy to witness.'

Jax came back, chocolate aloft. 'I'm ready to face Olivia.'

A car pulled up by the van, and Chris jumped out to curl Jax into his arms. Beth could hear him mumbling something and could see Chris looked more relieved than anything else.

Spencer's arm came around her shoulder, and she didn't mind snuggling into his side one bit. Jax had made a giant leap, even if it was done out of anger.

'We're going to head off to meet Bonnie and Leo,' said Chris, leading Jax to his car.

Spencer raised a hand. 'Sure. I'll get the bike back. There's more room in my van than your car.'

Jax turned to his dad. 'I have to give this to Olivia first.' He showed the chocolate, then proceeded to tell his dad how he spoke to the shopkeeper all by himself.

Beth was sure she spotted a tear in the man's eye, but he rolled it back, kissed his son's head, told him he was proud, then buckled him into the car. They waved goodbye, and she felt Spencer's body relax.

'I better get this bike back.'

'Hey, you okay?'

'It's just been one hell of a morning.'

'How bad was the meeting?'

Spencer shook his head. 'I almost called Annette a selfish cow.'

Beth gasped. 'No.'

'I don't know what happened, Beth. One minute I'm talking to Annette, the next I'm shouting at my mother in my head. I swear, just for a second I saw her face.'

'Oh, Spence.'

'It wasn't until I was driving here that it dawned on me just how much I want to shout at my mum. There are so many things I want to say to her, and yet, if she were still alive, I know I wouldn't say a word. I sure as hell don't want to talk to my dad.'

Beth pulled him closer to her body, hugging him tightly.

'Why is this crap surfacing now?' he mumbled into her hair.

'Probably because you're a parent now.'

Their heads shifted and noses brushed. A beat passed, then Spencer pulled back and gazed out to sea.

'I'm just going to pop in and see little man before I take the bike back.'

'Are you okay, Spence?'

He smiled as he stroked down her arm. 'Just one look at you and Archie, and everything is right in the world.' He winked, then turned to Berry Blooms, leaving Beth with goosebumps and a smile.

CHAPTER 29

Spencer

Spencer felt quite chuffed walking into the church hall with Beth and Archie for parent and baby group. It was his first time meeting everyone, and he wished he could introduce himself as Beth's partner, but seeing how nobody asked, just assumed, he didn't bring up the subject.

Beth was tugged to one side to browse over the items her friends had brought for the baby bank, and Spencer noticed the man called Edward was almost draped over her.

'Hello, you must be Edward,' said Spencer, tapping the man's shoulder. 'Beth mentioned something about a playdate one day for our kids.'

Edward smiled. 'Yes, it would be nice.'

Spencer widened his smile. 'We look forward to it.'

Beth turned to show him what was on the table. 'Most of this is from Edward.'

Lola moved to her side. 'That's because he's a shopaholic.'

Edward dramatically slapped his chest. *'Moi!* Never.'

Shelby had everyone sit on the playmats, telling them they could talk all things baby bank afterwards.

Spencer subtly perused the group as they placed their babies before them and started singing something about a floppy scarecrow, which seemed to go down well with Archie, who was wriggling and smiling.

Beth got him involved when it was time for the parents to stand to do a few yoga moves to help realign the spine. He had to laugh when one of the older babies crawled off. Shelby quickly lifted the giggling boy so his mother could carry on stretching.

Archie kept his eyes on his dad, and Spencer thought it best not to show him up by toppling over while attempting the tree pose, especially as Edward looked as grounded as a mountain.

They sat back down, and Shelby asked if anyone had any concerns they'd like to talk through, which came as a surprise, as Spencer wasn't expecting group therapy. He remained silent, listening to a woman speak about all things organic and how she felt a failure because she used the readymade food in jars.

Spencer wondered if he should be researching organic diets? He was sure he could secure a window box and grow something. Lottie was the one to ask. She practically had a whole allotment in her garden now. He'd have to start popping over more often to see what was on offer.

'Spencer, do you have anything you'd like to add?' asked Shelby, interrupting his thoughts on red bell peppers.

'Hmm?'

Beth offered an encouraging smile.

Spencer looked from her to Archie, then at Shelby. 'Oh, erm, I don't think so.'

'That's okay,' said Shelby. 'But feel free to bring any topic to the mats when you're here.'

Lola joked, 'Yeah, like Moira talking about haemorrhoids for a solid twenty minutes the other week.'

Moira frowned. 'Erm, excuse me, but we were talking self-care after labour, thank you.' She pointed at Edward. 'More relevant than Ed going on about designer baby clothes.'

Spencer glanced at Lester to see what he was wearing. The baby's dark romper looked like any other to him. Surely this wasn't something he had to look into as well.

Lola changed the subject. 'Ooh, I have a question. Has anyone put their baby's name down for the nursery yet?'

'Oh, I've never bothered until my kids turn two,' said a woman, opening her blouse to breastfeed.

'Two!' gasped Edward. 'I was told you should register with a school straight away.'

Lola raised her eyebrows. 'What, like as you come out of the registry office, nip straight to a school?' she said sarcastically.

Edward shrugged. 'Lester is enrolled in Clairmont.'

Spencer had no idea what that meant, but judging by the gleam in the man's eye, it was something to be proud of.'

Lola sank into the mats. 'Ooh, I wish I could afford to send my kid there.'

'You can pay monthly,' said Edward.

'Yeah, if I want to give up my rent.' Lola shook her head at him.

A conversation about private education went on for a while, only interrupted by Shelby telling everyone it was time to leave soon. That sentence seemed to mean something, as all parents snuggled their babies to their chests, Beth placing Archie on Spencer.

He went to ask what he was supposed to do, but a lullaby started to play from Shelby's phone, and some of the parents started to quietly sing along.

Beth leaned closer to Spencer, stroking Archie's hair while joining in with the song. Her chocolate eyes rolled his way for a moment, and he matched her warm smile before lowering his mouth to kiss his son's head. He wished he could lean over and kiss her head too but didn't feel it would be appropriate under the circumstances.

She continued to sing to Archie, and Spencer continued to melt into a pool of slush at the sight. As he glanced up, he saw Edward quickly look down at Lester.

Yeah, you keep watching, mate. This is my family. You can . . .

Lola suddenly snuggled into Edward's side, and Spencer witnessed the loving look they shared. If they were a couple, no one had told him. He honestly thought Edward's playdate line was code for trying to date Beth.

'Are they together?' he whispered close to Beth's ear, grazing her lobe with his lips by accident. Never mind yoga, a packed Zumba class had just taken place in his stomach.

Beth nodded. 'It's new,' she mouthed.

Shelby wrapped things up, and Spencer handed Archie to Beth so he could load the van.

'Are you two coming to the kindness festival?' he asked, watching Edward and Lola secure their babies in the prams. Now he knew Edward wasn't making moves on Beth, he felt he could be his friend.

'Yeah, we'll be there,' said Lola. 'We're taking turns to help Shelby shine a light on our group.'

'Great.' He turned to Beth, placing Archie in his car seat. 'You strap him in the van and open the back doors, and I'll grab this lot.'

It wasn't long before they were heading to the Hub, and Spencer noticed how squashed Beth was the other end of the three seats in the front of his van. Archie's car seat was pressing against his elbow as well.

'I might look into a family car,' he said quietly, as Archie was drifting off.

'I was thinking of buying one. I've been saving for a while. Thought it might be easier getting around with Archie.'

'We can go halves if you want. Do a bit of a car share.'

Beth laughed. 'The way we're going, we'd be in it together anyway.'

Spencer grinned. 'Ah, nothing wrong with that.' He pulled up outside the Hub, grabbed a box of baby clothes, and went straight inside to see Robson was on a shift with Alice.

Alice glanced in the box. 'Ooh, that's generous of people.'

'Wait till you see the rest.' Spencer motioned to the van.

'I'll help,' said Robson, following him outside, where Beth was pulling Archie's car seat out.

Spencer quickly took the seat from Beth, giving her back a gentle rub. 'Go and sit down. We'll sort this lot.' He placed Archie out of the way, leaving Alice to coo over him, then brought the rest of the donations inside.

'From the parent and baby group I attend,' Beth told Alice as she sat.

Alice started to unbox some items to place in the storage room. 'I just had someone come in earlier asking if we had breast pads.'

'Jan told me she and Henley have been in touch with the local health visitors, and they're going to give referrals to those in need, but I guess there will still be those passing that pop in on the off chance.'

Alice nodded. 'Word of mouth.'

'More people will hear about the baby bank at the kindness festival,' said Robson, carrying two bags stuffed with nappies and wipes.

Once everything was inside, and Beth said she'd help sort through the items, Spencer told her he had to go to the flower shop to do the accounts.

'I shouldn't be too long, then we can grab some lunch.'

Beth agreed, and he almost kissed her goodbye, only pulling away at the last minute when he saw Alice grinning at him.

Mentally shaking his head at himself at how much harder it was getting to stay platonic with Beth, Spencer headed outside.

'Hello, Spence.'

Spencer turned on the pavement to see an old school friend. 'Hello, Darren. You all right?'

'Yeah, all good. Just off to meet my missus in the pub.' Darren beamed at Spencer. 'Heard about you becoming a dad unexpectedly.'

Spencer smiled.

'Same thing happened to my cousin a while back,' added Darren, losing his grin. 'He wasn't told until the baby was born either. He bought one of those online DNA tests, just to be sure. Good thing he did, as it turned out he wasn't the father after all. What a shock that was. He—'

'Darren,' called out a female voice, and both men glanced down towards the bend in the road.

Darren raised a hand to the blonde lady calling him. 'There's my wife. Better shoot off.' He patted Spencer's arm. 'Keep well, mate, and congrats on the baby.'

Spencer said goodbye and watched his friend walk away. The thought of a paternity test wasn't something he needed to bother with. Archie looked like his sister, and why would Beth lie? Huffing to himself, he entered his shop.

Lottie was out the back, busy making bouquets with one of their staff members, Sarah.

'Hey, how's it going?' he asked, sitting at the table in the corner.

'We had a busy hour, then it went quiet for the rest of the morning. I've got two deliveries for you though. Any time after lunch will be fine.'

Spencer nodded as he opened up a spreadsheet on the laptop.

The doorbell jingled, and Sarah went out front to serve the customer.

'How was parent and baby group?' asked Lottie.

He peered over his shoulder. 'Did you know you can buy designer prams?'

She nodded as she laughed.

Spencer shook his head. 'Well, I certainly learned a few new things.' He turned back to the screen. 'Beth loves it there. You should see her, Lott. She was practically glowing this morning.'

'She's getting better, that's why. You have something to do with that too, you know.'

He glanced her way. 'I'm not taking her credit. She's been learning lots of coping techniques with Jan. Plus, everything's easier when you have help.'

'And love.'

Spencer made a start on the accounts, ignoring where Lottie was taking the conversation. He was having enough trouble lately thinking about being closer to Beth, and now a paternity test niggled. No, he simply wasn't going to think about that at all. But there it lurked.

Sarah and the customer's muffled voices could be heard out front, and Spencer hoped she'd stay there awhile, because he wanted to seek Lottie's advice.

'Lottie, can I ask you something?'

'Since when do you ask?'

He shrugged one shoulder and offered a half-smile. 'It's just personal.'

Lottie turned to face him fully as she nodded.

He glanced at the shopfront, making sure no one could hear. 'It's about Archie.'

Her eyes widened. 'What about him?'

'I just bumped into my old schoolmate Darren outside, and he told me about how his cousin found himself in the same situation as me.'

Lottie gave him a confused look. 'What situation?'

'Being told he was a dad.'

'And?' she whispered.

Spencer's stomach flipped. 'His cousin did a paternity test and it turned out the baby wasn't his.'

'Oh, I see. And now the seed has been well and truly planted in your head.'

Spencer quietly sighed. 'Do you think I should do one?'

'I guess that depends on you.'

'What if people think I'm an idiot for not taking one?'

'Since when do you care what others think? Anyway, how would they know?'

Spencer gestured towards the shopfront. 'I took Beth's word, but that was mostly because Archie reminded me so much of you when you were his age, and then I got to know Beth, and she's lovely and nice, and I don't think she would lie to me.'

'But it's bothering you now. I can see.'

'I believe Archie is mine, but it wouldn't hurt to be totally sure, would it?'

'I guess not, if it puts your mind at ease. Talk to Beth. See what she thinks.'

Spencer shook his head. 'No, I'm not letting her know. How am I supposed to bring that up now? That's something you do in the beginning. It might upset her if I did it now.'

Lottie offered a small smile. 'I don't know what to say, Spence. You're the only one who knows if this will play on your mind.'

It was something he could do by himself, perhaps. That way, he wouldn't risk Beth thinking he didn't trust her, and at the same time he would have the confirmation to wipe away the niggle.

No, I'm not doing it. Archie is my child.

Trying to shift the thought of testing, he turned back to the accounts.

Lottie came closer to him, resting a hand on his shoulder. 'You've fallen for her, haven't you?'

It was hard trying to add up while his little sister was pressing him for info.

'Why don't you tell her how you feel, Spence?'

The numbers on the screen seemed to shrink, and he wondered if he needed glasses.

'Have you opened up to her at all? It might be easier for you to talk about things like paternity tests if you had that kind of relationship. Perhaps tell her your birth name or—'

Spencer turned so quickly, he could have got whiplash. 'Have you told Sam my real name?'

'No,' she replied sheepishly, and that told him she had.

'You'd better not tell anyone else,' he said through clenched teeth. 'I didn't change that through deed poll for nothing.'

'So you haven't told Beth then?'

'No, I haven't,' he said, trying to focus on work.

Lottie moved away. 'Best you two don't get into a relationship,' she muttered, causing his shoulders to flop.

Don't take the bait.

'Why's that?' he asked.

'Well, if you can't be honest with her.'

'Erm, excuse me, I've never lied to Beth, thank you very much.'

'You won't tell her how you feel, your birth name, or talk about paternity testing. Hardly screams "team".'

Spencer slapped his chest. 'I'm not going to risk upsetting her unnecessarily. Plus it could make things awkward. Anyway, I might not bother, so there's no point bringing up the subject at all.' Perhaps he could go online to check it out. There was no harm in a quick peek.

'It's up to you if you want to keep things hidden, but one of my favourite things about my relationship with Sam is that we know everything about each other. The good, the bad, and the downright ugly. Sometimes I feel like we're one person, we're that connected. It's a nice feeling, Spence. If you just stopped closing doors on yourself, you might get to find out.'

Easy for her to say. She wasn't the one who closed her heart as a child, thinking it safer that way. The times he'd sat and analysed himself to the point of headache were more than he could count. He knew what he was like, and, yes, he closed many doors, but he used to let Rebecca in sometimes, even George. Could he really let go of the tight hold he had on himself?

He glanced at the laptop, knowing he could do an online search for DNA testing straight away. 'House of bloody cards, that's what I live in,' he mumbled, but Lottie heard.

'You used to, but then you got to grow up in a solid home. You just couldn't see it. Now, well, who knows what kind of world you see. I love you, Spencer. You've always been my favourite person. I just wish you'd see the beauty in life, then perhaps you'd stop being so afraid that something will always go wrong.'

'Things do go wrong.'

'Of course they do. That's life. But it doesn't mean we stop living because of it. You've pretty much lived your life like some sort of Groundhog Day, constantly looking for the bad.'

She had a point. He was looking for the bad just thinking about doing a paternity test. He could ignore the idea and carry on as he had been, but no. He was making his own waves, letting part of his brain tell him that there might be a chance Archie wasn't his son, because why would life be good to him?

Another part of his brain reminded him how he had made life good for himself. 'I changed after your accident.'

Lottie sighed. 'I know, and I see how much more you smile now, but I also notice your old self popping up to say hello every so often. I see it with you and Beth.'

'If my old self was up and running around Beth, I'd have tried to get her into bed by now.'

'Ah, so that's what's stopping you. You're worried if you get intimate with her, you might run away the next morning.'

Spencer scoffed. 'I'm not talking about intimacy with you.'

'Anyway, that wasn't what I meant. I was talking about your old ways stopping you from enjoying life.'

'I am enjoying my life, thank you.'

'You'll enjoy it a whole lot more once you're honest with Beth.'

'So you think telling her my parents named me Spaceman Spencer Jordan will miraculously change everything?' He jumped as a ball of ribbon hit his back.

'I think you opening up to her will change you.'

'She already knows about my childhood.'

'Everyone knows about that, Spence. Our family made the news.'

Spencer shrugged, feeling a tad deflated with his sister's interference. He happened to think he was doing quite well with his life, thank you. Everything was easy with Beth as it was. Wasn't it? There were those times when he wanted to kiss her lips, and then when they hugged he didn't want to let go. Why did he always have to think bad times were ahead? He knew why. He just wished he could stay in happy mode forever.

CHAPTER 30

Beth

With Archie snuggled in his cot, the dishes washed up and put away, and Beth and Spencer lounging on the sofa in their pyjamas, it was another average night at home, but as Beth reached out for the remote control at the same time as Spencer, and their hands met, she wanted to add something different into their routine.

'Can we talk?'

Spencer's hand was still on hers. 'Sounds serious.'

'It's just about us.' Beth gazed at their hands. 'About this.'

He too was looking in that direction, but then his blue eyes, so like her son's, slowly moved to her mouth, and Beth swallowed hard.

'We seem to have fallen into some sort of relationship,' she added, trying to stay focused on the subject, rather than the pull of energy she could feel between them.

'Not quite,' he said softly.

Beth had skills in breath control now, and she was secretly using them so she wouldn't show any nerves. 'It's just, well, we should talk about what's happening here.' She felt his finger twitch on her hand.

'What part?'

'All of it.'

He gave a brief nod.

'Perhaps we should speak about the future,' she added. 'Plan ahead a little.'

Spencer's forehead wrinkled slightly. 'Is this about schools for Archie?'

'No. I was thinking more along the lines of us.'

'We're doing all right the way we are, aren't we?'

'Yes, but are we just going to continue to live together and co-parent this way?' She watched him mull over her words as he relaxed onto his side, still holding her hand.

It was a strange feeling bringing the unspoken words to the surface. She had loads more she wanted to say, and now was the time.

'I want you to know I'm happy here, but I always knew this was short-term. I also know that when I move back to my place we'll need to set up a routine for Archie.' She cleared her throat, as her voice cracked on the last word. It was difficult to plan a future she didn't want, but how could she move in permanently with him unless he said so?

Spencer wasn't exactly joining in the chat. His bobbing head and lack of smile told her little.

'Say something,' she blurted, then chastised herself for sounding desperate. Pulling her hand from his, she sat back and folded her arms. 'I want this talk to be about honesty. I need you to tell me what you want.'

'You haven't exactly told me what you want yet.'

She thought back to what she had said, then realized she was holding back. 'I want this to be real. I want my family together, but I understand it's complicated.'

Spencer shuffled closer, placing his finger up to her cheek. 'It's not complicated, Beth.'

The fact her heart stopped beating was a sure sign something was complicated all right. She met his gaze, warm and inviting. 'Spence, I . . .' Words failed her as his face inched nearer.

'I want more.' His voice was hushed, almost sedating her. 'I want you.'

Beth lowered her head so it touched his. 'I don't want one night,' she whispered, praying he felt the same, as she couldn't bear it if he was only thinking of one thing when her heart was laid bare.

'If you want me too, you won't get just one night. I'll give you all my nights. You can have everything.' He gently raised her chin, and their eyes met once more, Beth seeing seriousness and passion.

There was something calming in that moment, so much so, she didn't want to move and break the spell. Just looking at him was enough. His hand lightly brushing the back of her ear, his other still holding her chin, the way his eyes told a thousand stories. Where were her heartbeats? Did it even matter? Did anything?

Spencer's nose touched hers, waking her gently from the daydream. 'Do you want me, Beth?'

Tilting her head slightly, she slowly placed her lips upon his, showing him exactly what she wanted. Within seconds, their kiss deepened, and Spencer lifted her, carrying her to the bedroom.

She gazed at him leaning over her as he placed her on the bed and watched him close his eyes as he rested his cheek in her palm. It was a side to him she hadn't witnessed before. One filled with affection and tenderness. Each gentle touch was making her feel safe and treasured in his arms.

Beth had never felt so overwhelmed by love before, and when Spencer nuzzled his face into her neck, trailing kisses up to her jaw, every part of her melted.

* * *

Sunlight poured in through the bedroom window, placing a golden hue over Spencer's relaxed face.

Beth smiled at him, still in bed with her, right where he promised he'd be. Even though she believed him when he'd said he had given himself to her, there was still a tiny doubt niggling at her until she drifted off to sleep. To see him by her side, copper locks dishevelled from her touch, was heart-warming on every level. He was her boyfriend now, and she could kiss him whenever she felt the need.

The need was strong, but so was the peace that came from simply watching him sleep.

A hushed groan and a stretch later, Spencer opened his eyes, smiling directly at her.

'Good morning,' Beth said quietly, seeing he still looked sleepy.

One side of his mouth quirked. 'It is definitely a good morning.' His croaky voice had her lips back on his once more, making him chuckle. 'Spaceman,' he mumbled.

Beth pulled back. 'What?'

'Spaceman Spencer Jordan. That's the name I was given at birth.'

'Your parents called you Spaceman?'

'Yep.'

Beth frowned. 'Why?'

'Might have something to do with them always being high.'

'Oh.'

'I legally changed it as soon as I could, but my aunt made sure everyone called me Spencer, as it caused me to get into some fights at my first school.'

Beth kissed his forehead. 'Why are you telling me this? Was it in your dream last night? Is that why it's on your mind?'

'Nope. Just want you to know everything about me.' He cupped her face, peppering light kisses along her lips.

'Are we really doing this?' she asked as she pulled back.

'We can do this all day if you like,' he replied, bringing her back to his mouth.

Beth laughed. 'No, I meant us being a proper couple, sharing everything.'

Spencer's smile was a mixture of mischief and warmth. 'Yeah, we're really doing this.'

Beth curled under his arm, wishing they could stay in bed all day, but Archie would wake soon, demanding their full attention.

'Why don't we go out for the day?' suggested Spencer. 'A trip to Looe, perhaps.'

Beth lightly stroked over his chest. 'We can check out the baby bank over there. Sam told me he spoke to the lady who runs the centre. He was after ideas.'

'Sounds like a plan.'

Beth leaned up on one elbow. 'It's our first family outing. Maybe we should just focus on us.'

'Hey, the baby bank is important to you. We can do both. It'll be good to see how they do things over there anyway. Could be helpful to see it for ourselves.'

Beth smiled as she kissed his cheek. The sun had not long come up and already she was having the best day ever.

Spencer turned his head, grinning as he cupped her face. 'I think we have time for a lie-in before little man wakes.'

'Shall we go back to sleep then?' she teased.

Spencer pulled her closer into his arms. 'Or . . .' he mumbled, kissing her.

* * *

'Ta-da!' said Spencer, spreading his arms out to Samuel's dark 4x4 parked outside the flower shop.

'Why are you showing me Sam's car?' asked Beth, lifting Archie higher to her shoulder.

'We're using it for our day out. It'll be way comfier.'

Beth couldn't agree more, squealing on the inside at having use of such a luxurious vehicle. She waited for Spencer to secure the rear-facing car seat, then place Archie inside, checking all the straps while the baby tried to lick everything coming close to his mouth. She offered Archie a soft play ring, which he grabbed with both hands and stuffed straight into his mouth.

'Right, I think we've got everything,' said Spencer, checking through the baby bag.

Beth laughed, taking it from him to place by her feet as she sat in the back with Archie. 'We're not going too far, and I'm sure there are shops in Looe if we do find we need something.'

Spencer clambered in the front, then turned to grin at her sitting behind him. 'We are definitely getting a car.'

Beth glanced around at the expensive-looking interior. 'I wonder how much these cost.'

'Knowing Sam, probably the price of a small house.'

She laughed as he started the engine. 'I doubt they're that much.'

Spencer pulled away. 'I can get one of these if you want, but I'd rather put my savings into a house for us.'

That came as a surprise. 'You've been thinking about that?'

'Archie can have a paddling pool in the garden. I thought that would be nice.'

Beth smiled, feeling it reach her heart. For two months they'd shared a little flat above a shop, grown closer, and now they were talking family cars and home ownership. She reached forward, placing a hand on his shoulder. 'It's something to work towards.'

Spencer tapped her hand before placing both hands back on the steering wheel. 'I know it's early days for us, but it's good to do a bit of future thinking.'

'I suppose, as it would take some time to save anyway.'

'We can afford one now, Beth,' he remarked casually, making her frown, as she was pretty sure she couldn't. How much did a florist make exactly?

Beth sat back, watching the world pass by her window. 'Not sure you know how much primary school teachers earn, but—'

'I was talking about my own money. I'm not saying you can't chip in. I'm just saying I have enough for us to buy a house.'

It was niggling at her but she didn't like to ask. Her dad always told her it was uncouth to ask people about their finances.

Spencer smiled at her through the rear-view mirror. 'I'm not loaded, but I got left some property.'

'Oh.'

'My aunt left her home and shop to us when she died, the flat above included. Lottie wanted to stay in the house, so I said it would make more sense for me to take the flat. I stayed with her on and off over the years, but the flat was mostly home. We never divvied up any money until she got with Sam. The flat isn't worth as much as the house, so Lott gave me the extra. We still share the business though.'

'Your aunt helped you in so many ways, didn't she?'

'Yeah, I guess she did. Not just her though. When George passed away, he left his house to Lottie and me. So I have half the money from that too. See, this is why I can afford to move us.'

'Oh, Spence, I don't want you spending all your money on us. I feel a bit bad.'

His laugh was quiet and warm. 'I can't think of anything better to spend my money on than setting up a home for my family, and I know Rebecca and George would be pleased to see the inheritance go in that direction.'

'I just feel uncomfortable about it all falling on you.'

'Doesn't have to. You can buy the car with your savings or use it to decorate the place. We're in it together, honey.'

Beth warmed at him calling her honey. She glanced at Archie, still happily chewing his toy ring. For so long she had assumed it would be just him and her, juggling life, coping as best they could, and now Spencer was in her life, offering all sorts of wonderful opportunities.

'Don't stress it, Beth. We can work on a plan later that makes you feel comfortable, okay?'

She nodded. 'Wow, we really are future thinking, aren't we?'

'I told you. I'm all in.'

It was nice to hear, but it was still early days for them as a couple, so she figured she'd just see how things went as they moved forward together.

She leaned forward once more to stroke his shoulder. 'Can you believe it's the festival in a few days? Where has the time gone?'

'I know, and the weather report says dry, so that's good. I reckon it's going to be a brilliant day.' Spencer sounded excited as he nattered on about the day, and Beth was happy to be part of the event. To feel her joy rise once more.

CHAPTER 31

Spencer

Spencer couldn't stop smiling as he walked around the kindness festival. So many people had turned up for the event and many stalls held all sorts of useful information.

Having spent most of the morning helping to set up, he was taking a moment to relax with a coffee and absorb the positive atmosphere.

Bonnie and Chris were in his eyeline, holding hands and laughing while their sons were drawing pictures with other kids in the Sunshine Centre's large tent.

With so much to be happy about, he just wished he hadn't done a paternity test now. It kept coming back to play on his mind, and it all seemed so simple online, so he'd ended up ordering a test, mostly to close down the niggle. Ever since he'd sent it off, he'd held regrets, more so for not discussing it with Beth. There wasn't much he could do now but wait for the email to come through. Perhaps then he would stop feeling so guilty about the secrecy and tell Beth what he had done. Or maybe not. He really hated the confusion.

The squeal of a child had him return to the present moment. Smiling, Spencer turned to see Samuel approach.

'Looks like you had the same idea as me,' said Samuel, raising his disposable coffee cup.

'I haven't even had a chance to say happy birthday to you. Happy birthday.' He tapped his cup on Samuel's. 'Nice day for it.'

Samuel glanced up at the clear blue sky. 'I'm too busy to think about it.'

'Lottie said you don't like a fuss. I'm the same. Not that she pays much attention to what I want, as you saw when it was my day.'

Samuel laughed. 'Yeah, she managed to talk me into dinner tonight with my sister and Felix.'

Spencer glanced over at Hannah and Felix snuggled together by the paintings they were selling for the centre. 'How's your sister getting on since you moved in with mine?'

'She's good. Loved up, as you can see.' Samuel sipped his drink, then glanced over at Lottie. 'Life's a lot easier when you've got a good partner by your side.'

It wasn't something Spencer had thought about until he fell for Beth.

Samuel turned back to him. 'What about you? You okay?'

'Did Lottie send you over to interrogate me about my relationship with Beth?'

'Sounds like her, doesn't it?' Samuel grinned. 'But no. I was just asking.' He patted Spencer's shoulder. 'I'm glad it all worked out for you, mate.'

Spencer could feel his smile deep within his heart. He'd never felt so complete before. Watching Samuel head over to Lottie made his smile widen. He was so pleased his sister had so much love in her life, and now he did too.

'Hey, Spencer,' called Ryan, jogging over. 'Dad brought me.'

Spencer looked around for the boy's dad. 'I'm glad he brought you. Where is he?'

'Looking around. I told him I'd be with Leo and Jax.'

Spencer gestured towards the large tent. 'They're over there. Oh, and Ryan,' he added as the lad went to run off, 'make sure you let your dad know you'll be here helping to clear up later.'

Ryan nodded. 'Yep.'

'Excuse me, Spencer, right?'

Spencer turned to see a middle-aged woman smiling his way. 'Yes, how can I help?'

'I was wondering if the Hub was still open today? I was going to pop in on my way home.'

Spencer nodded. 'Yeah. Jed and Luna are in there all morning.'

'Oh, I know them. That makes things a lot easier.' Her face flushed as she looked away.

'Easier?'

'My daughter just had a baby, and she's got no fella and is struggling financially. It's all falling to me to help, but I've not got much myself. Her health visitor mentioned a baby bank, so I was going to check it out. See what help was on offer.'

Spencer was feeling proud of Beth for setting up the baby bank, but he was also feeling sorry for the people needing one. He still struggled whenever someone came into the Hub for food, but just like always, he offered a warm smile and any advice he had to give. 'Definitely pop over.' He motioned towards Beth. 'Or go speak to that lady there. She's handing out information about the baby bank today. Oh, and let your daughter know about a parent and baby group over in the church hall.' He gestured towards the steeple of the stone-built church in the near distance.

'Yes, we just heard about that.' The woman thumbed behind her. 'We got some info from their stall.'

'It's so good there. Been myself with my girlfriend.' The mere reminder that Beth was now his girlfriend caused a hundred butterflies to take flight in his stomach.

'Thanks for your help,' she said, waving over at a young woman pushing a pram her way. 'I'll take my daughter over to the baby bank stall. Lucky you pointed it out. I missed that one.'

Spencer headed over to Shelby's stall to see if she needed any help, but she told him she was doing okay and that there had been a lot of interest in the parent and baby group. He smiled, pleased people near and far were seeing how much help was available in Port Berry.

Beth looked quite animated behind the tall white pop-up tent that made the information stand. He thought he'd see if Archie was awake before checking on anyone else at the festival.

Inhaling a waft of hotdogs, Spencer hummed along to muffled banjo music playing over the other side of the park. The slight skip in his step didn't go unnoticed by him, nor did the fact he couldn't stop smiling.

Beth had finished talking to the middle-aged woman and her daughter by the time Spencer arrived. He nuzzled his nose into her cheek, giving her a quick peck before looking in the pram to see Archie just waking.

'I'll take him for a walk with me to get some snacks. You fancy anything, honey?'

'Some juice please? Ooh, and a packet of crisps.'

Spencer gave her another kiss before heading off, peering over his shoulder to see her handing out leaflets. She looked so alive and brimming with happiness. So different to the woman who turned up on his doorstep. That day seemed years away now. Seeing Beth with colour in her cheeks and a smile on her face was the medicine he didn't know he needed.

There was a short queue for the food hut, so Spencer waited in line, exchanging pleasantries with the woman in front, before noticing Lottie heading his way.

'He awake now?' she asked, stopping at his side.

'Yes, and looking as adorable as ever.'

'Aww, he looks so content.' Lottie nudged his hip. 'And so do you.'

If there was anyone in the world that could be more excited for him than himself, it was his little sister.

'It feels good being settled with Beth and Archie.'

Lottie beamed, clasping her hands. 'I'm so glad, Spence. Honestly, I thought you'd never get there.'

He laughed. 'Get where exactly?'

'The life you deserve.'

'Hmm, well, I'm sure life can be just as lovely without partners or kids.'

'Of course, but I always saw you with a family of your own. It suits you.'

'Let's not get carried away. This is pretty new to us.' He knew full well he'd already discussed buying a house with Beth, but Lottie didn't need to know all their plans just yet.

'When you told me you'd got together, I wanted to throw a party, I was that excited.'

'Yes, I remember.' He smiled, reliving her squeal in the shop.

'Do you want some handy hints and tips from moi?'

'Not really.' He shook his head at her as they moved forward in the queue. 'But go on then, seeing how you're fit to burst.'

Lottie shrugged. 'Just keep things simple,' she said, giggling.

'That's it? That's your big relationship tip?'

'Yes. Love isn't complicated. People are. So if you just make sure you face everything together without adding complications, things should run smoothly.'

Spencer laughed. 'Good to know.' He tried to ignore the stir in his stomach as he thought about the paternity test he had done. Had he complicated things? Probably. 'I take it things with you and Sam are going well,' he added.

'Everything is wonderful.' Her dreamy eyes told him that was true.

'Go and find him then before you start missing him already.'

Lottie poked her tongue out, then headed off.

Spencer glanced at All Saints Church close by. In all the times he'd arranged flowers in there for someone's wedding, not once had he ever imagined himself standing at the altar. It was Lottie, with her whimsical outlook on love, making the idea of marriage appear. He laughed to himself at how much had changed for him, and all because he'd decided to become a different man.

Archie started gurgling and groaning as they neared the front of the queue, no doubt wanting his own feed.

'Hang on just a minute,' Spencer told him softly.

Archie started crying, his voice sounding as loud as the rest of the festival.

'Hey, hey, it's all right, little man.' Spencer picked him up for a cuddle.

Archie sounded even more frustrated, showing a whole river of tears as his little face flushed.

Spencer stroked over his back in small circles until he started to settle. 'We might think about opera singing lessons for you, son.' He pulled him off his shoulder to peer into his watery eyes, then kissed his head. 'You've got yourself all heated now, haven't you?'

Archie sighed, making Spencer laugh.

With a pram to navigate and a baby occupying one arm, it was quite the struggle moving forward on the grass, especially as a wheel hit a dip, but luckily a woman who was waiting her turn in the queue rushed to help.

'Oh, thanks. He didn't want me to put him down.'

She laughed. 'Probably because he couldn't see anything in there. Mine's the same. Nosey.'

Spencer laughed as he met Archie's eyes. 'Right, when we get home, we'll swap this carrycot for your upright number. You're ready now.'

Archie leaned forward, trying to eat Spencer's nose.

'Let's put you back down and turn your music on for a bit while I get your mum's snacks, then I'll carry you again, deal?'

As Archie didn't complain once his musical mobile was switched on, Spencer took that as a yes.

Someone was taking ages at the front deciding what they wanted to buy, so Spencer quickly checked his phone while waiting, in case Beth had sent a message asking for anything else. It was edging close to lunch, so perhaps a little more than crisps was in order.

Debra had the lunch sorted for the kids from the centre, so he didn't have to worry about them.

Lottie sprang to mind, purely from habit. He didn't have to look after her either. He smiled to himself at his sister trying to give him relationship advice earlier. He knew she was right about keeping things simple. Total honesty, team player, and not allowing any problems to tear them apart.

He didn't see himself as a complicated person, but there was one thing he hadn't simplified.

There were no messages from Beth, but he did notice an email from the paternity test clinic had arrived, causing him to freeze as soon as he read what it said. The sound of the festival faded away to a dull hum as every ounce of happiness left him within a split second. The phone screen blacked out, leaving him staring at his hand, and his stomach churned, waking him from a trance.

'You going to move up the line or what, mate?' said a voice from behind.

Waking with a jolt, Spencer left the queue and headed for Beth's stall. His heart started racing, causing a tightness to take control of his lungs. His fingers gripped the handle of the pram as though it were about to tip over the edge of a cliff, and the tension in his jaw was already giving him a headache.

'You okay, Spence?' asked Samuel as he passed him by.

Spencer didn't respond. He had tunnel vision for Beth. Unable to slow his legs or shake off the building anger, he marched across the grass.

Beth's smile dropped when he came to her side. 'What's wrong?' She quickly peered in the pram. 'What's happened?'

He went to speak but the words stuck in his throat, so he shoved his phone into her hand.

Beth glanced down at the email. She frowned, zooming in on the screen, then met his waiting eyes.

'How could you?' he whispered, his clenched teeth just about parting.

'No,' muttered Beth, looking back at the phone.

'What's going on?' asked Samuel, leaning on the other side of the desk.

Beth showed Samuel the phone. 'He's done a paternity test.'

Samuel took one look and his mouth flapped open. 'Oh.'

Spencer's attention was back on Beth. 'Why would you do this to me? I . . .' He took a step back as her hand reached for him.

'Spencer, when did you do this? Why didn't—'

'Don't talk to me.' He could hardly speak, let alone listen to what she had to say.

Samuel came around to his side. 'Spence, it's all right.'

Spencer took a breath as he looked at Beth. 'You didn't have to lie.' He had to get away from her. From everyone.

'Spencer, wait.'

There wasn't much he could take in. His head was spinning and his body shaking. He needed to sit, but where? He ran towards the pond, taking refuge behind a large white tent.

'Spence?' said Samuel, following him around.

'Don't say anything, Sam. I can't take this right now. I just can't believe . . .' He dropped to his knees, wanting to yell out. If he wasn't feeling so sick, a stiff drink would be on his to-do list.

'I'm sorry, Spence,' said Samuel quietly, crouching to his side.

Spencer went to say something, but bile hit the back of his throat, causing him to gag, and within seconds he threw up.

Samuel handed him a tissue. 'Let me take you home.'

Spencer scoffed, wiping his mouth. He slumped to his backside and stared at the sky. 'Doesn't feel much like home right now.'

'Look, mate, I'm sure there's an explanation for all this. There has to be.'

'I don't know.'

'Maybe she was just scared about being on her own.'

'That's no excuse.'

Samuel sat on the grass. 'I'm just trying to think of something.'

'It would make sense if I was as rich as you, but all I offered was a home.' Spencer shook his head. 'I guess that was what she needed.' He groaned, pinching the bridge of his nose with one hand while the other rubbed the back of his neck. 'I don't even know how to feel, Sam. So much of me is angry, but another part is too ill to think straight.'

'It's all right. You just need some time to get your head around this.'

Spencer breathed out a small laugh through his nose, feeling as though he might just cry. 'This must be what it feels like to be conned out of your life savings. Only, I've just lost a family.'

Samuel's face was full of sympathy, and Spencer didn't blame him for having little to say. He was still gobsmacked himself.

They sat there in silence for a moment while the festival continued around them as though no wrongs had been committed in Port Berry, but one had taken place, and it had ripped Spencer's heart to shreds. The last time he felt that lost was when he was eight and his little sister was taken from him.

'What do you want to do, Spence?'

He shrugged one shoulder. 'Pretend I didn't open that email.'

'How about you go speak to Beth somewhere more private? I'll look after Archie.'

Spencer shook his head. 'I can't look at her. She made me think I had a son. She lied to me.' He dipped his head, repeating his last words.

Samuel pulled out his phone. 'I'll send a few texts, let everyone know you're unwell and I've taken you home.'

'I don't want to go back there.'

'Back to mine then. Just until you feel you can face Beth again, because you're going to have to speak to her at some point.'

Spencer clutched his head in his hands. 'Not if I can help it.'

Samuel stood, tugging Spencer's arm. 'Come on, let's get out of here.'

Spencer straightened, then huffed a laugh, pointing at the back of the tent. 'Kindness festival, Sam. Of all places to find out I'm not the father of her child. Bloody kindness.'

Samuel's phone rang. 'It's Lottie. One sec. Hey, Lott, I'm—'

Spencer was busy staring at the sky, wondering who up there hated him to inflict such pain.

'Beth wants to talk to you,' Samuel told him.

'Not interested.'

Samuel got off the phone and grabbed his arm. 'Let's just go home.'

Spencer rubbed his chin, drawing in deep breaths of cake-infused air coming from the nearby tent. 'I can't believe this is happening,' he muttered, following Samuel away from half his stomach contents and quite possibly his soul. 'Wait. I have to speak to Debra. I—'

Samuel's phone rang again. He glanced at Spencer as he took the call. 'It's Beth. She's left.'

'Good. I hope I never see her again.'

'Lottie wants to speak to you.'

Spencer waved away the phone Samuel held out. 'Not now,' he mouthed, needing painkillers for his thumping head, not hearing whatever his sister had to say. 'I have a festival that needs me. I helped build this, and I'm not leaving because of *her*.'

'I really think you just need some time to yourself, Spence.'

'You know what, Sam, you're right, because I was doing just fine all by myself for years before she came along with her lies.'

Samuel flapped out an arm. 'Where you going?'

Spencer pointed forward. 'To do my job.'

'I'll speak to Lottie. Not sure what to tell her though.'

'Tell her I'm fine.' Spencer marched off, wishing he could fall face first into a tub of alcohol and drown his sorrows.

How could you?

Just for a moment, Spencer had no idea if he was still breathing. Numbness took hold, then a shiver ran the full length of his spine. He didn't know what to do.

'Spencer,' called Leo, suddenly at his side with Jax and Ryan. 'The donkeys are here from the rescue centre. Come on, let's go see them together.' The cheerfulness in his voice brought Spencer back to the land of the living.

The three lads dragging him across the park helped ease his racing heart. He couldn't be sure of anything much except he was needed by the Sunshine Superheroes. He had a job to do, a life to live, and Beth and Archie were just a dream that never came true for people like him.

CHAPTER 32

Beth

Racing back to her own home, Beth's adrenaline flushed through angrily from Spencer's unexpected announcement. She wasn't supposed to have stress in her life. Peace was needed in order to help heal, but stress ruled, making itself known. Her heart pounded and she couldn't think straight. Rage was the only thing working, using all the energy she had left to make it to the other side of her front door. Sweat built and air was limited as her stomach churned over and over.

Port Berry no longer existed. Nothing did. Just the palpitations, the hot flushes, and the never-ending agitation.

How Beth made it home so fast was beyond her. She parked the pram in the living room and dashed to get a glass of water from the kitchen tap. No sooner had the water touched her lips than a shiver removed the heat, and she started to calm her breaths, not wanting to feel so tightly wound, as it was no good for her to have high anxiety levels.

There were techniques she had learned, and now was the time to bring them out of her tool bag. The natural art of sedation.

'Come on,' she mumbled again and again, hoping her muscle memory would work.

Archie wasn't making any noises, which was helpful, as it was best he slept through her agitated state, as even though she was sure he wouldn't understand, she didn't want him to see her with beetroot cheeks, huffing and puffing.

Beth went to the bathroom to splash her face, the cool water waking her fully from the nightmare that had just taken place. What on earth was Spencer thinking? Should she have dashed away so fast? Perhaps things could have been sorted had they spoken.

With her head dipped, she shook her head at the mess they were now in.

'Calm,' she whispered. 'Calm is key.'

Jan had taught her so much, so she knew if she relaxed first, she could then figure out what to do about the situation.

Beth felt disappointed she had left the park now, but she had to get away, as she was fuming that he wouldn't speak to her.

She made her way to the sofa, telling herself it would get sorted soon. She just needed to process, and no doubt Spencer would want to talk to her at some point.

'Argh!' she growled through gritted teeth.

Why had he taken a DNA test without telling her? She wouldn't have minded. If the shoe were on the other foot, perhaps she would have taken a test too, but for him to do it behind her back, then not speak to her afterwards, was all a bit much.

She started to settle a touch, but her mind was still filled with questions. She flopped back, covering her face with her hands while taking a long calming breath.

Tiredness hit hard, acting as though it were doing her a favour. It wasn't rest she needed, it was control of her crumbling life.

There were two options. She could call her cousin and ask to stay with her for a while so she could avoid everyone in Port Berry, which she was sure would be okay with Pearl, or she could call Jan to tell her about the stress hijack she had stopped from taking her down.

Jan won and was quick to answer her phone, and once Beth explained what had happened, Jan reassured her everything would be okay. She offered to come over, but Beth was shattered, not to mention perplexed. All she really wanted was to talk to Spencer, but she had more chance of having a dinosaur come over for tea.

After a long chat with her therapist, she stood, adopting one of Leo's superhero poses. Enough was enough. Even though she knew about her condition now, it was still exhausting having to battle the monster, but one thing she knew thanks to Jan was not to cower away. Stress would always be part of life. At least she coped well enough when challenged, and she felt quite proud of her achievement.

Anxiety had tried to rise, but her techniques dampened the flames, and it was good to know she had the ability to calm herself.

She wasn't going to sit around twiddling her thumbs or going over what she should have said to Spencer.

'Do you know what, flat, it's time you became a home.'

She would tackle Archie's bedroom, because one way or another, she wasn't reverting to her old ways. A new woman had emerged from the darkness, and she was stronger, wiser, and more confident.

She went to the kitchen, thinking it was probably best to have a wipe round before starting anything. It had been a while since she'd been home, so some dust had accumulated, which wouldn't do. She'd have to get some food in later as well.

'Right!' Slapping her hands on her hips, she scanned the area, thankful there was still so much she hadn't taken to Spencer's.

His hurt face flashed through her mind once more. All the pain was right there in his eyes.

Would he answer if she called? Should she try or leave him alone? It didn't feel right leaving the wound open, but what choice did she have if he didn't want to listen?

Beth sighed. 'What a mess.' And she didn't mean the kitchen. She couldn't blame Spencer for his actions, but after the bond they'd built together, she did expect a little more from him. At the very least a chat.

Archie murmured, so she went to check on him. He wriggled, then went back to sleep. It was settled. She'd clean the kitchen, sort his bedroom so it was ready to be decorated, feed and change him when he woke, then they'd pop down to the local shop and get some food.

As for Spencer, it was his move to make, as she couldn't force him to speak to her. She glanced at the front door as though willing him to knock. Her phone vibrated, bringing a rush of excitement, but it was just a message from Lottie, asking if she was okay and could they talk.

'Nope.' Beth placed the screen downwards and got to work. It wasn't Lottie she wanted to speak to. The talk that was needed was going to be saved for Spencer only. Just like Jan had taught her, energy was precious and should be saved for important moments.

Knowing all too well what lack of energy felt like, Beth knew how to manage hers now. There was no way she was wasting any in the wrong areas. And with energy in mind, she went over to the sink to pull on a pair of pink rubber gloves.

* * *

Archie's room was an empty shell, and an online search found the perfect wallpaper. With that ordered, it was time to get some groceries, but first she needed to look up something else.

It didn't take long to do some research into paternity testing offered online. Even without knowing which company Spencer had used, she got the gist of the process and could see how things might go wrong. And with that in mind, she ordered some testing kits herself.

She just hoped Spencer got in touch with her so she could sort the issue.

Not wanting any more anger to surface, Beth got ready to tackle the shops.

Just as she got her son snuggled in his pram, someone knocked on her door, causing her stomach to flip. Glancing at the clock, she could see it had been a good few hours since she bolted from the festival. Surely it wasn't over already. No, it was too early. Perhaps it was a neighbour at the door. Maybe a parcel had been left with them while she was away.

To Beth's surprise, Lottie and Samuel were there, both looking awkward but friendly enough. 'You'd better come in.'

'It was my idea to come, not my brother's.'

Samuel rested a hand on Lottie's shoulder. 'We wanted to make sure you're okay.'

Beth saw the strong team before her, taking on life together. She had hoped that for her own short-lived relationship, but the first sign of trouble, and she was left alone. She mentally shook her head at her thoughts. As annoyed as she was, Spencer was not to blame. Anyone would have reacted the same way. She was the traitor who had stabbed him in the back. At least, that was how he would see it, she was sure.

'I'm just heading out to get some food.'

'This won't take long,' said Lottie.

'Look, I know what you're going to say. That—'

'Archie's my nephew.'

That wasn't what Beth thought she would say, and it left her speechless for a moment.

Lottie gave a slight nod. 'I believe he's family. I believe you.'

'Why?' was all Beth could think to say.

Samuel smiled. 'Part from the fact he's Lottie's double, we've got to know you, and we're struggling to believe you're a liar.'

Beth warmed at their trust. 'Thank you, and I want you to know I didn't lie. I looked up online testing places, and during my search, I discovered results can sometimes be wrong. Labs can make mistakes, but so can the person who performed the test. Anyway, I want you to know I've ordered five testing kits from different places, all fast delivery. Should arrive first thing. I want to carry out the tests myself.'

'In case Spencer messed it up,' said Samuel.

'Oh, I know someone messed something up, because there is no way anyone else can be Archie's father. It's just not possible.'

Lottie moved forward. 'I do believe you, Beth, but my brother is all over the place right now. When he calms down, he'll see what's staring him in the face, and these new tests will help settle him, I'm certain.'

'Do you think you can get him to do more tests?'

Lottie nodded. 'I think it's for the best. Like you said, things can go wrong. If you like, we can do the tests at my house. Neutral ground, and all that. I can do them with you both watching, if that helps.'

'Thanks, we can do that. And I just want you to know I'm not mad at Spencer for not believing me. I was just thrown by it all. I'm annoyed he didn't speak to me about this though. I'm not sure why he thought he couldn't.'

'He thought it might upset you,' said Lottie.

'Did you know?'

'I knew he considered the idea after a friend of his told him a paternity horror story, but I didn't know he had gone through with it. I guess it must have niggled at him.' Lottie clenched her fists. 'Ooh, I've a good mind to sue that DNA place.'

'Spencer could have easily contaminated part of the procedure. As soon as I read about it, I knew more testing was in order to help him see that. Also, it helps if the mum takes a test too, which, obviously, I didn't,' said Beth.

'We'll get this sorted, Beth.' Lottie offered a warm smile.

Beth sighed. 'I think if the next five tests come back negative, I need to see a doctor to find out if there's another way, because Archie *is* your nephew.'

Lottie bobbed her head. 'I know, Beth. Truly, I believe you, and I'm so sorry this has happened. I can only imagine how awful you must feel. But please know, we're on your side, and not because I want you and Archie to be our family, but because I believe in my heart of hearts you are.'

'I really appreciate that. Thank you.' Beth took a slow and steady breath. Lottie and Samuel both had kind eyes, and she was so grateful for their friendship and their trust.

Lottie nodded. 'Come straight over as soon as the tests arrive.'

'I wish we had them now.'

'Me too, for my brother's sake mostly. He's in so much pain right now.'

'He won't speak to me, but please tell him I'm not lying.'

Lottie raised her chin defiantly. 'Oh, I will. There's one thing you have to learn about Spencer. He can be his own worst enemy at times. I'll not take any of his stubbornness, not when I know it's for his own good.'

'He should have a clearer head by morning,' said Samuel, looking hopeful.

Beth smiled at them. 'I'd do anything to prove I'm not lying. Even if Spencer didn't want to be with me, I want him to know Archie is his son. I know the tests won't hurt my son. It's the results I'm worried about, after the last one.'

'There was obviously some sort of glitch,' said Lottie. 'And by this time next week, that will be proven.'

'I do hope so, because I honestly have no idea what to do if every test in the world doesn't match father and son.'

'It'll be all right, Beth.' Lottie raised her hands. 'I'll do the tests in front of you both, and we can all see that each and every step of the process is done correctly. I'll sterilize the table, wash my hands four times over, make sure everything is super clean. Nothing will go wrong.'

Beth breathed out a small laugh, not really finding anything funny. 'Let's hope not.'

'I'll try to get him to call you tonight.' Lottie glanced at Samuel, who smiled her way.

'It's all right,' said Beth. 'As long as he turns up at yours tomorrow.'

Lottie's hesitation wasn't exactly encouraging. 'I'm sure things will be different by morning. He had a shock.'

'He wasn't the only one.'

Lottie looked to Samuel again.

'We'll let you get on,' he said, thumbing towards the door. 'Unless you need us to stick around. Help you with anything.'

'Thanks, but I'm okay.' Beth was looking forward to some peace and quiet.

There wasn't anything left to do till morning. Putting it to the back of her mind for a while was the rest she needed. Whatever happened after five DNA tests were sent off was out of her hands. All she could do was pray Spencer got the confirmation he deserved.

When Lottie and Samuel left, Beth glared at the ceiling.

Why me? One reckless drunken night, and now look. Dodgy DNA results and a broken heart.

She walked over to the pram to meet Archie's bright eyes. 'I should have named you Silver Lining.'

He offered a little smile, warming her immediately.

'Whatever happens, son, you and me are going to be just fine,' she whispered, gaining herself another smile.

CHAPTER 33

Spencer

Sitting in Lottie's kitchen had never made Spencer feel awkward before, but having his sister, Samuel, Beth, and Archie all staring his way was rattling every part of him. Anyone would think he was the one who had done something wrong. Well, he wasn't having it. Nope. They could all get stuffed. Except Archie. The baby was the only one with a shimmer of love in his eyes, and it was heartbreaking to look at him.

Spencer sniffed as Lottie unwrapped the first box, pulling out a leaflet.

'Okay, before we start, did you do what I asked?' Lottie glanced at Beth first, then Spencer.

Even though she was speaking to him as though he were five, it felt good to have her to focus on, because his eyes kept wanting to wander over to Beth all the time, and he wasn't about to acknowledge her presence. It was way too hard just being in the same room with her. Besides, it wasn't as though she had spoken to him. She hadn't said anything but a polite hello to Lottie and Samuel.

'Yes,' he told his sister. 'I haven't eaten, had a drink, brushed my teeth or anything in over an hour. I'm good to go.'

Lottie turned to Beth.

Beth nodded. 'Me too, and I have Archie's bottle of water ready to give his mouth a rinse before we start.'

Lottie pointed at the sink. 'Go rinse your mouth first, Spence.'

He went off to do as he was instructed, realizing he hadn't done that before. He tried to think back, but it was a bit of a blur, what with his mind in a muddle at the time.

Lottie started to read the instructions out loud, checking things off. 'My hands are clean, yep. All mouths are ready for swabbing, yep, you've both signed the consent form, yep.'

'I didn't last time,' said Beth, sounding slightly bemused.

Spencer swallowed hard. 'I did it by myself, as I thought I had parental responsibility, seeing how I was told I was Archie's father, and the place I used only wanted a signature anyway.'

'Never mind that now,' said Lottie. 'Let's just sort this properly once and for all.'

'Besides,' said Beth, 'I was going to talk to you about adding your name to the birth certificate. As far as I'm concerned, you have parental rights.' He was sure there was a slight angry undertone to her words.

Spencer sat back down, keeping his gaze firmly on the containers that held the long-stemmed cotton buds, while Beth gave Archie to Samuel before heading off to rinse her mouth.

Samuel gave the baby some water.

'I'll do Archie first,' said Lottie, once Beth had returned to her seat and held her son again. She broke the seal, then without touching the part that was about to enter his mouth leaned forward. 'Right, so I just have to twizzle this between the bottom lip and gum.' She smiled at the baby. 'Sorry, lovely. Might tickle a bit.'

Everyone watched her take the swab, then seal it back in the tube, and Spencer wondered if he was as careful. Could he have accidentally touched the cotton tip and contaminated it? He took a silent breath as his sister came at him with a separate swab to rub around the inside of his cheek. She swirled it around about ten times, then sealed that one away too before turning to Beth for her turn.

'One down,' she mumbled.

'Do we really need to do five?' he asked.

'I'm happy to do twenty,' said Beth, looking only at the table.

Spencer had no words for her, so shut up altogether.

Lottie placed everything in the prepaid tamper-proof envelopes, ready to post, then opened the second box and once more followed the instructions to the letter.

As soon as it was over, Spencer rushed to the street door, feeling the need for fresh air. It was hard being around Beth and not holding her. His heart felt torn in two. He was so sure she wasn't lying to him, but the test told him otherwise. He just couldn't think straight.

'Spencer,' she called, sprinting to his side on the doorstep.

'Look, I'm sorry I didn't tell you about the first test. I wasn't—'

'It's not that. I don't care.' She tapped her chest. 'I just want us to talk.'

He lowered his eyes, unable to meet hers and not kiss her. The pain was too much, and the confusion worse. Why was he even putting himself through more testing? Could he take the hit again? Lottie was so sure he'd messed it up last time. Now, he couldn't think straight, and being so close to the woman he thought he loved was making the situation harder. He turned to walk away, but she grabbed his arm.

'Please, Spence, don't run away.'

He stared out at Berry Hill and at the seagulls. 'I'm not running,' he said softly. 'I have to collect the boys from the Sunshine Centre. We're searching for fossils.' He felt her hand slip from his sleeve, and he missed her touch already.

'Okay. But I just want you to know something before you go.' He heard her breath catch, but he didn't turn. 'I didn't lie. Hopefully you'll see that when the results come back.'

Some of the test centres offered one- to two-working day results, and Beth had paid for the quickest, so it wouldn't be long before he knew for sure if Archie was his son, but after the last test, he wasn't holding out much hope, and Beth's words were meeting a wall guarding his heart.

'I have to go.' Spencer walked slowly down the steep hill, inhaling the sea-salty air in large clumps. He daren't look back in case she was watching, but suddenly he could hear footsteps behind him, then arms clutched his body as she embraced his back, causing him to stand stock still.

You're killing me, Beth. You're actually killing me.

'Take this with you,' she said quietly, then released him, and whatever spell was keeping him in place was broken.

Without saying a word, Spencer walked away.

The drive over to Penzance settled Spencer a touch. Looking out at wide green fields and quaint farmhouses had him thinking about family life. It was Easter soon, and he could just see himself hunting colourful eggs in the park with Archie. It was a nice dream.

A sign caught his eye, and with little thought, he pulled up next to someone's gate so he wouldn't be in the way of any traffic. He jumped out of his van and walked over to a man attaching an orange *For Sale* sign to a post.

'You interested?' asked the man, following Spencer's gaze down the short driveway.

Spencer scanned the small brown-brick cottage. 'I remember the woman who lived here. Kathleen. She passed a while back now. How come this place is only going up for sale now?'

The man lowered his hammer. 'Family have to wait a while before selling an inherited property.'

'Yeah, I know about that stuff, but it's been ages.'

'They did have it on the market, but no takers. Rundown, you see. They took it off for a while, as one of them decided they'd take on the project, but that fell through, and now they're trying their luck with us again.'

Spencer narrowed his eyes as the clouds moved away from the sun. 'How bad is it?'

'Structure's all right. Just old. Unloved. You know how it goes.'

He nodded, stepping up to the small dark picket fence that made the entrance. Pink, purple, and blue came to mind. Potted flowers placed out front, a paddling pool at the back. 'Three beds, isn't it?'

'Yep. Do you want a quick peek while you're here?'

Did he? He wasn't entirely sure why he had stopped. 'If that's okay,' he found himself saying.

'I'm an estate agent, of course it's okay.' The man told him his name was Geoff as he handed out his card. 'Recent price drop, just so you know.' He leaned in his open car window and came back with a flyer. 'Here, take this.'

Spencer glanced down at the info about the old house, remembering entering a few times as a child with his aunt.

Geoff rattled off house prices, comparing Kathleen's old home with others in the area while he went from room to room, splaying his arms left, right, and centre.

It made little difference to Spencer what the man was going on about. All he could hear was Archie's content sounds and see Beth's smile. Had things not gone so wrong, they could be viewing properties together.

He remembered the last time he was in the house. Rebecca had brought Kathleen some groceries, as she wasn't well and there was no one else to help her since her children had grown and moved away.

'Bit of plastering,' said Geoff, coming back into focus.

'Hmm? Oh, yeah.' Spencer laughed to himself at the attention the place needed. 'And the rest,' he mumbled, heading for the front door. He shook hands with the man, then went back to his car, still wondering why he had bothered to check out the home for sale.

With the engine purring, and his hands clasping the steering wheel, he took a deep breath and lowered his head to his fingers for a moment.

'Bloody hell!' he muttered, feeling agitated on every level. Snapping out of his haze, he made his way to the Sunshine Centre, as the boys would be waiting. He didn't feel much in the mood for fossil hunting, but it was planned, and the children were looking forward to another badge.

It wasn't long before Spencer swapped his van for the centre's minibus and was heading to the seafront with buckets and spades and three eager lads. It was nice to see how much more they smiled since he first met them.

'Right, now the chance of finding a fossil is slim, but if we can find some unusual shells, that'll be good enough,' he told them as he parked.

'Or sea glass,' said Leo, gasping at the thought.

'Knowing my luck, it'll be an old boot we dig up,' said Jax, collecting his spade from the back seat.

Ryan laughed. 'Skeleton bones.'

'Pirate treasure,' said Leo.

Spencer shook his head as he followed them down to the shingles, thankful it was a lovely day and the sea was calm. The gentle whooshing sound soothed his weary soul, and the boys laughing brought back his joy. Before he knew it, half an hour had passed.

Jax pulled him over to a small pool nestled by a circle of rocks someone had built up by a wall. 'Do you think they tried to make a castle for a fish?'

'Probably just someone playing with—'

A yell ripped through the air, coming from the shoreline. It took a moment to notice Leo's red cape flapping in the breeze.

'Leo,' shouted Spencer. Following the boy's pointing finger out to sea.

'It's a dog,' said Leo. 'Looks like it's struggling to swim.'

Ryan went to move closer to the sea, but Spencer pulled him back. 'But I can save it,' said Ryan.

'I'm sure you can, but you're not going out there.'

Leo frowned at Spencer. 'Can I go?'

Spencer shook his head. 'No one's going in the sea.'

Jax started to coax the dog to the shoreline, patting his knees and whistling.

The little dog was paddling furiously as wave after wave rolled over its head.

Spencer knew he had to help, as the poor thing looked exhausted. 'I'll go.'

Leo gasped dramatically, then clapped as Spencer waded into the cold water, glad the dog wasn't too far out.

Jax was still calling the dog, and Ryan asked if he should call the coastguard.

Spencer told them not to move, then tried to walk a bit faster, reaching for the dog as the rolling waves splashed against his stomach.

The children cheered as the dog was whipped up into Spencer's arm just as another dark wave rolled their way.

Spencer was relieved the sea wasn't too choppy as he plodded to the shoreline, lowering himself and the soaked dog panting in his face.

Leo tugged his cape so it draped on the animal. 'It's all right. You're safe now.'

The dog licked Leo's hand, making the boy smile.

Ryan flopped to his side. 'He's so small. He must have got swept away.'

The boys started to fuss the dog while Spencer scanned the beach for an owner.

'He looks fine now,' said Jax.

'You need a good sleep,' Leo told the animal, stroking its brown fur.

'Hello. Hello,' a high-pitched voice squealed.

They all turned to see a young man running their way.

'It that my baby?' he cried, approaching.

The dog jumped up, tail wagging.

'Your dog was drowning,' said Leo, standing as the man bent to his pet.

'He ran off. I only let him off the lead for one minute. Didn't think he'd get far on his little legs, but then he saw another dog, and zoom, he was gone. I've been looking everywhere. I had no idea he came down here.'

'Spencer saved him,' said Jax proudly.

Spencer half smiled, glad the dog was okay, but fed up with his legs being soaked through to the bone.

'Your dog isn't a good swimmer,' said Leo.

The man cradled his pet close to his face. 'Thank you so much for saving Tiny.' He turned to his pet. 'What were you thinking going in the sea?'

'Maybe he chased a seagull,' said Jax.

'Or was paddling and got swept out,' said Ryan. 'It's not the same as a swimming pool, you know. There's all sorts going on out there.'

'Barracudas,' said Leo, scrunching the damp part of his cape to his chin.

Ryan frowned at him. 'I meant the undercurrent.'

'We're just glad your dog is okay,' said Spencer.

'Thank you once more.' The man let the boys stroke Tiny again before he headed off, looking slightly teary.

Leo glanced at Spencer. 'Do we get a badge for that?'

'For what?'

'Saving Tiny.'

Ryan laughed. 'Spencer saved him.'

Leo lifted his cape. 'I helped keep Tiny warm while he was in shock.'

'I think Tiny was more out of breath,' said Jax.

'Can we have a paddle in the sea now?' Leo asked Spencer.

Spencer shivered, needing dry clothes and less drama in his life.

'Are you all right, Spencer?' asked Ryan.

'Cold, but okay.'

Leo stepped closer to offer his cape, making Spencer smile at his kindness.

'Thanks, Leo, but I think we should head back to the centre now.'

'I agree,' said Ryan.

'Me two,' said Jax.

'Me three,' said Leo.

Spencer glanced at his wet bottoms. 'Right, let's go.'

They trudged to the minibus in silence, which was a small blessing, as Spencer was having one of his stress headaches. Just when he thought his day couldn't get any worse.

'I need to tell Debra so she can put it in the incident book,' said Leo, clambering into the vehicle.

Ryan frowned. 'Tiny's not a member of the centre.'

Leo shrugged. 'Spencer had an incident.'

Jax chuckled as he sat down. 'Spencer saved a dog. He's a hero.'

That was the last thing Spencer felt like. He'd gone behind Beth's back, refused to talk to her, hardly looked at Archie earlier. He was pretty sure heroes didn't act that way.

The corner of Ryan's mouth curled. 'I think we're all heroes in our own way.'

Very profound.

Spencer mentally shook his head as he started the engine. It had been one hell of a day, but suddenly the fog in his head started to clear. Leo had the skills to calm himself with breathing techniques, and Jax had spoken to a shopkeeper, and now Ryan was willing to go back into the water, even if it was to save a dog. Inspiration hit hard. If the kids could find ways to navigate their problems, then so could he. It was time he faced his own insecurities.

CHAPTER 34

Beth

Having left Archie with Lottie and Sam for a couple of hours, Beth went to the Hub to get on with the shift she had promised to do. Just because her head was a mess didn't mean she would leave Alice to volunteer alone. Good thing she went, because Alice looked tired.

'Why don't you sit for a bit, Alice, and I'll finish sorting the noticeboard.'

Alice pulled down some flyers, rearranging them so everything on the board could be seen. 'I'm better standing today.'

Knowing Alice had fibromyalgia, Beth wondered how she was really coping. 'Are you in a lot of pain?'

'Not too bad. I had a rough night thanks to neck pain, but I've got what I call the finger bruise at the moment, so sitting isn't that comfy.'

Beth approached to glance at her hand up by the board. 'What's wrong with your fingers?'

Alice chuckled. 'Not them. It's just one of my symptoms. Basically, I have these small tender spots, about the size of your fingertip, either side of my spine, just by my bra line, and when I lean back in a chair, it feels like I'm pressing on a really painful bruise.'

'Ooh, that doesn't sound good.'

'Doesn't feel that great either.'

'Is there anything I can do to help?'

'A cuppa would go down well.'

Beth headed to the kettle, thinking more along the lines of rubbing some pain relief cream into her friend's back. 'How long has it been hurting?'

'All morning, but hopefully it'll go away soon. These don't seem to last long with me. Couldn't tell you about anyone else, but they come and go on me in the same day.' Alice shook her head as she stepped back to admire her work. 'Funny old condition I've got. Still, I'm better off than some, so mustn't grumble.'

'Oh, you grumble away if you want. Nothing wrong with that.' Beth placed some choccy biscuits on the table.

Alice smiled. 'I have my moments; don't you worry about that. But all in all, I just get on with it. Part of my life now.' She turned to the door as it opened. 'Ooh, hello, Roxy. Your mum said you'd pop in. One sec, I'll just grab her food package.'

The tall blonde woman, chewing gum, came over to snatch a biscuit. Beth watched as she removed the gum, wrapped it around her finger, then stuffed the biscuit into her mouth. 'Mmm, I haven't had any brekkie today.'

Beth offered a plate of pastries. 'You can have one of these if you like.'

'Ooh, ta,' said Roxy, picking one out.

Alice came back with a box of food.

'Is it right that you have some baby clothes?' asked Roxy, taking the box, chewing gum hitting its side.

'Yes,' replied Beth.

'My mate Lola told me. She heard about it from the parent and baby group at the church hall.'

Beth smiled. 'I'm friends with Lola.'

Roxy lifted the box to show her flat stomach. 'Might need some help myself soon.' She shrugged as best she could while juggling the box and a croissant.

'Well, we'll be here,' said Beth, helping her with the door. At least she hoped she would still be around helping the Hub with the baby bank and anything it needed.

'You all right, Beth? You've got a faraway look in your eye.'

Beth turned from the view of the sea. 'I was just thinking about Spencer.'

Alice held a sympathetic smile. 'Everything okay?'

'We fell out.'

'Oh, sorry to hear that.'

Beth went back to making the tea. 'It was a misunderstanding. I'm hoping we'll sort things in the next few days.' *If those paternity tests do their job properly.*

Alice pulled out a cloth to give the windows a wipe. 'I'm glad I'm single.'

It was a sharp reminder for Beth that she was too now. She placed the tea on the table, then picked up another cloth to help clean the door.

'Have you ever been in love, Alice?'

'Only once. Long time ago now.'

'Haven't you been with anyone in a while?'

'There was this one man, but he was horrible, fooled me at first.' She inhaled loudly, making Beth turn. 'Glad that's over.' She flapped her green cloth at the pane. 'Some right nasty people out there. Whatever happened with you and Spencer, just know his heart isn't bad. He just keeps it under lock and key.'

Beth could understand why, if her own heartache was anything to go by. She went to speak, but someone was at the door, waggling a carrier bag. She quickly opened it to say hello.

'Just dropping off some long-life milk,' said the man, handing her the bag.

'Thank you so much.' She waved, then headed straight to the storage room to unpack the bag.

'Alice, that labouring job still on the board?' said a deep voice, causing Beth to poke her nose around the door frame to see who had entered.

Alice pulled down a card, passing it to a young man. 'Here you go. Best of luck.'

The door closed and Beth came out to take a sip of tea. 'Come and sit for a bit. You can turn the chair around so you're not leaning on the back.'

Alice did, reaching for a biscuit. 'I'm looking forward to lunch already. Said I'd eat with Nan later.'

'Can your nan really see into the future?'

'Well, she's hardly ever wrong.'

Beth wondered what her own future held. Just for a moment back at Spencer's, she was starting to see a clear picture, but now it was just haze. 'Has she told you what's in yours?'

Alice's laugh was muffled around the rim of her cup. 'She won't say much about me. Told me the fella I went with was a rotten egg, but I had to find that out for myself the hard way, as you do. 'Part from that, she can be tight-lipped when it comes to her own.'

'Do you have any plans?'

'I'm looking into opening my own B & B. A home and business for Benny and me. I often help out up the road at the Seaview, and the lady who owns the place, Mabel, has taught me all I need to know.'

'Oh, that was nice of her.'

Alice smiled warmly. 'Yeah, well, she's like family to me.'

'It's nice how close you all are around here.'

Alice nudged her elbow. 'Ah, it's all about choosing the right circle for yourself. Makes all the difference.'

'I've never really been much of a circle person. I guess mine is small.'

'Got us lot now, don't forget.'

Beth appreciated the kindness she had found in Port Berry, and Alice was right, having such a positive circle had made such a difference in many ways.

'What are your plans, Beth?'

Sorting her flat, she figured. Going back to work after maternity leave was over. Looking for a new job. One that gave her more time with her son. Now it was put to her, she felt perhaps she should plan ahead, but with Spencer not talking to her, not much mattered.

'Ah, like that, is it?' added Alice, as Beth still hadn't answered.

Beth shrugged. 'I've never been much of a dreamer. I guess my future will be similar to my past, with Archie added into the mix.'

'It's not about dreaming. Change happens all by itself as life moves forward, but we can control some parts. Look at me, I live with my mum, nan, and nephew above a newsagents. It's a bit of a squash, so I plan to move out, and having a home that's a business kills two birds with one stone. Ooh, that's kind of a horrible saying.' Alice frowned. 'Anyway, my point is, planning isn't dreaming. It's figuring out how to get from A to B.'

'I guess I just need to really figure out what my B is.'

Alice grinned. 'I'll hit you with the interview question.'

'What's that?'

'Beth Horton. Where do you see yourself five years from now?' Alice said in a sharp high-pitched tone.

Beth smiled. 'Okay. Let's see. I would like to be in a new job, own my own home, and live happily ever after with Spencer.'

'Ta-da! Now you know your path.'

Beth chuckled as Alice got up to open the door for an elderly man. Her friend made it all sound so simple, but could she really pour her energy into building the life she wanted, or should she just settle for the one she had?

I've had some changes. Archie, living with Spencer, the parent and baby group, and this place.

Beth glanced over at the framed affirmations on the wall. She'd come a long way in a short time, and her confidence had turned a corner. She felt different to who she was before she got pregnant. Stronger somehow, but also gentler on herself.

Alice was leading the gentleman over to the soft, green, high-back chair, offering him a cuppa.

Beth knew some people only came into the Hub for some company. She scanned the old man's worn features while he nattered away to Alice, wondering what his life had been like. She left them to it, going into the storage room to unpack some baby clothes.

The generosity of the local residents had been incredible, and Beth was so glad she was helping others.

Talking about the future had inspired her somewhat. She pulled out her phone and sent a quick message to her old work colleague, asking for information about jobs at the private school where she worked. After everything her friend had said about how she was getting better pay and working fewer hours, she was interested in working there herself.

Beth's phone rang almost immediately.

'Oh, hello, Joy. I wasn't expecting you to call so fast.' She heard her friend laugh.

'It's so weird. I was just talking about you with my boss. An opening is coming up, and I put your name forward, as I knew you were interested.'

'Oh, yes, very much.'

'The job doesn't start until after your maternity leave, so the timing is perfect for you, and she told me you can send your CV directly to her. I'll text you her email address. I'd do it straight away if I were you.'

'Thanks, Joy. That is perfect, as Archie will be in day care by then. I'll send my details right now.'

'Go on then. Let me know how you get on.'

Beth hung up the call and quickly pulled up her CV to double-check all was in order, even though she knew it was. She had easy access to it on her phone, so all she had to do was attach it to the email and press send.

Here's to my future.

She sent the email and relaxed. It was out of her hands now.

'Hiya, chick,' said Ginny, entering the storage room. 'What are you grinning about?'

'I've just applied for a new school job.'

'Ooh, do you want me to help you practise interview questions? I think there's one where they ask you what biscuit you'd be.'

Beth giggled. 'A crumbly one.'

Ginny sat on the small stool in the corner. 'Nah, you're more a chocolate finger. They're pretty tough when dunked.'

She definitely felt like she'd been dunked a few times. 'Well, at least I know what to say if I do get asked.'

Ginny grinned. 'I fancy a bickie now.' She called out to Will to put the kettle on.

'Will's here too?'

'It's our shift, chick.'

Beth glanced at her phone. 'Blimming heck, is that the time? I'd better go pick up Archie.'

'Come and have dinner with us tomorrow night, if you're not busy.'

'That'll be nice, thanks.' Beth gave Ginny a warm hug, then went out to the front to say goodbye to Alice.

'Hello, Beth. I just saw Sam and Lottie with Archie, at the tea shop,' said Will.

'Thanks. Now I have an excuse to buy cake.'

'I'll walk with you,' said Alice, opening the door. 'I'm going that way.'

Beth smiled to herself at her surroundings. The sky was blue, the salty air refreshing, and her new friends made her feel part of something wonderful. Her phone buzzed in her pocket, and she quickly grabbed it, thinking it was Lottie letting her know where they were. 'Oh!'

Alice clutched her arm. 'What is it, Beth?'

'Sorry, I didn't mean to sound so dramatic. I was surprised, that's all. Look.' Beth showed her the screen. 'I've been offered an interview. Tomorrow.'

'That's great. Well done, lovely.'

'Ooh, I feel a bit flustered now.'

Alice gave her arm a gentle squeeze. 'You'll be fine. You already know what biscuit you are.'

The two women burst out laughing as they turned the corner of Harbour End Road. Oh, it was good to feel alive.

CHAPTER 35

Spencer

Leo was the first to tell Debra what a hero Spencer was for saving a drowning dog, telling all he should be on the news.

Spencer shook his head as he entered Debra's office. 'I'd rather just get changed.' He had a spare tracksuit in his locker there, in case of emergencies. He never thought one would be him entering the sea.

The boys headed off to the arts and crafts room, leaving Debra glancing over Spencer's damp clothes.

'Are you all right?' she asked quietly, closing her office door. 'You've been through a lot with the boys. How are you coping?'

'I won't lie, I've had my moments when I thought I might not be cut out for this after all, but we all changed at some point or other, and progress has been made all round.'

'You're a good mentor for them.'

Spencer scoffed. 'I wouldn't go that far.'

'I would. I've seen the way they look up to you. You're doing a great job.'

Spencer left the office feeling a lot better, then quickly grabbed his things and got changed, wanting to see how the boys were getting on.

'Can we make Easter bonnets?' was the first thing Leo asked.

'Next week,' said Spencer.

Bonnie had turned up to collect her son. 'And there's the Easter egg hunt, Leo.'

Leo beamed as his mum led him and Jax out to the car park.

Spencer followed with Ryan, knowing someone would be along soon to collect him.

He hesitated by the main door, pondering his next move. Beth was on his mind, and so was Kathleen's old house. He just wasn't sure if he should speak to Beth before the test results came back, but on the other hand . . .

'Ryan. Over here,' Annette called, then gave a small wave to Spencer from her car.

He returned the gesture as he watched Ryan leave, then went off to pick up his bag of wet clothing and let Debra know the kids were with their parents and he was leaving.

It didn't take long to get to Beth's flat, and Spencer had championed himself all the way, going over his lines, making sure he wouldn't forget anything important. It was quite the blow to find she wasn't there.

With still so much sitting on his chest, he made his way home to see if he could spot her. Perhaps she was sitting outside the Jolly Pirate, having something to eat. It certainly was a nice day for it.

He parked and checked his flat first, just in case she was there, after all, she still had a key. No sign of her, so he went for a walk, popping his head in the Hub.

'You looking for Lottie, chick?' asked Ginny.

'No. Beth.'

Ginny thumbed down the road. 'Last I saw, she was heading to my tearoom.'

'Thanks.' And with that, he was off, turning his long strides into a slight jog.

Lottie was outside with Samuel, eating chocolate fudge cake with one fork between them.

Spencer ignored his sister feeding her partner. 'Have either of you seen Beth?' The way they were gazing into each other's eyes, he'd be surprised if they'd noticed anyone.

'She left a little while ago,' said Lottie. 'I think she was going to the park on her way home.'

Spencer left them to their shared cake, setting off back to his flat. Just in case he saw her on his way to the park, he wanted to have Archie's car seat in the van, as there was somewhere he wanted to take them, if she was willing. At least he wanted to be prepared.

There was hardly anyone about on his drive to Anchorage Park, which did make looking out easier, but still no sign of Beth. He pulled up to ring her, hoping she'd answer and let him know where to meet her, but his call went straight to answerphone.

Just as he started to walk across Old Market Square, he saw her leaving the park. 'Beth,' he called, raising an arm.

She stopped pushing the pram and looked up.

Spencer sprinted her way. 'Hey,' was all he managed, wondering where his big speech had disappeared to.

'Where you off to?' Her smile was soft, warm, reaching into his heart.

'I was looking for you.'

'Oh?'

'I want to, well, the thing is . . .' He gestured over to his van. 'I'd like to show you something.'

Beth nodded. 'Okay.'

He walked by her side, then sorted the pram while she strapped Archie into his seat. There was so much he wanted to say, it was getting muddled in his head and not reaching his mouth. He couldn't blurt it all at once, but something had to be said.

Beth smiled as she put on her seatbelt. 'Where are we going?'

'Not far,' he replied, pulling away. 'There's this old cottage, used to belong to a woman called Kathleen. She passed away last year.' He was rambling, he knew. 'Anyway, when I saw it was for sale, something made me want to take a look. Here it is.'

Beth was staring out the side window as he pulled up close to the picket fence. 'Oh, it looks in need of a lick of paint.'

Archie had fallen asleep already, so Spencer left him in the van, as they were only standing by the bumper.

'I saw us here, Beth. You, me, Archie.'

She glanced his way, her expression unreadable.

Spencer met her eyes. So many feelings hit him at once, he felt quite lost.

'I'm sorry you're hurting,' she said quietly, taking his hand. 'I wish I could make your pain go away. Please believe me when I tell you I didn't lie. Archie's your son. I promise you.'

Spencer took a steady breath, raising their linked hands to his chest. 'I don't care about those tests anymore, Beth. I know you didn't lie to me. I can feel it in my heart and soul. I was the one in the wrong putting us through all that. My insecurities got the better of me, then my brain scrambled, and I stopped listening to my instincts. I love you both so much.'

'I love you, Spencer.'

With one look, he could see the sincerity deep within her eyes. A strong awareness of their attachment flooded him, overwhelming his senses.

Beth leaned into him, curling her arms around his back. 'I just want our family,' she whispered, her voice mingling with the gentle movement of the leaves in a nearby tree.

He dipped his head so his chin rested on her mousey hair, and he closed his eyes for a moment as he held her. They were his family because together they had made it so, not some test or need for company. They had helped each other, grown together, and fallen in love.

Her embrace tightened slightly as she raised her chin to face him.

'I believe you,' he said softly, meaning every word. Somehow, some way, he just knew. 'I promise, I believe you.'

Beth was staring at him, face relaxed, eyes gentle. Her hand curled around the back of his neck, lowering him slowly towards her mouth, and Spencer's heart cradled hers as their lips met.

Their soft, gentle kiss quickly heated, causing them to stumble into the fence. They laughed as they straightened, then Spencer gestured towards the house.

'What do you think, Beth? It's affordable. Just needs some love.'

She snuggled under his arm as she looked up the pathway. 'Can we peek through the windows?'

'Sure. I've already been inside with the estate agent I saw putting up the sign. It's definitely a project, but not too much of one.'

'Let me put Archie in his pram, then we can walk around.'

Spencer helped set up the pram, then opened the small gate in need of new hinges.

Archie stirred but soon settled again as soon as Beth started to push him along.

The front door was pale blue and the framework chipped, but it still held a welcome.

Beth peered through a small square window and cooed. 'Oh, Spence, do you really think we could live somewhere like this?'

'Yeah, we can put in an offer if you're ready now, but if not, we'll make a home wherever we end up in the future.' He glanced up from the pram to see her smile.

'Let's have a nosey round the back.'

He followed her along a side path in need of a good groom, then scanned the garden while she looked through the pane in the back door to take in the kitchen. All sorts went through his mind. A shed, greenhouse, perhaps a pergola, maybe a parterre. No doubt Lottie would come over with her green fingers and get stuck in. He imagined some raised beds along one fence, filled with herbs or vegetables.

Beth grabbed his arm, making him jump out of his daydream. 'I want us to put in the offer.'

He grinned. 'Yeah, you sure? This is the first house we've viewed.'

'It made you stop and take a look and bring me here. It's where you looked me in the eyes and told me you believed in me. Everything feels right. I know it's old and in need of repair, just like us, but—'

'Oi, cheek!' He tickled her ribs, and Beth squirmed away. 'We're not old yet.'

'No, we're not, so let's take this on while we're fit enough to deal with it all.'

Spencer laughed. 'Well, I was thinking we'd hire some experts to do most jobs.'

Beth squealed, clapping her hands in front of her chest. 'Ooh, Spence, I haven't told you. I have an interview for a new job tomorrow. It's fewer hours and better pay, and best of all, less stress, as I won't be working with a lot of children.'

'That's great.' He lightly tapped her chin. 'Looks like we're on a new road.'

'Maybe we were always on the same road, and this is just the part where we get to walk it together.'

'In that case, this is definitely the best part of the journey.'

Beth nodded. 'The company makes all the difference, doesn't it?'

Spencer kissed her head. 'It certainly does.'

'Let's go home and have something to eat. I need to prep for my interview, and can you get the ball rolling on this place?'

'I can do that.'

Beth hugged him tightly. 'I missed you.'

'I'm sorry about—'

'Hey,' she said, cupping his face. 'It was a shock, and it hurt us both. I want us to move past that now, else we'll always live in that moment. One of the things I learned from Jan was how to let go. Let's just put our energy into what's happening now for our future.'

Spencer gave a slight nod. 'Sounds like a good plan. But, Beth, I want you to know that I'm not interested in the test results. I'm not letting that tell me what I know in my heart. I never should have done it in the first place, and I'm sorry, and—'

'We're moving forward, Spence. No more apologies. Let's focus on our future as a family.'

They shared a kiss before heading back to the van, where he watched Beth glance over her shoulder and smile at the old cottage, and something told him their offer on the place would be accepted.

CHAPTER 36

Beth

Watching the kids run around the gardens of the Sunshine Centre, searching for colourful toy Easter eggs for their small wicker baskets, was making Beth smile no end. She sat back in a patio chair beneath a red canopy while Spencer bounced Archie in front of a large ornamental rabbit over by the entrance to the nature reserve.

It was hard to believe it was the middle of April. February seemed years ago not months. The changes during that time seemed unreal, and Beth was so thankful for the life she was living now. No more dark clouds over her head, no shivers and shakes keeping her awake, and no more feeling alone.

Had someone told her what was in store when she moved to Port Berry, she wouldn't have believed them. Just the community spirit alone was heart-warming.

'You look deep in thought,' said Matt, sitting down by her side.

Beth smiled. 'Oh, I was just having a surreal moment. It just blows me away sometimes when I think about how much my life has changed since moving to Port Berry.'

Matt chuckled. 'Tell me about it. I have those all the time, and it's been a year now since I moved here.'

'They're a friendly bunch, aren't they?'

'Best circle of mates I've ever had.'

Beth bobbed her head. 'Me too.'

Matt glanced over the small wooden table between them. 'When you've been stuck in one long dark tunnel for so long, then you come out the other end somehow and the light is so beautiful, it feels like magic.'

Beth grinned. 'Do you think Port Berry is enchanted?'

Matt chuckled. 'If it is, then my Sophie was definitely a magical potion that helped raise me to the next level in this game of life.'

'Aww, Matt, that's so sweet.' She smiled at his blush, then followed his gaze to Sophie. 'I hear you're getting married this December.'

'Yeah, that blows my mind. I still can't believe how blessed I am.'

Sophie waved him over, and Beth watched him walk into his fiancée's embrace. It was lovely to witness such love, and her heart warmed even more when she spotted Spencer approaching.

Just like Matt, she too felt blessed.

'Hey, is that my lemonade?' asked Spencer, pointing at the blue glass on the table.

'Yep.' She smiled at him as he sat, Archie on his knee.

Her phone buzzed, showing the last email to come through from the paternity test clinic. Spencer hadn't wanted to know about them, but she had looked when alone, smiling as each one proved he was the father.

'What are you grinning about?' Spencer asked, peering over at her while Archie tugged on Spencer's *Best Captain Ever* badge sewn to a lanyard, gifted to him by the children.

Perhaps she should share the news, even though he had proven it didn't matter. They loved each other and Archie so much, and life was good. She knew Spencer believed her, but part of her really wanted to share the results with him.

She leaned closer, offering a warm smile. 'Last paternity results just came back. Another yes to you being Archie's dad.'

'I believed you. I put my name on Archie's birth certificate.'

'I know, but I still wanted to show you. You're a good man, Spencer Jordan, and we're lucky to have you.'

'I'm the one who is blessed.'

She reached over the table to stroke his arm. 'I can't stop smiling at how happy we are.'

He smiled. 'We're doing all right, you and me, aren't we?'

'I'd say. With our offer on the cottage accepted, and me getting a new job, life is blimming well brilliant right now.'

'Don't forget our new car.'

Beth's heart warmed some more. 'I hope whoever buys your flat finds our kind of happiness.'

'They might already have it.'

She gazed around at all the love she could see. Happy families, laughing children, snuggling couples. 'Do you ever have that feeling like your heart might just explode from all the joy inside you?'

Spencer gave her hand a gentle squeeze. 'Every time I look at you.'

Beth kissed his knuckles as she giggled. 'Smooth line, Spence.'

'Hey, I was being serious.'

She placed his hand to her cheek, and he lightly stroked her skin with his thumb.

'Come on, Beth, let's have a dance.'

Laughing, she stood, cuddling into her family, and swayed to the muffled sounds of something about bunnies hopping. Spencer started to sing along, making her laugh some more.

Archie gurgled as though joining in, and Beth couldn't hold herself back from kissing his chubby cheek. She then turned to give Spencer a peck on the cheek too, but he moved so their lips met, and he grinned on her mouth.

'I've come to the conclusion that you're my best friend,' she whispered.

He nudged her nose with his own. 'Is that right?'

Beth smiled. 'You make everything better.'

'No, Beth, you did that all by yourself. You made the changes you needed, and you helped yourself.'

His words hit home. She really had taken all the steps Jan had shown her, and her life had only changed when she got up and did something about it, but he was part of the process. He had shown compassion and understanding, given her an extra set of hands, and a group of new friends.

She gazed deeply into his cool blue eyes. 'You are so loved,' she said softly.

He pulled her closer, kissing her cheek. 'So are you, Beth.' He kissed Archie's head. 'So are you both.'

THE END

ACKNOWLEDGEMENTS

This story is dedicated to everyone on a healing journey. You are powerful, resilient, problem-solving masters who know how to survive the deepest, darkest pits of hell. Remember that next time you doubt your strength.

Huge thanks goes out to the Choc Lit/Joffe Books team for their help, support, and encouragement for the Port Berry series and my author journey. Much appreciated.

Also sending a cheer to my readers who are a constant support to my author journey. I want you all to know that I'm so completely and utterly grateful to each and every one of you.

As always, sending lots of love and light your way. Keep reading. It's good for the soul.

ABOUT THE AUTHOR

Hello, I'm K.T. Dady. I write uplifting love stories filled with friendship, family, and community set here, there, and everywhere, as love happens anywhere and under all sorts of circumstances. But whatever challenges my characters face along the way, there is always a happily ever after.

Feel free to join my newsletter over at my website, where you can download a free Pepper Bay short story that you won't find anywhere else. Newsletters go out once a month and often contain free gifts, previews, and writing tips among the news. Head over to my website at ktdady.com

If you enjoyed reading my book, please leave a rating or review on Amazon or Goodreads. It really helps to bring the story to more readers. Thank you so much.

You'll also find me on my social media accounts.

Instagram: @kt_dady

Facebook: @ktdady

THE CHOC LIT STORY

Established in 2009, Choc Lit is an independent, award-winning publisher dedicated to creating a delicious selection of quality women's fiction.

We have won 18 awards, including Publisher of the Year and the Romantic Novel of the Year, and have been shortlisted for countless others. In 2023, we were shortlisted for Publisher of the Year by the Romantic Novelists' Association.

All our novels are selected by genuine readers. We are proud to publish talented first-time authors, as well as established writers whose books we love introducing to a new generation of readers.

In 2023, we became a Joffe Books company. Best known for publishing a wide range of commercial fiction, Joffe Books has its roots in women's fiction. Today it is one of the largest independent publishers in the UK.

We love to hear from you, so please email us about absolutely anything bookish at choc-lit@joffebooks.com.

If you want to receive free books every Friday and hear about all our new releases, join our mailing list here: www.joffebooks.com/freebooks.